Loves Lost and Found

Loves Lost and Found

E V Radwinter

Matador
9 Priory Business Park,
Wistow Road, Kibworth Beauchamp,
Leicestershire. LE8 0RX
Tel: 0116 279 2299
Email: books@troubador.co.uk
Web: www.troubador.co.uk/matador
Twitter: @matadorbooks

ISBN 978 1 8004 6484 1

British Library Cataloguing in Publication Data.
A catalogue record for this book is available from the British Library.

Printed and bound in Great Britain by 4edge Limited
Typeset in 11pt Minion Pro by Troubador Publishing Ltd, Leicester, UK

Matador is an imprint of Troubador Publishing Ltd

To mum.
Forever in my heart.

one.

I hope you are sitting comfortably

I got love wrong.

Often, if the truth be known.

As a consequence, I realised that whilst we all get our hearts broken at some time in our lives, it is the way that we cope, and survive, that heartbreak that defines us. Like everyone, I have loved, been loved and lost love, and now I live in hope, so much hope, that I will never experience the last of the trilogy again.

Walking is my escape, my physical and mental break from the mundane, a chance to take joy in the beauty of nature. And, as it happens, walking is how my life changed forever and it is where this story begins.

My name is Chloe. I rather vaguely describe myself as being too old to be in the first flush of youth, but not yet of an age to experience the hot flushes that come to all women eventually. Unfortunately I am not the type of person to stand out in a crowd. Instead I prefer to be in the background making myself useful and ensuring everyone around me is happy. My family has described me as having a larger than life personality which, apparently, makes me attractive in my own unique way. However, I lack confidence in myself. I am a little below average height and above average weight, with shoulder-length wavy fair hair. Apparently my most distinctive features are my eyes which twinkle, I am told, especially when I release my raucous laugh. I am passionate about the causes I believe in, my family mean the world to me and, I believe, my best quality is my loyalty. I work in communications and I have to confess that I am a determined, successful and hard-working, career-minded person. Some, if not all, of these characteristics may well be part of the reason why lasting love has eluded me.

That aside, my career has provided me with the means to live on the edge of an attractive medieval town in middle England. It has a cacophony of quaint higgledy-piggledy houses in pastel shades, walls and roofs at unfathomable angles. I often pause to ponder how they have managed to remain standing after so many centuries without having a horizontal or vertical line amongst them. The town has a bustling market twice a week and is nestled into a valley surrounded by green fields and copses.

The day that marked the beginning of a vibrant and new chapter in my life was a beautiful spring Saturday, not the first sunny day of the year, but the first that offered hope for the summer to come. Apart from that it was an ordinary day, the sun shining, a cooling breeze, the birds singing; flowers were beginning to flourish as the warm rays hit the cold earth, the buds on the trees were unfurling into bright green leaves and all around smelt fresh and new as nature awoke after a harsh winter.

The day was too glorious to spend cooped up at home so I set out for a walk. The first hour was uneventful – two hills to power up before dropping back down to more level ground. The walk was mostly along roads, cars and lorries rushing by so close that I could feel the wind blast at me as they passed, requiring a quick reaction to hold down my top for fear it might take flight.

I continued along a minor road, through woods which provided some blessed, shaded relief from the sun. The light was dappled where the sun filtered through the evergreen leaves, the rays brilliant as they danced across the puddles that remained from the rainfall the night before. Around the bend and the trees receded to reveal a stately home, built early in the seventeenth century, set back from the road.

As I was passing the house, I was absorbed by the sight of the sandstone façade reflecting back the sunshine which engulfed it. A short distance further on I turned right, away from the road, towards the meadow that runs along the edge of the walled grounds of the house, passing across the estate farmland. The little-used footpath provides a shortcut and by this stage in the walk, most importantly, an almost level route back to the town.

I had trodden this path many times over the years I had lived in the town. Despite the amount of time spent walking along paths adjacent to roads, it was still a favourite walk of mine. However, this was the first time the walk would impact on the future direction of my life.

The path starts out as a concrete slab road that leads to a couple of the estate farmhouses. The road runs a short distance, passing a field with a dilapidated World War II machine gun post, the concrete exterior still intact but now overgrown with weeds. It then crosses a narrow stream, where the water gurgles and bubbles over the stones that make up its bed. Beyond that the road continues over a concrete bridge into a chaotic farmyard, with wooden barns which have seen better days, filled with old, long-forgotten machinery and equipment, and on hot days the smell of rotting manure can be pungent. Before the bridge the walker turns off the road and down onto a narrow muddy path that runs between the stream and the estate's stone and flint wall.

It was just before the road and path separate that I heard a vehicle coming up behind me at speed. I stepped to one side to let it pass, assuming it was a farmer returning home. In fact it was a police van. I was surprised to see it on this road. *What on earth has happened at the farm?* I thought as my mind went into a flurry of imagined scenarios. I could see through the windows that the van was full of police, so whatever had happened at the holding must have been significant.

I expected the van to pass by me and make its way into the farmyard. However, it ground to a halt just ahead of me and one of the policemen in the back got up, made his way to the door, slid it open and got out. Laughing inwardly, I wondered if they were lost and were stopping to ask for directions. How ironic that would have been.

As the policeman rounded the front of the van, I felt a strange feeling of recognition, or was it the ice-cold fingers of déjà vu gripping my heart, so intense I shivered. It stopped the breath in my chest, and then, just as quickly as it had descended upon me, it was gone. I was slightly perturbed, unsure of what I was feeling or why. I couldn't work out what was happening. There was no time to dwell on it though as he was here, standing in front of me, smiling sheepishly.

At a guess I would have placed him a few years older than me. His hair was cut short, dark but greying at the edges giving him a distinguished appearance. He looked trustworthy, although that might have been the uniform which his body filled to perfection. He was ruggedly handsome, the sort of man I had previously fallen for. He had a strong chin and cheekbones, a face you could happily stare at for hours. And yes, he was tall, but then at five foot one and a half inches, almost all adults, and some adolescent boys, are taller than me.

As I looked behind him, I could see all eyes in the van fixed on us and I wondered if some practical joke was about to be played on me. I felt a little uncomfortable alone as I was on this track, with a van full of policemen watching me, one of them seemingly lost for words.

It felt like the stand-off of silence might go on forever. *This won't do*, I thought, *I have a coffee to buy in town and a walk to finish.*

"Can I help you?" I asked inquisitively in the most confident voice I could muster at that moment.

"Well, I hope so," he replied in a deep, firm voice of authority that you would expect from a man in his profession.

"I saw you on the road, just back there." His voice grew quieter as he turned his body to point in the direction I had come from. He turned back to face me, and continued, "It's the strangest thing. I think I know you," his voice just starting to betray a little nervousness in where this conversation might be going. "I was taken aback, you look so familiar, but I just can't place you. I had this overwhelming need to find out. Before I knew it I had told Graham, the driver, to turn around. I just knew that I needed to speak to you. We are en route to a meeting and it took a while to convince my colleagues. But then we couldn't see you. You were no longer on the path and we knew you couldn't have gone too far, well, not unless you had jumped into a car and sped off." The words were tumbling out of his mouth, like a gushing tap. I remained silent and let him ramble on.

"Luckily one of my eagle-eyed colleagues spotted you and here we are, but now I don't know what to say. I feel I know you, but I don't know why or how. Sorry, I'm rambling now, I'll shut up. I don't know what I was expecting from this," he confessed.

"Maybe we could step away from the van a little," I suggested. "It's a little off-putting having all your colleagues staring at me."

He glanced over his shoulder to take in the scene, nodded in agreement and smiled. As he drew closer I could smell his aftershave. I hesitated for a moment as I recognised the distinctive and heavenly scent of Eternity. He put his hand on my elbow to guide me away. The instant there was contact a shot of adrenaline spiked through my body. Maybe it was the aftershave, or the firm, assured way he held me; maybe it was just the proximity. Whatever the reason a flash of memory brought me out of the storm of confusion that had been tumbling around my mind and into the clarity of understanding.

"I know how we know each other," I said quietly, stopping and turning to him. I glanced over to check we were out of earshot of the van, then looked him in the eye.

"But first my name is Chloe," and I proffered my hand in a slightly over-formal gesture. He responded in kind and a firm shake ensued. He looked at me confused, but adhering to tradition replied, "I'm Edward. Ed."

"Nice to meet you again Ed," I said as we let go of each other's hands. He tilted his head to one side after I said 'again'. Obviously if he had recognised me then we must be meeting again, but clearly he was still unsure as to when or where our first meeting had occurred.

I continued quickly, to put him out of his misery, "We met in Nottingham. You had just finished your police training and were out celebrating. I had just graduated from university and was also out celebrating. We got chatting and…"

At this point the fog evidently lifted from Ed's memory. His eyes widened as his smile grew and he took up the recollection.

"And we got chatting, we drank too much, and one thing led to another. I didn't want it to be just that one night, but we got split up. I looked for you but I… well, obviously, I didn't find you. Not a very good start for a policeman's career," he said with genuine regret in his voice.

"It's okay," I reassured him, "I'd have liked it if you had found me, but it's not exactly held me back. So how have you been over the intervening years? You're still a policeman, I see."

At this point there was a toot of the van's horn and Graham tapped his watch impatiently from behind the wheel. As the van did a far-too-rapid three-point turn for the narrow road, Ed said, "Look, I hate to go, like I said we are en route to a meeting and it wouldn't be good to turn up late. But I'm not going to go without taking your number. I'm not going to mess up this second chance." I felt my heart flutter, a feeling long suppressed and unexplored in me.

Ed typed my number into his phone and jogged back to the van. As he climbed in, he turned back and gave me a heartfelt smile and wave, and then he was gone.

I turned slowly back to the path, a huge smile on my face.

This is my favourite part of the walk, shaded by the trees that have grown above the estate wall to provide a canopy. The path leads to an ancient stone arched gateway that would have previously contained a heavy oak door, long since rotted away, one of the few remaining clues that once a monastery stood on this land.

The rest of the walk passed quickly as I made my way along the side of the river, across the meadow, emerging into the town where I bought a massive coffee (a passion of mine). As I took the last few steps towards home I realised that the last half an hour had been a blur, my mind racing – hopeful possibility, moments of doubt. I didn't have a chance to ask if he was married. *Why am I even thinking about that? But of course he is*, I thought. *Most men, and especially the good, handsome ones are. Why didn't I look for a wedding ring? Would he have asked for my number if he was married? Then again, he didn't ask about my situation either.* In truth the conversation was just too short, there simply hadn't been time.

He had stopped because he recognised me but didn't know why. Maybe he took my number because he felt guilty, or to save face in front of his colleagues. Who knew? *If he's married then he won't call*, I thought. Either way it was nice to feel alive again, to feel the rush of excitement at the prospect of a new relationship, and heaven knows it had been a long time since that had last happened.

Now, as I paused to think about it, it had been several years. Not that I had been counting, nor had I been looking for a man in my life. A succession of disastrous relationships had left me rather raw and of the opinion that it would be better to be alone than to enter another bad relationship, another set of years wasted whilst wanting to escape it but not knowing how.

I was surprised to find myself hoping Ed would call. Oh, those giddy early days of nervous anticipation, of constantly checking the phone for non-existent messages, hoping that a message had come without knowing it, even though the volume was on full and it was never far from my hand. *Oh blessed phone, please ring.*

Calm down, I told myself. *It's only been two hours and he is probably still in his meeting.*

It was no good, I would have to find something productive to do for the afternoon, as much as I loved sitting in my little garden, lounging on the wooden steamer chair and soaking up the heavenly warm rays of sunshine, the cool breeze rustling through the shrubs that surrounded my garden and the beautiful red ornamental cherry tree that stood proudly in the centre. The birds were busily chirping a happy tune nearby, but it was no good because sitting and doing nothing meant it allowed my mind to wander. Usually this was my sanctuary, the place to let my mind switch off from the worries of life, of work, of everything. But now, sitting there, sipping my coffee, my mind kept wandering back to Ed and I found myself starting to daydream about what might be.

No, I told myself, *this will not do*. Reluctantly I rose from the lounger and made my way to the front drive, which was just big enough to fit my car on. Unfortunately, though, the weeds were starting to take over the gravel.

Time for some gardening I told myself as I reversed my car back onto the road and went to find my trowel and bucket to put the unwanted greenery in and, of course, my trusted knee pad. No one wants to kneel on gravel, any more than anyone would want to walk bare foot on it.

They say that gardening is therapeutic, relaxing and of course good exercise. All of which is true, but as it required little brain action it allowed my mind to, yet again, wander, which is exactly what it did until finally I went and got my trusty retro radio. Amazing how music can distract the mind. I sang along, in my head, to the songs blaring out from Radio 2. Luckily for the neighbours I declined to sing out loud. On hearing me singing, one boyfriend had covered his ears and groaned quietly. A little harsh, but understandable. I really wouldn't know a tune if it jumped up and tapped my cheek.

It took a couple of hours of back-breaking bending, pulling, turning, scouring to clear all the weeds. They would be back soon enough. A combination of warm sunshine and regular downpours had provided them with the perfect conditions for growth, and grow they did.

It had been hot work. As I finally stood up I surveyed the drive to ensure I had removed every last blighter. I wiped the sweat from my forehead with the back of my arm, as my hands were protected by dirty gardening gloves. Looking down I saw my arm was glistening with sweat, but it was a good sign, it shouted back at me that it was the result of a job well done.

Time for a shower, I thought, looking down at the dirt spread across me. I tidied up the tools and put the weeds to one side while I moved the car back onto the drive. Once everything was back in its allotted place I sat in the back garden to cool down before heading to the bathroom.

two.

The past can haunt the present

That evening, sitting in the cool of my garden, I tucked into my low-carb Tom Kerridge-inspired salad. I had my phone for company, thinking about what a surreal day it had been and wondering if, in fact, any of it had happened at all or if indeed it was all part of my overactive imagination. That had got me into trouble more than once in the past.

I reminisced about when I was living in Nottingham, after graduating. I had tried to start a career and had applied, as had thousands of graduates across the country, to the prestigious John Lewis partnership management scheme. I had successfully progressed through the first two rounds, but then the process ground to a halt for me and I had to rethink my options.

I had contemplated moving back to my parental home and looking for a job in London. I do sometimes wonder how my life might have been different if I had taken that path. If I had my time again, knowing how it has worked out, that is probably the decision I would have changed and lived a different kind of future. But I didn't return home. The decision was made following my experience of working in London during my gap year between finishing school and starting university. That year had started with an intensive three-month secretarial course, part of which was to learn to type. I have to say that was one of my smartest decisions, developing a 'life skill' as they would say today. Whenever I have relocated I have gone straight to the nearest temp agency and signed up.

After the secretarial course I applied to several London firms. I felt I wanted a career in marketing, advertising, the media – something creative at least. I was desperate to work for the great, iconic institution that is the BBC, but whilst my typing speed was up to their exacting standards, my shorthand simply was not. I could do the theory, I just couldn't do the speed. I was lucky though, as an advertising agency was happy to take me on as a secretary for eight months before I started at university.

I loved the job, the pressure, the excitement, the adrenaline, and I loved the glamour of working for a prestigious company. I was not afraid to put in long hours and I learnt a lot about business. However, I also discovered that I didn't like commuting in and out of London every day. On a normal day it was bad enough – the cost, the overcrowding, the oppressive heat and humidity on the tube in the summer months. Unfortunately while I was working there it also coincided with train and tube strikes that went on for weeks. So, at the age of eighteen, and having only just passed my driving test, I now found myself driving into the centre of London. Terrifying but essential if I wanted to keep my job.

No, I had thought, alone in my flat in Nottingham, *returning to work in London is not for me.*

At that point fate had dealt me a lifeline. My professor, under whose tutelage I had achieved a 2:1 in Geography and who later told me that he thought I would achieve a first, except I was having too much fun in my third year, got in touch. He suggested I might like to consider studying for a PhD. I was thrilled. It had never occurred to me that it was an option, let alone that I might be clever enough to undertake such an academic challenge. Dr Chloe certainly had a ring to it. My parents were thrilled of course and very proud, so I returned to university.

To cut to the chase I never became Dr Chloe. Despite numerous attempts I failed to get any significant funding, other than a few jobs around the university tutoring, working in the library, and discounted fees, none of which covered the rent, let alone food bills or heaven forbid entertainment. As a result, after just one year of full-time study I got a job – 8.30am to 5pm at work then straight to the campus where I continued my research during evenings and weekends. It soon became apparent that the research would take too long. By the time I finished the PhD part-time, the theory would have been either proven or disproven in the real world, and besides I was enjoying work and decided not to continue my studies.

However, now that I indulge myself in dwelling on memories I have to confess that I cringe with embarrassment just at the mere thought of the trouble I got myself into during my postgraduate time. It was then that my overactive imagination got me into trouble, not just once, but indeed twice.

In my first year of study, I shared an office with two older postgraduates. Sophie had made friends and had her own social circle, so we seldom met outside the office, and besides, her research often took her away for months at a time.

The other person in the office was Neil. A quiet, considerate person. About average height for a man; short, mousy-coloured hair. I guess I would describe him as a good-looking nerd. Not traditionally handsome, or striking, but he had an air of quiet confidence and there was certainly something about him that made you look more deeply. He was slender, if a little too thin for my liking, and he wore a uniform of a plain shirt, the collar always buttoned down, and the bottom hem tucked with neatness and precision into the top of his unexceptional jeans. On a rare show of exuberance the top button of the shirt was undone, revealing just a hint of the hairy chest that lay beneath.

I am not sure if it was because he was quiet or because he appeared to be shy, either way he didn't seem to have much of a social circle, so I started inviting him out with my crowd who were made up of a handful of the hardcore who had stayed on after university and knew the best drinking holes and clubs to while away the weekends.

My friends took to him immediately. He listened rather than imposed his personality; he considered his contributions to conversations but had a wicked sense of humour that bubbled under the surface and occasionally, with an imp-like glint in his eye, he would let it shine.

The more time we spent together, particularly outside the campus life, the more I started paying attention to him – the man not the colleague – and slowly but surely I found myself falling for him. He was one of those people that slowly grows on you; not the thunderbolt type that erupts into your life, but someone who creeps up on you and suddenly they are all that you can think about. And stupidly I let myself start to believe that his interest in partying with us, his smiles and laughter, were because of me.

I liked a tipple back then, I still do if I'm honest. Today it's ice-cold Pinot Grigio in the warm summer months, Prosecco for celebrating at any time of year and in winter a Shiraz, especially with a hearty roast dinner. Back in the day it was pints of dry cider.

As with all tales that involve alcohol it was my downfall. In my drunken fog, in that state of disengaged rational thought and decision making, I launched myself at the poor innocent man. I guess, because we never discussed it, that out of pity, or shock, or not knowing what to do in such a socially awkward situation (at a guess he had never been confronted by a drunk friend launching herself at his lips), he reluctantly returned my kiss. I was in heaven. I thought, *Finally, here is a decent man, someone I would be proud to introduce to my family.*

But the euphoria was short-lived. The following Monday, whilst working in the office Neil quietly suggested a coffee. My heart was in my throat. I was embarrassed by my actions on Friday, but hopeful, so hopeful, that my imagination had been right and that the feelings were mutual.

Hope, so much hope, in the silent walk to the canteen. Hope, so much hope, as we ordered and made our way to a quiet seating area by the window. Silence. Awkward, embarrassing, painful silence as we both looked out of the window at the view across the university lake, surrounded by trees and decorated by the elegant swans majestically swimming around the lake searching for food. It was like a mirror of what was happening in the room: on the surface all was calm and peaceful and serene; beneath the surface the swan was paddling for its life, as was I internally.

My mind was racing, unsure of where to start, what to say, what he was thinking, what he would say. It was killing me. I wished a hole would miraculously open beneath me so I could fall into it and disappear.

In the end it was me who had to break the silence. Well, I guess that was only right given it was my actions that had brought us to this hellish impasse. "Look, Neil, I'm sorry, I shouldn't have done that on Friday." I paused. "It was ill-judged and very unladylike to say the least. I'm sorry, it won't happen again."

I wanted to apologise. I meant what I said, that it wouldn't happen again. However, if the truth be told I wanted nothing more than for it to happen again, and again, and again. All I wanted was for Neil to instigate a kiss by wrapping his arms around me and pulling me in close.

Instead he was a gentleman. In truth I had expected nothing less. "I appreciate the apology, thank you," he said in his soft, unassuming tone. "To be honest I've been worrying about what to say to you all weekend."

I felt ashamed at that point. Not only had I acted appallingly, but poor Neil had been wrestling with what to say to me. And, of course, it dawned on me that these were the words of a man struggling to find a polite way out of the situation, not of a man looking for the words to ask me out on a date. I did the only honourable thing and fell on my sword.

"Look, Neil, like I said I shouldn't have done that. If I'm honest, and I apologise if this seems cruel especially after how I treated you, but you are not really my type. I was horribly drunk and behaved inexcusably. I'm genuinely sorry. I really hope we can remain friends and that it won't be awkward in the office?"

Crisis averted, the relief on his face was palpable. He smiled. "Thank you Chloe, no offence taken and yes, I'd like to stay friends."

Of course you would, I would say to myself when just a couple of weeks later the real reason, or should that be desire, to remain friends became abundantly clear. As I returned from a night out with friends I opened the front door straight into the front room of my tiny flat and found my flatmate Sam, who had gone home early, in the arms of Neil, who had coincidentally left not long after her. Not only was she in his arms but also they were fully engaged in a passionate kiss. One of the kisses I had imagined being destined for me. A kiss so all engrossing they didn't even hear me enter the room, let alone see me standing there, taking in the scene before darting into my bedroom to escape the soul-destroying passion unfolding before me.

Anyone would think, or hope, that that was the end of my wild imagination, but sadly not.

The following year a new postgrad joined our motley crew. He was in the office next door and was more of a wham-bam-thank-you-ma'am, thump-you-in-the chest, fall-in-love-in-an-instant kind of a man. Fred was gorgeous, goooorgeous. He was tall, all rippling muscles honed from hours in the gym every day. He had short, dark hair, a natural tan gained from an active life and a smile that would melt the coldest of hearts. And mine was not cold, mine was warm, no hot, very hot.

We had more in common than you would think. We were both specialising in human geography and yet we shared a passion for geomorphology – how the environment affects how we live, how we mess it up and then how nature gets its revenge. We had once spent an afternoon talking about flooding, batting ideas back and forth, which Fred summarised: "So, the pressure to find places to build new housing often results in developments going up in spaces previously ignored as they were difficult to build on or because it was inappropriate, like the flood plains of rivers. The thing about flood plains is they flood, so eventually home owners find their homes swamped with dirty water. The second thing about flood plains is they are designed to slow the progress of the water into the river, slowing it down as it seeps through the soil to find the water table. However, when you cover it in bricks, concrete and tarmac, there is no longer a mechanism to slow and absorb the water. It still needs to go somewhere and so it rushes at damage causing speed to the river, which is already full. The river floods, and the water continues downstream, gathering speed and flooding the next community and the community after that."

And so went many of my conversations with Fred, putting the world to rights, discussing the issues and potential solutions. It was not all nerd talk though. We went to the cinema, we went out for dinner. I fell hook, line and sinker in lust; he remained faithfully committed to his childhood girlfriend who was back in his hometown situated a little way outside Bristol, as revealed by his accent. I guess that was one of the things I liked about him: he was open and friendly, and great fun to be with, but he was loyal to his girlfriend, going home to visit her as often as he could. Maybe it was his unavailability that was part of the attraction, the exquisite pain of unrequited love.

We did get drunk, and I had, in private, let my imagination run wild. Hope sprung eternal as I created this little world where we could be in love with each other; I even created a little white cottage, with slate roof and roses growing up the side of the porch. No doubt if it had gone on much longer there would have been an imaginary marriage and children and a happy ever after. If truth be known he knew how I felt about him, and I knew he knew, but he was the perfect gentleman and we never spoke of it and soon he was gone. He missed home, he missed his girlfriend and being a postgrad was not working out as he had hoped. He escaped Nottingham and went home, and in the letters that followed the move, I discovered that he had trained, and subsequently entered, the teaching profession.

He was the first of three men called 'Fred' that graced my life: one, the first one, I had lusted over; the second I had loved; and the final one I ended up loathing. Still do, even after all these intervening years. Some men that have left my life I wonder where they are and on occasions have been known to use a search engine to answer my curiosity. Others, like Fred 3, I've never wanted to know, nor did, or do, I care.

As a child I always assumed that one day I would be the archetypal cliché – married, with 2.4 children, a dog and a four-door family car on the drive. I never thought about it much or even questioned it, I just knew that one day I would be the stereotype. As I grew up, however, I began to realise that it just was not that easy.

Luckily I had never acted on my dreams about Fred 1, the ones I had created in the privacy of my mind. The moral? Whilst imagination and creativity are good, alcohol and action are not.

Back to the present

So back to the tale, which I carelessly drifted away from some pages ago. To recap, I was in the garden enjoying a glass of ice-cold Pinot. I cannot say it was particularly relaxing though, as my neighbours a few doors away were having a party. It had already been going a few hours and by now the guests were well lubricated. The more they drank, the louder their voices became, the more the volume on the music system was cranked up. It was a depressing cycle of ever-increasing noise. Made all the worse for not having been invited to join in. Not that I would have. Without going into details, relations between us had been hostile for years.

As the party went on, a second music system was set up. At one end of the garden the adults were listening to 80s music – fine in my book – whilst at the other end the 'kids' were blaring out 'banging' tunes. Literally all I could hear, or indeed feel, was the bang, bang, bang of the monotonous rhythm. Then again I really know nothing about what constitutes good music.

One more shriek from the party and my patience finally gave out and I retreated inside to find some solitude.

I sank down into the sofa. It was old and saggy but it was comfy, and it was familiar. I flicked on the TV. I didn't really care what was on, the less challenging the better, just some pictures and some noise to drown out the bedlam which was seeping into my home from outside. I turned up the volume on the TV and settled back into the sofa with my wine.

My relaxation was suddenly shattered by the buzz of my phone. It startled me and I stared at the screen, holding my breath, hoping this was the text I had been waiting for all afternoon and evening.

I reached over gingerly, hoping, but scared to check. A torrent of thoughts crashed my brain. *It might not be him. If it is, he is probably making an excuse to walk away, but what if…? What if he wants to talk? To meet? To… who knows.* I sighed. The only way to find out was to read the text.

Bracing myself I unlocked my phone. It didn't provide an answer to my first question. As my phone display sprang to life it showed 'unknown' above the text. *Could it be?*

Deep breath, calm down, in fact just calm down and read the text, I told myself.

'Hi Chloe,' it read. 'It was great to bump into you today after all these years.'

Too formal, I thought. *Here comes the 'but' or the excuse.* I read on.

'I've only just got back from dinner with my colleagues following our meeting. I know it's too late to meet tonight but are you free tomorrow for a coffee or lunch perhaps? It would be good to catch up. Ed'

Oh my giddy aunt, it's him, he wants to meet up. My heart felt like it was going to beat out of my chest; my palms went sweaty. *He wants to meet me!!!!* Then the doubts, the inevitable doubts. *He just wants to meet to talk, to catch up, nothing more.* I needed to stop my imagination from running wild. That uncontrolled daydreaming would result in the inevitable destruction of anything potentially good. *Don't think this is anything more than a polite, friendly gesture from a blast from the past,* I told myself.

Yes, I thought, *obviously my answer is yes, but how quickly do I reply? I don't want it to seem like I've been waiting by the phone for hours, even though, in truth, I have been. Then again he wants to meet tomorrow, so I can't leave it too long, and besides I will be heading to bed soon,* I considered as I hit 'reply' on the message and stared at an empty text box.

It had been so long since I had been in this position and I didn't know what the etiquette was these days.

If he had, as he said, sent a text as soon as he escaped from his colleagues then the least I could do was reply.

'Hi Ed, I would love to, lunch is good for me, where would you like to meet? Chloe'. I read and re-read the message several times, deleting it, rewriting it, eventually hitting send before I could overthink the situation.

Don't expect a reply tonight, I told myself. *Maybe I should have held off sending my text. Maybe I should have pretended to have a life and either be too busy to reply tonight or claim to have a prior engagement.* In truth I was too old to play games. I gave myself a stern reminder that an old acquaintance had invited me to lunch, which I accepted, and that is all that had happened.

As I climbed into bed I plugged in my phone to charge. I didn't want it to run out of juice before the all-important reply.

I shut my eyes, smiling, feeling hopeful and contented for the first time in an eon despite the party that was still raging outside. Just as I started to drift into blissful sleep, my phone sprang back into life. It was another message from Ed. 'Tomorrow it is then, how about 12.30pm in the Market Square, we can decide where to eat then?'

Perfect, my sleepy brain thought as I typed the reply, 'See you then'.

three.

So begins the beginning

Well, I tried to sleep, I tried very hard. I tried 'mindfulness' although I have never read anything about it so don't know the specifics – the how and the what. I tried going to my calm place, my happy place, my grandparents' house. I imagined driving off the ferry in Stromness, Orkney. I listened to the sounds of the curlew and the wind. I imagined the sting of the horizontal rain as it hit my cold face. I thought about the drive over the hill, turning right towards Kirkwall. I imagined passing the loch on the left, and off in the distance the Odin Stone and the Ring of Brodgar. None of my Celtic forefathers were on hand to help me get to sleep. I continued along the road, over another small hill with the only trees on the island nestled in the river valley beside the road. Down into Finstown and turn left. Those last couple of miles so ripe with memories. Across the ancient stone bridge over the river where many summers ago, my father, brother and I went fishing.

Lying in bed, awake, I imagined continuing along the road, the hills on the left, the sea on the right. Up ahead, nestled into the hillside for protection from the weather I could see my mum's cousin's farm. And ahead, just to the right of the road, now bathed in sunshine, the white house shone as a beacon of hope and love. My grandparents' house. At least it was, many years ago. Now it's preserved in my memories. It's my happy place, my go-to place for love and laughter and carefree summers. My grandparents had chickens and we would search for eggs for breakfast. Wild cats and their kittens lived in a store at the back of the house. It was originally an outside toilet, but that was long gone and now a small hole had been cut roughly in the bottom of the rotting door to provide access to shelter and protection from the harsh Orkney winter weather. My grandfather, a farmer, or crofter, of many years, allowed them to live there to catch vermin and protect his animals.

During the summer he would borrow someone's pony so I could ride round the field that wrapped around the house.

There was a swing in the door of the garage that was rolled down from its storage place and allowed hours of fun swinging back and forth, back and forth, whilst the family sat in the sheltered spot, enjoying any sun, endless tea, conversations and love.

That was my go-to sleep place. On a good night I never arrived, having drifted off to sleep several miles before. Not that night though. That night I arrived, unpacked, played, chatted, remembered my grandparents, my amazing grandfather with his weather-beaten face, the few remaining strands of white hair combed over his bronzed scalp and the smell of the ever-present cigarette which miraculously hung from his lips as he talked. He was strong, very strong, as someone farming in these northern reaches has to be. And my grandmother, so meek, so mild, so steady, so strong. It always amazed me how she kept her hair dark even to the end of her days. Maybe it was because she wore a tea cosy on her head – at least that was what I thought it was as I grew up. Or maybe she had a secret stash of hair dye. Either way her hair is of no consequence. She was the matriarch that held the family together.

I remember hours spent in the kitchen, all the grandchildren and parents lined either side of the long kitchen table, the adults drinking whisky and the kids on pop as granny stirred the stew and we waited so patiently for it to be ready. I'm not sure if the stew took that long, or if it was an excuse to drink more whisky and talk. Orcadians have always been fabulous hosts. Eventually the melt-in-the-mouth stew and newly-pulled-from-the-garden boiled tatties were served, with lashings of butter across the broken skin. Oh, just thinking about those days fills me with happiness even after all these years.

This tale, however, ends in both a sad and a beautiful way. My grandparents were very much in love, having passed their fiftieth wedding anniversary some years before. One April my gran had a stroke and was taken to hospital. The family gathered around. After a couple of months it was clear she wouldn't recover and came home to die. My mum, aunt and uncle travelled north (all of them living in or around London at the time) to care for her.

All this time, ever since my gran took ill, my grandfather was slipping away. He had no intention of living without his wife, his life. By the time my father, brother and I arrived in Orkney that summer, grandfather was in hospital. We visited him there, but he was visibly removing himself from this world. Back at their home I went in to my gran's room to read poetry which, as a former teacher, she loved.

Early one morning my father knocked on the door of the room my brother and I were sharing.

"Granny's gone," he said. "Would you like to say goodbye?"

My brother was adamant that he did not, under any circumstances, want to do that. But I felt differently.

"Yes," I replied timidly, having never seen a dead body in real life before.

Holding hands we entered my gran's bedroom. She looked so peaceful, like she was asleep.

"Goodbye, granny," I whispered, and leant in to kiss her cold cheek. "Goodbye, I love you." Granny was the first, but not the last, person I loved that I kissed goodbye after they had passed.

A few days later my grandfather passed. I didn't get a chance to say goodbye, but as a teenager, in the space of a week, I lost both my grandparents, and attended two funerals.

Orkney is not known for wall-to-wall sunshine, but on the day of both funerals the wind died down and the sun shone. I remember now how the sun bounced off the mill pool lock on the left of the funeral procession, the bank to the right resplendent with summer flowers. There were tears of course, so many tears, so much pain and sadness. I was amazed at how my mum held it together, having lost both of her parents so quickly. I don't know how she did it.

My father stood firm, strong, silent beside her. That must have helped. Through all this sadness what I took away was how much, how very much they must have loved each other and I knew that if I found just a fraction of that love in my life, how lucky I would be.

Back to the present

Love – that was what was keeping me awake that night, the endless churning of the same argument, swinging from hopeful anticipation of the lunch, to reminding myself that it was just that, lunch; from wanting love to return to my life, to never wanting to feel the pain of separation again. It was hardly surprising I couldn't sleep.

I must have eventually drifted off and awoke several hours later to hear the dawn chorus start. It always amazes me that as the first semblance of life-giving light appears in the east, what starts out as a few birds, tweeting their welcome to the new day, builds so quickly into a cacophony of noise, every bird in the neighbourhood shouting their greeting and competing for attention.

As the sun slowly rose I tried to get more sleep. It came, although only fitfully until eventually I could stay in bed no longer.

I showered, dressed and made up in a turmoil of thought and anticipation. The sun was shining on the patio and I decided to join the birds, still merrily chirping about goodness knew what. Sitting there, mug of strong tea cupped in my hands, I looked around my pretty little garden. It hadn't been much when I bought the house some five years previously, but now the flowers and shrubs I had planted were growing strong and making their presence known. As they now began to fight each other for space in the borders I would have to decide which ones to keep and which ones would need to go. It would be hard though, having planted and nurtured them for years, but it would have to be done.

For a north-facing garden it got a surprising amount of sun. I closed my eyes, soaking up the warmth. I played over and over in my mind what time I would leave the house to walk into town, which was not far, only a few minutes' stroll. I thought about what I would say, how long I would wait if he didn't turn up, what we would talk about.

In the end I realised I was waiting for the sake of waiting. I packed a bag and headed into town early. I planned to wander around the bookshop, pick up some historical thriller. Hopefully one of my favourite authors had published something juicy. With book in hand I would head to the nearest coffee shop for a large latte and a table in the sun.

I did do most of those things but not as I had imagined or planned as I walked into town that day.

I made my way into the bookshop, an increasingly rare site on a high street these days – an actual bookshop with real pick-them-up-and-flick-through-them books, even an assistant or two to ask questions and garner recommendations. Online might be quick and cheap, but nothing beats the real thing.

As I stepped inside I heard a voice behind me. "Morning Chloe, you couldn't wait until lunch either then?"

I turned, or more accurately, spun around to find myself face to face, or rather my face to his chest, with Ed.

I breathed in the smell of Eternity. My heart was thumping so loudly I could feel it reverberating in my ears and I was worried Ed would sense it too. I felt the temperature rise in my face. Ed now found himself looking down at a red-faced, embarrassed fool. This was not in any way how I wanted to come across.

He must be regretting suggesting this now. I wouldn't blame him if he just turned and walked away, I thought.

Instead he smiled at me deeply, giving me time to regain my composure.

"Morning," I finally managed to say and returned his smile. "As it's such a lovely day I thought I would buy a book and grab a coffee."

"That sounds like a great idea," Ed said. "I arrived early and was just wondering about how to occupy my time when I saw you cut across the square and head down here. So what sort of book are you after?"

We wandered over to the fiction section, but my mind was no longer on books. "I'm a fan of historical murder mysteries, that sort of thing," I rambled on.

"You'll be a fan of C. J. Sansom then," Ed suggested, and guided me over to the 'S' section.

I turned to face him. "Yes, I've read all of his books. I think they're terrific, real page-turners. But I don't think he has anything new out."

We both looked blankly at the full shelves, not really looking at the books, more using the time to gather our thoughts.

"Shall we skip the book and head straight for coffee? It's a little early for lunch," I suggested. He smiled and we left the shop in silence.

"I didn't ask yesterday, but do you live near here or are you just visiting for the meeting?" I asked, both fingers crossed, hoping it would be the former.

"Actually, I'm afraid I'm still up in Nottingham so I'll be heading back there this afternoon."

My heart sank; this really was just a catch-up on what our lives had become over the intervening years.

I guess the disappointment must have shown. I have always been told my face is very expressive and paints a clear message of exactly what is going on in my mind.

Ed reached down and took my hand, pulling me to a stop. I turned towards him, nervous, but excited by his touch.

"I'm glad that wasn't the news you were hoping for, I was going to build up to this if it seemed appropriate. I have to be honest, I've been trying to find the right words and nothing ever seems to be right somehow. And here we are two hours before we were meant to meet and you've already told me what I was hoping to hear, or in your case, see."

Now I was puzzled. I was not sure where this was going as we stood staring at each other in the middle of the street.

"You see," he continued, "the meeting yesterday was about a job, well, a promotion actually. It would mean moving down here, well, about fifteen miles from here. When I saw you yesterday it felt like fate, like everything was finally falling into place."

He paused, reaching down to pick up my other hand. "What do you think?" he asked quietly as he stroked the back of my hands with his thumbs.

I was beaming from ear to ear. I don't think he really needed me to answer his question, and his cheeky grin gave away that he knew exactly what I was thinking, but clearly he wanted to hear it from me.

"I would love that, if you were nearby. Do you think you'll accept?" I asked, holding my breath and biting my bottom lip.

"Yes," he said, "I already have, I start in a few months."

With that he dropped my hands, put his arm around my shoulders and led me off to the coffee shop. We must have looked deluded as we strolled across the square, this tall man and short woman, in silence, but beaming from ear to ear with sheer heavenly delight, a happiness I hadn't felt in years, if ever. No, I had felt it before, which is how I knew this was something really special.

The last time I had felt this giddy excitement, had, strangely, also been in Nottingham. That seems to be the place that most of these ramblings emanate from. Strange that, given that Nottingham had a reputation as a city that had six or even eight women to every man. Although I believe that had been the case when the lace industry was at its peak back in the nineteenth century, but was probably now an old wives' tale rather than a true reflection of the city's recent gender make-up.

I had, as we have already established, stayed on after university and by this point in my life I had a job and a flat on my own. I had a small circle of friends, mostly boys, and weekends were spent drinking and dancing the nights away.

One fateful Saturday night the boys said they would be bringing along someone new. They were all off to a music festival soon and they thought it would be good for everyone to meet before then. Not that I had been invited to go with them to the concert and nor did I want to. Camping is definitely not my thing. Hot tents, miles to walk to get to the loo, queues for showers. Give me an en suite, a bar and a restaurant, that is more my kind of thing.

The boys arrived in a taxi at the allotted time and I jumped in. A quick 'hello' to those I knew and a shake of the hand to the new member, Fred number 2. Conversation flowed and we were soon in the city centre and disembarking from the taxi. I had to get some cash out, as did Fred 2, and as we banked at the same place we agreed to meet the others in the pub, instructing them to get pints in for us if they got to the bar before we joined them.

Fred 2 was a decent amount taller than me, but not much. He had a strong build – another gym junkie, by the looks of him. He had floppy black hair which he frequently pushed back from his eyes and a wicked smile. He was well dressed in jeans, a checked shirt and brogues. He was well spoken and he was handsome. Of course, it does occur to me at this point that saying someone is handsome is a moot point. Obviously they wouldn't be a 'love interest' if I didn't find them attractive.

Back to Fred 2. He had boyish good looks rather than rugged, or chiselled, or striking good looks. He worked as an accountant for a company that manufactured some specific car parts which I have long since forgotten. He lived in the same town as his job, some fifty miles away from me, in the heart of the Peak District.

As we walked over to the pub we talked about where we were from. It turned out that Fred 2 was a year younger than me. He had been brought up in a village not far from my parents, his sister was the year above me at the school I attended and his parents played tennis with my aunt and cousins at inter-club matches. What a weird coincidence. And how weird that over all these years we had never met and yet in Nottingham, via friends of friends, here we were.

I have to confess in terms of the boys all getting to know each other it was a bit of a flop. But for me, on the other hand, I did a lot of getting to know Fred 2. Not that anyone seemed that bothered.

We did our usual circuit of the pubs, ending up inevitably in the old student nightclub. More of a village hall than a state-of-the-art club. But they played good music, the drinks were cheap and they had well-lit rooms where you could chat, away from the thump of the music and dancing.

I felt something was going to happen with Fred 2, there was this electricity flowing and sparking between us. Neither of us could stop smiling, our friends had long since stopped trying to engage us in conversation, their nudges and winks had ebbed and now they were just indifferent.

As the night drew to a close I sensed the opportunity might pass us by. Fred 2 lived too far away to be part of our weekly outings, which meant I didn't know how often, if ever, he would be out with us again.

Fred 2 leant in and whispered in my ear, "Fancy a dance?"

"Yes," I agreed and we made our way through the crowds to the dance floor. I was not going to make the first move. I had made the first move before and got that very wrong, and somehow Fred 2 seemed quite shy at this point, his earlier confidence and bravado escaping him now.

The lights came up. Home time.

We found the rest of the crew and made our way outside

to join the hubbub of drunken young people looking for one of two things: a taxi or food. It took a while but eventually we managed to flag one down – a taxi obviously, not food.

Sensing the disappointment in us, one of the boys, Mark, suggested I went back to theirs for a nightcap rather than dropping me off en route as they usually did. I leapt at the chance. Maybe tonight was not going to be a washout after all.

We talked for hours, and one by one my friends disappeared upstairs to their beds. Eventually it was just Fred 2 and I left on the sofa. We were both exhausted and had little left to say, but that dizzy scent of anticipation, the tingles of desire were still present, dulled by the booze and the hour, but still present. He leant in close, I didn't move, he moved in closer, so did I and then there was pure, unadulterated animal passion. It was the kiss to end all kisses. It held such promise and such knowing.

Nothing happened more than a kiss. I do, after all, have some morals. We awoke late the next morning, curled up on the sofa, fully dressed.

"Morning," he whispered in my ear. I snuggled back into his chest and his arms wrapped around me.

"Morning," I replied.

Back to the present

That was how it started all those years ago, a whirlwind romance. The trouble was, here now with Ed, it re-awoke all those old feelings and I was petrified.

Yes, yes, I know, you don't know unless you try, but having had my heart broken before and having only barely survived that, those old fears began to resurface.

Luckily, given the option of me metaphorically sinking or swimming, I had chosen to survive and grew strong. I chose a life with men who couldn't break my heart rather than experience that again.

But here I was with those intense, addictive feelings surging through me. Was I really going to do this, was I really going to risk this again? Of course I was, who wouldn't? I couldn't help myself.

We arrived at the cafe in the corner of the market square. It was a cafe during the day and a delightful Turkish restaurant at night. The family owners always made a fuss of regular customers, ensuring they felt valued and therefore ensuring they would return time and time again. Occasionally the cafe was frequented by one of the local famous clientele enjoying a meal with friends or family.

Today one of the owners was standing in the door and smiling at his new guests.

"Is it alright if we sit outside?" I asked.

"Of course, of course," he replied.

We ordered a couple of coffees and then pulled out the chairs, the metal legs scraping across the stone paving. We sat down at a small round table, sitting with our backs to the large cafe window, facing the sunshine as we looked over the town square, which was bathed in spring sunshine.

I took a deep breath, drew in the atmosphere. There was nothing better than whiling away the hours people-watching. It was a Sunday morning and the square was busy: some people were rushing around trying to grab last-minute items before heading home; others were taking life at a much slower pace, ambling in and out of the high street names and local independent stores laden down with shopping. I watched a couple whom I imagined had been married for many years, as they both looked relaxed in each other's company and yet sat in silence. I noticed through the slats of the bench that they were holding hands – pale, veiny, wrinkled hands but united in love. I smiled. *I hope I have someone to hold hands with at that stage of my life*, I mused.

Ed saw the smile and followed my line of sight.

"How romantic," he said softly. "Oh, to be in love at eighty." He turned to me with that knowing look that he had reflected exactly what was going through my mind again.

"Oh, indeed," I replied, turning to face him.

"Where do we start after all this time? There seems almost too much to catch up on," I said, trying very hard to come across as relaxed and chatty but feeling anything but.

"Well, I guess we start at the beginning and work our way forward. But before we do, I think that maybe we should cover one very important topic first."

I felt my heart leap to my throat. I felt dizzy, my eyes lost focus. He must have, yet again, picked my thoughts, and smiled reassuringly, no doubt guessing that I was worried he was about to tell me he was married. Well, 'is' married at the time.

As he opened his mouth to speak our waiter arrived in front of us carrying a small tray with our drinks. We both looked up and smiled at him as he placed the drinks on the table, and then thanked him as he turned and discreetly made his way back into the cafe.

We sat in silence for a moment, the momentum lost. We stared at our drinks and aimlessly stirred them for no reason – neither of us took sugar. Ed was the first to speak.

"Where were we?" he teased. We both knew full well where we were. We were on the cusp of discovering the one thing we were both desperate to know. The one thing that was going to make or break the day.

He looked me in the eye. One of those smouldering, hold-your-breath looks. My heart pounded. *At this rate I will be having a heart attack before lunch*, I thought.

"Look, it was amazing bumping into you yesterday." My heart sank, sank so low I could feel the pain. He didn't pause for breath, but rushed on, "I don't know what your situation is, I can't imagine you are single, and I don't know where this might go or what it might be, but I'm single and…" It had all come out in a rush and suddenly his voice trailed off, looking at me, almost pleading with me to help him out of the hole he now found himself in.

"Me too," I said softly. Smiling at him, I reached across the table and touched his hand.

"Me too," I repeated.

He turned his hand over and took hold of my palm. As he stroked the back of my hand with his thumb he said, "Good." The confidence returning to his voice, "Now that's out of the way, let's catch up."

The hours flew past. Once the conversation floodgates were opened it was impossible to push against the weight of the flow and shut them again. As we sat in the sunshine outside the cafe, chatting, eating, drinking, at some point during the afternoon, coffee was replaced by ice-cold white wine that slipped down our throats, cooling our warm bodies but warming up our effervescent conversation and feelings.

He had been married for a number of years, had one

child, and he and his ex-wife were still friends. He was open about the relationship, admitting that in the end they just grew apart. She had since remarried and had two more children, one of whom, the eldest, Ed was godfather to.

"It just makes it so much easier to be friends," he explained. "At birthdays and Christmas we can all get together and it makes the kids happy to have us all around."

"If only all relationships could end so well," I acknowledged. Certainly mine hadn't always been so amicable. In fact on one occasion I had to take the drastic step of getting a job on the other side of the country just to escape from an ex.

That was a toxic relationship on reflection, and hindsight is a wonderful thing. He never really wanted to be with me in the first place. It had taken me some months to realise that, and years more before I finally ended it. For months he kept trying to wheedle his way back in and so I made the decision to move to get as far away as possible, and it worked – he was out of my life permanently.

Ed was lucky to have been spared such baggage from his relationship.

By late afternoon, as the waiters started clearing tables and moving them inside as they prepared to close on that Sunday afternoon, we realised it was probably time to leave. Neither of us was ready for the day, or date, to be over so we made our way to the Common that had stood for time immemorial behind the square. The Common is a large open grassy area, and on a beautiful sunny afternoon it was crowded. There were couples getting to know each other, leaning in close so no one could hear the sweet nothings they were whispering in each other's ears – not that anyone was close enough to hear, it was more the intimacy it permitted the courting couple in this crowded theatre of townsfolk.

Further down the Common a group of friends were playing football. There were no marked edges to their 'pitch' but balled-up coats and jumpers marked where the goals stood, their shouts and laughter as the game proceeded distracting as well as entertaining.

There were families playing games of frisbee and catch, whilst friends sat on benches or on the grass chatting animatedly about goodness knew what.

We found a relatively quiet spot out of earshot of our fellow 'Commoners' and sat down on the warm grass to continue our conversation. At some point Ed must have made a decision about his planned return home, as rather than preparing to leave he became more and more settled in.

It was far too soon to end the 'date', and the pubs and bars were not open yet, which would be the logical place to continue it. So the Common is where we were and where our chatting edged slowly towards becoming a relationship. As the conversation continued we grew closer, not just metaphorically but also physically, edging closer and closer as we talked about every detail of our lives between our two chance meetings.

Ed had obviously been a policeman ever since we first met. He had slowly progressed through the ranks, trying his hand at different specialisms. Now I reflect on it he was rather sketchy on the details of what he actually did day to day. He talked about the team, about the opportunities and the admittedly risky but at times exhilarating job, but he never quite touched on any details or any specifics.

I, on the other hand, was effervescent about my jobs. I had worked either as a PA or as a communications and marketing manager. I loved to look after people and I loved to write, so both jobs were ideal for me.

I had worked across a number of industries and I gave Ed a brief insight into each one – why I did or didn't enjoy them. From the happiness and creativity of working for a British toy manufacturer to the boring, rule-restrictive insurance industry, which was the kiss of death to creativity. From an events-based job at a shopping centre which involved recruiting Father Christmas each year and tens of thousands of pounds spent on Christmas decorations to draw in the crowds. A year spent on the south coast working for a small group of hotels – the stories from that may be the subject of another book, *What the Communications Manager Saw*! And on and on the jobs rolled – international marketing and research agency, and finally two education charity jobs. And that was where I was now, at a charity, working long hours, not just because the job demanded it but also because I had nothing, or more importantly no one, to come home for.

By the time I finished telling Ed the tale the sun was getting low in the sky and a cool breeze was picking up. I kept lifting my hand to pin my hair back as it tickled my nose. As I did so, Ed caught another strand of hair that had flicked across my face. As he leant forward to restrain it by pushing it behind my ear our faces were so close we were almost touching. It was an electrifying feeling. We paused. Looking each other in the eye we inched closer, closer, closer still. I shut my eyes in hopeful anticipation. And then it happened. The most glorious of kisses, passionate, warm.

It went on and on, it offered hope and promise. It filled my entire being with life-giving endorphins. I never wanted it to end. But eventually, slowly, we pulled apart, then leant back in to give a reaffirming peck on the lips. We lay back on the cooling grass, enjoying the last few rays of sunshine. Listening to the birds singing in the trees along the edge of the Common, we watched as other sun worshippers packed up and started to make their way home. We lay there, smiling, holding hands and dreaming.

It's strange, I thought, *how different kisses can be and how different their meaning can be.* Thank goodness Ed was a good… no scrub that, a great kisser. I should have remembered that from the night we first met, but I had not. As we lay there I mused how strange it is that we have all sorts of subject and life lessons in school, but we are never taught how to kiss. We study maths to understand how to survive in our capitalist market. We study history to learn from the mistakes of our forefathers. We learn languages to communicate with, and understand, other cultures. We study science to make the world a better, healthier place. We even learn about reproduction in biology and sex education. And yet we never learn how to kiss, thereby leaving it to nature to determine where on the scale we are. From downright disgusting, like those who use their tongue to replicate the actions of a toothbrush, running their tongue over your teeth – not only wrong but also very awkward – to the other end of the scale: the ecstasy kiss, tongues clashing, lips locked, a pressure, an urgency, a rising of the blood in the loins, the desire. Ed's kiss.

Ed rolled onto his side, facing me, and I mirrored his actions.

"Can I be honest?" he asked, smiling sheepishly at me. "I'm not ready to call it a night yet. It's still early, do you fancy finding somewhere to get something to eat and making a night of it?"

Wow, I thought, *two meals on one date, or should that be two dates?* I couldn't think of anything, anything at all, that I would rather do than spend the evening with this amazing man. I didn't say this of course, I tried to sound relaxed and simply went with, "Yes, I'd love to."

We rose from the grass and as we made our way back into the town, Ed leant down and picked up my hand, a small, but significant romantic gesture. As we headed back to the square to find somewhere to get some food we chatted about everything and about nothing.

It sounded like the simplest of ideas, to find somewhere to eat, but in this small town, most places had shut after the Sunday lunch service and, save the illuminated menus on their exterior walls, the buildings were shrouded in darkness.

Luckily one of the quieter pubs, tucked away on a side street, was still open and had empty tables, so we made our way in. There were enough people enjoying an evening meal to give the place a bit of atmosphere, but not so many that it made conversation impossible, either due to the noise or the proximity of the diners at the next table.

We talked and talked, until eventually, and for the second time that day, we were conscious of being the only ones left in the pub. We paid the bill, actually Ed insisted on paying and I accepted graciously. We walked out into the cold night air. I now regretted not bringing a coat, but then when I had left home that morning I had no expectation that we would still be out so late, and on a school night.

We stood outside the pub in awkward silence, neither of us knowing where to go next. Every part of my being longed to be in his arms, to be engulfed in another passionate kiss, but this was not the right place for that, far too public. Even though the street outside was deserted, the staff in the pub were no doubt watching this uncomfortable situation unfurl.

"Shall I walk you home?" Ed asked tentatively.

"I would love that," I replied, possibly a little too eagerly, displaying my relief, excitement and happiness all at the same time.

"Which way?" he asked, laughing at me. We had been talking so long and being together felt so natural and so comfortable that I had forgotten he didn't know where I lived.

We set off but at a slow pace, neither one of us wanting to bring the night to an end, but both eagerly and nervously awaiting the time to part.

It was only a short stroll back to my cottage. I can remember every step as if it was yesterday. Strolling, hand in hand, occasionally making furtive glances at each other. At my front door, we turned to face each other.

"Thank you," I blurted out. "Thank you for an amazing day. It's been so great to catch up and..." I trailed off, not wanting to say too much or too little, not wanting to appear too keen or not keen enough. It had been a long time since I was last in the early heady days of a relationship and was hazy on the etiquette at this stage.

Ed leant down to me and whispered in my ear. His warm breath, his proximity made me shudder.

"Thank you too," he whispered.

I turned my face to him. One second, two seconds, three seconds. Time slowed. A millennium of time passed as we stared at each other. I could hardly breathe. Short, gasping breath. Expectant, oh so expectant. I could feel the long-suppressed desire rising hot and urgent inside me. All-consuming desire. And finally we released our pent-up need for each other. We kissed, a fury of tongues entwined, the sweetness of the taste of him, the passion of the embrace, his solid, strong body pressed against mine. I could feel my knees begin to tremble.

Finally, reluctantly, we dragged our unwilling, heaving bodies apart.

He took a step back, making it clear this ended on the doorstep. But he looked me in the eyes, holding both of my hands, and asked, "Can we do this again, soon?"

I nearly fainted with relief and excitement, and far too quickly and with little respect for the old-fashioned dating rules I gushed, "Yes, yes, that would be wonderful."

He pulled me back into him, holding me tight. We kissed once more and then, reluctantly, he turned and as he started walking down the path between the drive and the wild flower bed he turned. "I'll call you," he promised.

I stood and watched him go through the open wooden gate at the end of the path. He turned to close it, looked up and gave me a hearty wave, turned and was gone.

OMG, I thought as I unlocked the door and entered my little home. *OMG, what a day*. I flopped onto the sofa, tired but far too wired to sleep. As I sank into the soft cushions I felt, for the first time in ages, content. Happy at last in my own skin.

In truth it had been a long time since I had felt this way,

since I had felt happy being me. It was not just the lost loves, the bad jobs, the loneliness, the feeling of inadequacy when it came to my shape and my looks.

I don't believe for one minute that you need a partner to make you feel good about yourself, but sometimes I struggled, particularly when I was stressed and tired from not sleeping properly. I sometimes felt despair when I had to cope with so much on my own, because I worried that my friends would be tired of listening to my moans. Well, sometimes it all became too much and I would slip into the fog, struggling to find the goodness in life.

At times like that I referred to my happy list to remind me of what makes me smile, makes me happy, like:

- A riot of bright yellow daffodils in spring.
- Cuddles with my pet.
- The earthy, almost iron, smell as refreshing rain falls on baked, dry earth.
- Rainbows – my aunt believes they are loved ones looking down on you.
- Cherry blossom in spring.
- Curling up on the sofa in front of a roaring log fire in winter.
- Feeling the sun on my face.
- Barbecues and ice-cold white wine on a hot summer evening.
- Holidays.
- The sight of bright red poppies in a field of green corn.
- The sound of waves crashing onto the shore.
- The smell of a freshly opened jar of coffee.

Now, though, I didn't need my list, I had the glow of a new relationship. I wanted to be alive, to feel alive. I felt my lifeblood rising. I felt excited and terrified. I felt the adrenaline coursing through my veins.

four.

Lessons from the past

Then the wait began. I hadn't expected it, or anticipated it for that matter. It may have been some years since I had last dated, but I remembered that appearing overly keen is not the right move. But I hated the uncertainty, always had. My imagination would run wild – *He's changed his mind, he never really felt anything anyway, I don't care, oh, I do so care.* The thoughts swirled round and round in ever-decreasing, defeating circles. I was not physically wringing my hands but I felt like my stomach was tied in sickening knots.

I had, in the first few days, been convinced he would call, but as the days passed by, my confidence began to waver, then the doubt crept in, then the inevitable: I gave up hoping.

As much as I wanted to know one way or the other, I was resolute that I was not going to call or text him. But that didn't stop me checking my phone every few minutes just in case I had missed a notification. But I never did.

Work that week was particularly hard. Not that the work was as stressful as usual, not because of the long hours I put in or the workload I had to surmount. Hard though, because my mind was elsewhere and I couldn't afford it to be. The only joy that week was one morning, driving into work, with low mist hovering above the open fields, I spotted two majestic pheasants standing proud in the field bathed in early morning sunlight. I love nature. There is an idea about pheasants which is that they prove the theory of survival of the fittest, as the stupid ones foolishly believe they are more powerful than the mighty motor car and inevitably fail to make it across the road. The clever ones either wait for the cars to pass or simply fly over the road.

However, even that heart-warming moment on the way to work was not enough to distract me from my phone. In the end I did a deal with my colleague at the desk opposite me. My phone would go in her desk drawer at 9am and I could only check it halfway through the morning, at lunchtime and halfway through the afternoon, only getting it back at the end of the working day. None of that, of course, stopped me trying different tactics and excuses to check it more often, but luckily my colleague was more than happy to play along and made me wait until the allotted time. I think deep down she enjoyed the power. Whatever the reason it worked, and slowly I became more convinced that it really had all been part of my overactive imagination yet again. I was focusing better, throwing myself into my work, now more as a distraction than anything else.

And still nothing.

Monday became Tuesday.

Tuesday became Wednesday.

And still nothing.

Wednesday became Thursday and then despondency descended.

Just as well, I thought to myself as I walked the mile from work to where I parked my car. I didn't have to leave my car there, but it was better than sitting in traffic – stop, start, stop, start, crawling the last few yards into work. It was also relaxing and helped me set out in my mind my priorities for the work day ahead of me. And of course it was good for my fitness, my mental health and my waistline.

The walk back to the car at the end of the working day was equally good. Finally released from the shackles of my desk, it was good for unwinding and putting to bed any worries of the day and, of course, to stretch my legs after having been stuck in front of a computer all day.

That week, however, was different – none of the preparing for, or unwinding from, the days, this week my mind was preoccupied.

What did I say or do wrong? I asked myself. *How had I misread the signs again? Had he just been leading me on, unsure how to get out of it having met me again after all these years? What was wrong with me?*

Luckily by Thursday, though, I had mostly put this to one side, reminding myself of the promise not to subject myself to this again. Feeling safe and happy in my little cottage that night I poured a large glass of Pinot and settled back into the sofa to watch something that would entertain but not tax my brain in any way.

Bliss. My calm, even keel restored. *At least it didn't go any further before he changed his mind. That would have been so much worse*, I mused.

My reflections were rudely interrupted, my inner sanctum shattered, by the trill ring of my phone as a message was received.

My hand shot out and then stopped just short of the low coffee table in front of me where the phone lay. I leant further forward, resting my wine glass on the table and hesitating for a moment just staring at the phone. My logical, reasonable brain said, *It'll just be a bill update or notification of some sort.* But my heart was singing, *What if, what if it's Ed?*

I desperately wanted to look but I dreaded the disappointment. *Maybe I should leave it for a while, better to be hopeful than disappointed. Better not to know*, I thought.

All these thoughts tumbled through my mind, over and over. They tripped over each other and got muddled in the process. There was nothing else for it, I would just have to pick it up and find out one way or the other.

Hope or disappointment?

Disappointment or hope?

I held my breath as I picked the phone up. I could see it was a text message but couldn't make out who from. I unlocked my phone and the screen came to life.

I pressed the text button.

I yelped with joy. There, in front of me, I saw 'Ed' and the message read: 'Hey you! How's your week going?'

I had waited all this time, just a few days in anyone's book, but it felt like a lifetime when waiting to hear the news I was so desperately waiting for. And after all that waiting, just six words, no kiss, no 'shall we meet?', just six simple, noncommittal, unemotional, measly, simple words that you would send an acquaintance. Even a friend would get more than that, surely? Maybe I had been right all along and I had misread the situation. Maybe the kisses were down to me and not mutual after all. On the other hand, maybe he was not sure how to start this conversation. Maybe he had been struggling with the wording or unsure of how I was feeling and so started with a casual check-in. *Well, I will never know unless I reply*, I told myself.

The time received showed as just ten minutes ago. Was it too soon to reply? Would that look too keen? Would that look like I was waiting, waiting, hoping and praying he would get in touch? Which, in truth, was exactly what I had been doing, but that was not the message I wanted to send back.

I slowly started to craft my reply. Delete, delete, delete, delete. It took several attempts, a good few minutes before I sent an overly simple reply: 'All good, how are you?' There, he sent six, I replied with five. At this rate it might be a very short conversation, literally. *Back in your court*, I thought, surprised at myself for using a sporting analogy when I was the least sporty person alive.

I didn't have to wait long for a reply, but this time it was not the short bleep of a new text, but the sound of the phone ringing. I snatched the phone off the table, did a double check on the caller and with the biggest smile ever answered the phone.

"Hi, Ed, it's great to hear from you."

We talked for hours, again all the nervousness, confusion and concern drifting away after our initial exchange of pleasantries.

It turned out that Ed had resigned from his current job as soon as he went on shift on Monday and it had caused a flurry of activity. Firstly they had tried to keep him, offering training, promotion, more money. But Ed explained to them, and as he told me my heart soared, it was not just the promotion, the new challenge or the money, it was the opportunity of a new life and the possibility of a romance with someone who had always felt like the one that got away. I couldn't believe what I was hearing. There was no game play, no second guessing, no hoping or not knowing. He wanted to be with me. Simple. Clear.

With only a few months until he changed jobs his boss wanted to ensure they got the most out of him and that everything would be ready for a handover. That, he explained, was why he hadn't been in touch before. He wasn't sure if or when he would be able to get away and he didn't want to make promises he couldn't keep.

How amazing, how rare to have someone that genuinely seemed to care about the other person's feelings. I felt a tingle of excitement course through my body.

We also talked about my week so far. I left out the bits about my colleague guarding my phone and about how many times I had checked it each night. Instead I focused on my work and what I had achieved that week, including the fact that a conversation with a trade magazine editor had resulted in my organisation being commissioned to write a series of best-practice articles. It was a massive accolade to the reputation of the company and my boss had been thrilled. I had to quickly devise a plan for what we would cover in each edition, who would write it, edit it and sign it off in order to meet the publication deadlines.

We talked like we had never been apart. So open, so chatty, no awkward silences, no apprehension. Easy.

Natural. That was until we started to draw the conversation to a close. We both had work the next day and needed our sleep.

The tightness in my chest returned. Would he ask to see me? How do we end this?

"So, you," he said, "when can I see you this weekend?"

I hesitated. Clearly we were not playing games, but did I really want him to know that I had absolutely nothing in my diary other than cleaning the house, doing the weekly shop and generally doing chores? But why lie? Why pretend I had plans if all I wanted to do was see Ed, be with Ed, feel the warmth of his embrace, his kiss, his presence?

"Anytime," was my simple reply, delivered quietly and unconfidently. "Anytime," I repeated, hoping for a speedy and positive reply.

His voice matched mine, quietly and softly. "How about I take you out for dinner tomorrow and we go from there?"

I could hardly get my words out, I was so shocked with excitement. "Perfect," I said. "When and where?"

"I'll pick you up at 7pm if that is okay with you?" he said more confidently.

"Perfect," I replied, kicking myself for my short, repetitive responses that didn't do justice to the way I was feeling, but unable to order my mind into anything more eloquent.

"7pm tomorrow then," he whispered. "I can't wait," he continued.

"Me too, me too."

*

Friday I was at work. I went through the motions. I was there but it was all a bit hazy, like a dream sequence in a 1980s film. My mind was elsewhere. I was planning what to wear, what to say, imagining what might happen on this, our second date.

Luckily my boss left early on this particular Friday, and I was finally and thankfully able to give up the pretence of concentrating intently on proofreading a report. To be thorough, I always read a page forward, as a normal person would, to ensure the content makes sense. However, when you do that your brain usually fills in the next word in the sequence, making it hard to notice small errors like 'leant' instead of 'learnt'. So when I got to the end of the section I would reverse my direction and read backwards one word at a time to pick up formatting and spelling mistakes. Unfortunately I just couldn't focus for long enough to be certain I was spotting errors. After ten minutes I would realise I had not taken in any of the words and had to return to the beginning and start again.

By 4pm all I was able to do was tidy my desk and do some filing. It was an activity that was long overdue and provided me with the perfect excuse to disengage my brain from work. But without the need to focus my mind it wandered further and further from the workplace.

At 4.45pm I gave up altogether and slipped out the door before anyone noticed. I managed to escape unnoticed, not because of my stealth-like abilities but because those few that remained would shortly be heading in the same direction. Well, it was Friday after all.

I walked back to my car, twenty minutes in the heat. I hadn't thought this through. Now I was hot, sweaty and later than I needed to be if I had, for once, driven the whole way into work. Too late to change that now. I put the air conditioning on full blast and made a conscious effort to focus on every mile of the journey home along the pretty country roads. I smiled as I saw the fields of green crops, dappled with the bright red of the poppies that had seeded themselves across the open space.

Back at home, finally, I took a deep breath. I had an hour until Ed arrived. I fought the temptation to raid the fridge for a cold glass of Pinot, for courage of course. But I had learnt an important lesson on that some years before.

Yet another romance that didn't last the distance due to my incompetence when it comes to relationships. It had started online. We had liked each other's profiles and got chatting via email, safe and secure hidden behind the site's firewall and anonymity protocols until we were sure we wanted to take it further and exchanged phone numbers. Emails turned to texts, which turned to phone calls, which after a couple of weeks turned into a date.

We had arranged to meet in London after work on a Friday. At that point I was working half an hour outside the city, and Friday nights at work were when everyone let their hair down, let the week's stress dissolve – time to catch up with friends in different departments over a few drinks in the staff bar.

On this particular Friday I popped into the bar at work for a glass of Dutch courage before running for the train. Just the one, mind.

We met outside Costa on the concourse of Waterloo station. Very public, and I had told everyone I knew where we were meeting and who he was, just in case. He was every bit the man he had described in his profile, which was rare, really rare. One liar – let's not beat about the bush or hold back – said he had never been married, had no children and was of a similar age to me. The only truth on his profile was the fact that he was a man, although I didn't hang around long enough to check that fact out. He had recently had the stereotypical 'love' and 'hate' tattoos removed from his fingers. He was single but had been married and was living with his daughter and grandchild!

Another liar was the person who claimed to be taller than my diminutive five foot one and a half inches, and as he walked towards me I kept expecting him to get taller. But he never did.

Why do people lie on their profile? Eventually the truth will out.

Moan over, back to Costa at Waterloo. David was a tall, well-built, rugby-playing type, short dark hair, well spoken and well educated, in fact everything I had hoped for. We had a fantastic evening walking around London, popping into bars for a drink, having dinner and ending up in a club, as it was the only thing still open. We didn't dance, we found a quiet spot and a comfy sofa and sat drinking and talking until the small hours.

He was, actually, the perfect gentleman, hailing me a cab and giving me the money to get home – quite some distance out. Before I got into the cab we leant in for a brief but passionate kiss and a promise that he would call.

The following week we again met after work on Friday and again I had a glass of wine before leaving work. Only this time I let my nerves get the better of me and I'm ashamed to confess that I bought another drink on arriving at Waterloo.

At this stage of the evening I felt fine, just my tongue had been loosened and I didn't feel as nervous or as boring. However, just after we ordered our meal, I started to feel sick and it got stronger and stronger, eventually forcing me to apologise and go to the loo. It didn't help. On returning to the table, to a slightly concerned David, I apologised again and said I would have to leave, running out of the restaurant leaving this gentle giant to explain to the waiters that we wouldn't be eating after all. As I made my way home I realised that in fact I had a low blood sugar, an occasional occurrence for a type 1 diabetic, and that was what had been making me feel ill. I ate some glucose and started to feel better, but by then it was too late for the relationship. I never got the chance to explain. I never heard from him again. Another one had slipped through the net and this time it was a good one.

Back to the present

So on that night, my second date with Ed, I was not going to fall foul of the same misadventure. I did a blood test just to be sure and was reassured to find it in the normal range.

I headed up for my shower. Once clean and just as important cool, I set about picking an outfit. By the end, anyone would have been justified in thinking the house, or at least my bedroom, had been ransacked. There were clothes everywhere and worse still, I was starting to feel hot again. Time to calm down and think this through.

I sat on the edge of my pine double bed and surveyed the disaster around me.

He stopped to talk to me when I was wearing scruffy walking gear, I'm sure he won't mind what I wear tonight, I reassured myself.

I bent down and picked up the second item I had tried on, a black and white princess-cut dress with thin straps, a bodice that emphasised my one asset (or should that be two) and then a long flowing skirt. I selected some black, high-wedged-heel canvas shoes – not exactly the most fashionable but very comfortable nonetheless, and they did give my calves a good shape, should my skirt ever have occasion to rise up during the night's escapades. And of course they would raise me up closer to Ed's gorgeous lips and addictive kiss.

Dressed, with Oscar de la Renta *eau de parfum* dabbed on my wrists and chest, and with my face covered in war paint, I headed downstairs to wait and to practise looking cool rather than the desperately eager person I was feeling.

My hands were sweating. In truth I felt my face burning up, sweat beading on my brow. I was shaking slightly. *A glass of wine would really help right now*, I thought. *Short term only though*, I remonstrated with myself and turned on the TV to distract myself. It was a solution, of sorts, and at least it helped pass the time.

7pm came and went and my heart sank. Surely he couldn't have bailed at this point, or was he being fashionably late?

I didn't have to wait long. My phone trilled, shaking me back into reality. I glanced at the screen with trepidation. It was Ed. I unlocked the screen. It was a text. It was short, to the point and a complete relief as it read, 'Sorry, I'm on my way, I'll be there soon.'

OMG, I thought, *I'm not sure I like this rollercoaster. I'm not sure I can put myself through this again, not after the last time.*

With Fred 2, of course, the rollercoaster had been the same – the ecstatic highs, plummeting to the depressive lows and everything in between. With Fred 2, however, the first proper date had been more of a surprise. He had gone to the music festival with the boys, so I hadn't expected to see any of them that weekend.

I was curled up on the sofa watching TV on the Saturday night. I was a little sad about not going out, but I had a glass of wine in hand. I was surprised when there was a knock at the door, but not overly concerned about my shabby appearance given everyone was away. I opened the door and there in front of me were my mates all beaming at me and in the centre was Fred 2.

They piled into my front room. At that point I was living in the ground floor flat of a large Victorian villa on the edge of the city. I had my own front door, although the other flats had a communal entrance on the other side of the property. I had two very small rooms at the front – a study and a spare room, only large enough to squeeze in a bed but no room to walk around it, let alone have any additional furniture. There was a tiny kitchen with half-height, cowboy-film, wooden, swinging bar doors. Next was a massive sitting room, with a large bay window overlooking the garden – not that I ever went out there. Down in the basement were the bedroom and bathroom, but I had long since moved out of the bedroom as the mould took over.

It had started as mould on the back of the wardrobe and spread to my clothes. There were large mushrooms growing out of the carpet near the emergency exit window, and the last straw was when it started growing on my bed and I developed a permanent cold. At that point I saved what clothing I could and started sleeping on a fold-down futon in my living room. Luckily it was not my job to fix the problem as I was renting the flat which, other than the health issues it presented, I liked as it was convenient for work, friends, shops and bars, plus I couldn't afford to move.

As the boys settled in they explained that the venue was flooded so they decided to come home for beers instead. And here they were, full of beans and happiness, and looking at me to join them.

I quickly changed (in the privacy of the spare room), threw on some makeup and was ready to join the party.

Fred 2 and I had kissed on that fateful night when we first met and we had stayed the night together – not that anything physical happened, we had just fallen asleep, while talking, curled up in each other's arms.

The following week we talked every night on the phone and he had promised I would see him one Saturday. In hindsight I think that because I was younger and was more confident, I was more inclined to believe what he said. Also, as my friends were involved and he was theoretically staying with them, it never occurred to me that he would lie or let me down, well, not at that stage.

Following the unexpected turn of events on the first time we met and the unexpected second meeting, then it became very expected. We saw each other the next weekend, and the next, and our relationship developed and our feelings deepened, and then the rollercoaster started.

Back to the present

But on that day, as I sat waiting for Ed to turn up, the rollercoaster was already at full speed and I was experiencing the terrifying highs and stomach-churning lows. How much I could take was yet to be seen, but for now I was excited, I was almost trembling with anticipation. I couldn't stop smiling.

I was brought back to the present from my ruminations by a loud, confident knock at the door.

My beaming smile was mirrored by the face that greeted me when I opened the heavy oak door to Ed.

"Evening," I said, stepping aside to let him in to my cottage-style front room.

"Evening," he said, pausing to plant a cheeky kiss on my cheek, instantly putting one of my fears to bed. Clearly we both knew the direction this evening would go and immediately relaxed.

I practically flew across the room, I was so excited, like a giddy child who had an ice cream in one hand and a bunch of brightly coloured balloons in the other, skipping through the park on a sunny afternoon with my family and looking forward to the walk around the lake; feeding the ducks, looking out for squirrels and when the ice cream was finished, holding on tightly to my father's hand.

That was how I was feeling as Ed took a seat on the sofa, leaving plenty of room for me to settle in beside him. But one thing at a time, first it really was time for that drink.

I poured us both a large glass of chilled Pinot Grigio. My favourite white wine is a Chablis or at least a petit Chablis, but they were both more than my budget would allow, not that I'm a skinflint, but it's nice to sometimes keep something as a treat, something to look forward to.

I carried the glasses through to the sitting room, handing a glass to Ed, who took it and thanked me. I curled my feet up under me as I took the spot next to him on the sofa.

"To your good health," I said, still unable to wipe the inane grin off my face.

"And yours," he said. He lifted the large, heavy wine glass in acknowledgement, pausing for a moment before putting it to his succulent lips and taking in a considerable gulp. To my great relief he swallowed silently. There is nothing that annoys me more than noisy eaters and drinkers. How can you make such a din just swallowing a mouthful of liquid? Enough of my gripes, Ed was not a 'urg-urph-umer'. The only noise in fact was an almost audible sigh as the nectar slipped down his broad, manly neck. Clearly he had been waiting for a tipple as much as I had. To confirm this he said, "Ahhhh, that's good, I've been looking forward to this, oh, and of course seeing you, all day," he added in haste.

I laughed at his awkwardness and to show him no offence had been taken. His face relaxed and we started chatting in a more natural way.

He was obviously unable to go into details about his work, but by all accounts it had been a challenging few days even for an experienced officer. He had been late in arriving at my home which, he hastened to point out, he hated. I mentally chalked up another massive tick in Ed's book, not that I was keeping a record, not yet anyway. I'm unsure where my hatred of tardiness originated from.

It could be because my parents were late for everything, which inevitably resulted in the blame game rolling into an argument, followed by apologies to our hosts when we turned up late, again. I, on the other hand, made it a point to be early for everything. If I hit traffic the palpitations would start as I recalculated the timings in my head to reassure myself I would still make it on time.

I guess as a police officer, being punctual must be an important factor and characteristic. He explained that, on this occasion, his lateness had been due to having to complete the tedious recording of everything that had happened during an investigation. He could not, would not, leave without completing his duty, no matter how much he hated being late.

I forgave him, obviously. In truth there really was nothing to forgive.

As we sipped our wine, now relaxing into the evening, no longer feeling the need to gulp down the anaesthetic wine, I talked a bit about my day. It seemed foolish, or even childish, somehow to talk about the mundane office-based jobs I had been doing when he had, for all I knew, been putting his life at risk. I hoped, as we sat chatting, that one day he might be able to confide in me more, to let me into that part, the bigger part, of his life. Maybe with time that would change. For now though, it would have to wait, and as we had a table booked at a restaurant in town we finished our drinks and made our way there.

As we walked, hand in hand, Ed stiffened up a little and I asked if everything was okay.

"Ah. Well. There is something that I should mention. It's a little awkward but I think it best to get it out in the open at the start of the evening. You know, in case I need to do anything about it."

I could have curled up and died. My heart was racing, my palms began to sweat. *What on earth is this confession going to be?* I thought. Just a matter of minutes before I had been praying he would be able to confide in me, and here he was about to do exactly that and I was rapidly turning into a hedgehog, rolled up in a ball.

He pulled my hand, bringing me to a stop, and turning in to me he smiled reassuringly.

"You see," he continued, "I still live up North, I don't move down for another month or so and obviously was hoping we would have a few drinks and see where the night takes us. I thought about booking a room in a local hotel, but it turns out there's only one in town and it's full. I…"

I could see he was starting to flounder and luckily I could see where this was heading. Calmness returned. I smiled reassuringly, almost laughing at his nervousness. I put my palm flat against his hard chest for reassurance and said, "You can stay with me. If you would like to of course?"

Ed had obviously been holding his breath, as I felt him let out the most almighty sigh, at the end of which he replied, "Yes, I'd like that, I'd like that a lot."

I was relieved he had broached the subject so early in the date. It got it out of the way, we both knew where we stood and now we could relax without the impending awkward moment on the front doorstep at the end of the evening. It did of course beg the question as to where he had stayed after our last date. But there was no point looking back, tonight was all about the future.

Ed had booked one of the high-street Italian chains.

I understood his choice. We had eaten at the Turkish and a pub before so it made sense to try somewhere new. The restaurant was on the corner of two streets in the town centre, with windows on three sides giving it a commanding view of people coming and going. And besides, beyond the opportunity for people-watching that it provided, the food was always delicious and there were lower-carb choices so I didn't have to break my low-carb rules. The atmosphere was also good. It was not one of those noisy places where diners had to compete to be heard. It meant we could continue our conversation, catching up on life, who we were, our loves and pet hates.

Our loves chimed – long walks, warm fires, family, the smell of a barbecue, sunshine and spring flowers.

Our pet hates were also in line, from rude drivers who didn't say thank you when you went out of your way to let them in, or being cut up by equally ignorant and unobservant drivers. Bins not being collected on time, potholes that remain unfilled even when a crew has been out and filled in all the holes around it.

We talked about his ex-wife and how he genuinely felt happy to see her so happy. He shared stories about his son, funny anecdotes from his childhood and how proud he was of all that he had achieved. That he never let adversity get him down. He battled through any obstacles put in his way in order to achieve his goals. Ed described how alike they were, both in personality and in looks, and how even in a crowd of people they were easily identifiable as father and son.

He admitted, with genuine sadness in his voice, how he sometimes regretted not having more children. But his goddaughter helped and as they were all really close it was almost like having a second child.

The questioning now turned to me. Had I ever wanted children? It felt like a slightly edged question, so I paused for a moment to gather my thoughts before opening up. "Yes, but in all honesty the opportunity has never arisen. Obviously I've been in relationships before, but none of them lasted the distance. In truth I always thought that by now I would be married with children, living happily in a little cottage." *Well, one out of three is not bad*, I thought to myself. I had been smiling the whole time I spoke, not wanting him to either be worried by what I said, or even worse, feel sorry for me. *I hope he doesn't think I'm desperate*, I thought, before shrugging as I finished off, "Fate had other ideas."

I looked down at my hands, avoiding eye contact, a little concerned I may have said the wrong thing and uncertain of how we got here, or for that matter how we would get out of it.

Ed reached across the table, moving the tiny flower pot that housed a fake, pink flower and the candle that spent more time extinguished than alight, and took my hand in his.

"Fate has a lot to answer for," he said softly, looking into my eyes, "after all, it separated us too soon after we first met. Then again, it's not all bad, as I'm pretty sure fate played a large role in us meeting again last weekend. Maybe fate can provide a rocky path at times, often without clear directions, but at other times it will give a massive…" and at this point Ed let go of my hands, opening his arms up wide to indicate how massive, almost taking out an innocent waitress carrying food to a nearby table. He did all this while saying, "… sign, that says, 'here you are and here is where you're going' and for that," Ed picked up my hands again, "I, for one, am really grateful."

Phew, disaster averted. We sat there in silence for a moment, only letting go of each other when our food arrived.

I'm always nervous eating in front of others. I have a terrible habit of being clumsy and often drop food on, what as others have described as, my ample breasts. I was extra careful this evening, not wanting to make myself look like the type of person you really didn't want to be seen in public with. For all the good and positive signs earlier in the evening, I was still a little on edge that somehow I would end up ruining it as I had done so often before.

I laughed slightly and Ed, looking up from his meal, asked what I was chuckling about.

"Well, I probably shouldn't tell you this as you'll get a bad and lasting impression of me," I said, still laughing.

"Go on," he said slowly and cautiously.

"Well, I'm a little bit, well, actually a lot, clumsy."

Ed looked amused and encouraged me to tell more.

"Well, there was one time when I was in the office, I was sitting in a high-backed wheeled chair which had no arm rests. I was working on a project and accidentally dropped something on the floor next to me. Now, most normal people would stand up, bend down, from the knees of course, and pick it up. Not me. Without a second thought, I leant over the side of the chair, stretching down to pick up the piece of paper. But as I reached, and stretched, I guess I overbalanced the chair and the next thing I knew I was on the floor, chair still under my bum, and I was rolling around in fits of laughter. Luckily my colleague at the next desk also found it hilarious and just managed to ask if I was okay through her fits of laughter, but I don't think I ever really lived it down."

Ed's first reaction was to look concerned either at my complete lack of common sense or out of a duty to care for my wellbeing. Either way, his face began to soften and he soon joined me in laughing at the recollection.

There were many more examples of my clumsiness, but that would have to do for tonight.

The conversation continued to flow as we finished our meal, drank our wine and enjoyed each other's company.

Ed was, as expected, a true gentleman, picking up the bill despite my offers to go Dutch. We walked slowly back towards my house, arm in arm. No need to make a pretence of extending the evening by going to the pub. No need to make excuses to stay together for longer. No need because we knew we had all night and, as it turned out, most of the weekend as well.

It was getting dark as we walked up the path. The witching hour. There was something magical about this time of night and something was definitely in the air. You could feel the electricity sparking and jumping between us. Our bodies were touching in as many places as was possible as we walked side by side, the hairs on my arm standing to attention as the tingle spread throughout my body.

As we entered through the front door I flicked on the lights. Ed mirrored my actions, but in reverse, switching the lights back off. As he softly closed the door behind us he pulled me into his arms. We stood there in silence, staring into each other's eyes. Our bodies now touching all the way from shoulder to toe. I could feel his chest heaving beneath his shirt. Smelt his aftershave. I closed my eyes, every sense alert to his presence. It felt like forever, the tension growing, the addictive sense of anticipation growing to a crescendo. And then it exploded. Our lust was unleashed. We were tongues, arms, hands. We were eating each other alive like we hadn't eaten for a month and the only thing that could sate our appetite was the other person. We drank each other in like we had been walking in a desert for an eternity and the other person would provide the succour we needed.

Now, I wouldn't describe myself as a prude, but nor am I a 'kiss and tell' kind of girl either, so I'm afraid that I'm not going to spell out exactly what happened next. So, I will cut to the next morning.

five.

Letting the sunshine into my life

In my humble opinion there is nothing better in the world than slowly waking up to find a warm, strong body spooning behind me. I smiled and pushed back into Ed's body. His arms pulled tightly around me, squeezing me, conveying his reassurance and happiness.

"Good morning, gorgeous," he whispered into my ear.

Gorgeous, he called me gorgeous, I screamed inside my head. It had been years since anyone had called me that, let alone since I had actually felt gorgeous.

"Morning, handsome," I purred in response.

We lay there, our bodies entwined, snuggling into each other until our senses, newly invigorated by sleep, awoke and nature once more drove our bodies to find ecstasy in each other.

We whiled away the morning in pretty much the same fashion, taking restorative naps followed by reawakening our passion. Finally, sated, we showered. Not together unfortunately, my shower just was not big enough.

Ed and I sat down at the breakfast bar. He tucked into

some toast and whilst bread is definitely not part of my low-carb diet, I decided that after the night's activities my body needed to replenish some of the lost energy, but what a way to lose it. I had made some strong coffee. I cupped my hands around the warm round bowl of a mug, looking up to take in the sight of Ed devouring his food.

We didn't say it, we didn't need to. We just knew that we wanted to be together, to be in each other's company. Inevitably we would have to part, but for now, it was just now. Just us. No one and nothing but us.

Having spent the last fourteen hours in bed we felt the need to get out of the house for a while. Not that we had much energy, but we needed a change of scene, and more than that we needed time to rebuild our energy and prepare for what more was to come.

We held hands as we headed into the noise, the hustle and bustle of town on a Saturday. The market was in full swing. "Two pahnd a paahnd, two pahnd a paahnd, strawbebberies, two pahnd a paahnd," the greengrocer was shouting. The smell from the fishmongers was pungent on that sunny day. It was enough to turn the stomach, but even that didn't dent my happiness. The flower stall was a riot of colours, scents, shapes and sizes. People perused the choices before making their selections and walking away with arms full of flowers wrapped up in brown paper.

Each stall provided its own feast for the senses. A stall selling pork products had a sideline in selling hot food – burgers, bacon or sausage rolls. The ironmonger's array of new and old tools scattered across trays on the paved market square. Coffee stalls, clothes, footwear, jewellery, every requirement catered for.

Away from all of this we started the gentle climb to the next village. The path separated from the road, rising above it, sheltered from the noise by a covered walkway, shrouded by trees and bushes. It was quiet. I could hear my heart beating, not from the exertion of the walk but from the proximity of our bodies. We didn't talk much, both so content just to be next to each other, happy in that moment, our moment, our bubble.

We weaved our way up to the top of the hill, pausing at the top to look back across the town with the stunning church spire rising high above it. It looked so peaceful down there, the noise of the market dispersed in the distance between us. Holding hands we drank in the view and appreciated the cooling breeze, before turning back to the path and continuing on through the village, which was more of a sleepy hamlet.

We passed the tiny red brick church, barely more than the size of a large front room. It had a turret with grey slates rather than a spire. On we trod to the meeting room, a small, modern building set back from the road next to the children's play area.

We turned away from the road onto a footpath that meandered around a field and turned us back towards the town. There had been little or no rain for over a week and the path was dry. With a crop of green corn rising from the dark brown earth on one side and a thick, prickly hedgerow on the other, we were forced to walk in single file. Ed took the lead, holding back branches that overhung the path and letting me pass through. We walked on in silence across two fields until we came to a small copse that provided some shelter from the sun and from any eyes that might be watching our progress.

I felt a shiver traverse my entire body as Ed came to a halt in front of me. Turning slowly he beamed down at me, putting his arms around my waist and back and drew me in close and we started to kiss. At first slowly, lovingly, like old lovers, tongues tied in our protected world. But as time ticked by the kiss became harder, more passionate, more urgent. We sank to our knees and lay down in the long grass, providing more screening from the path, creating our own world. Nothing and no one else existed right at that moment. We were pulling at each other's clothes, desperate to be united once more.

Sometime later, sated and curled up in each other's arms, Ed gently kissed my nose, a small touch that was so intimate and hinted at a relationship much longer and further developed than just this one amazing week. He suggested we reluctantly move on. I could have stayed there forever but Ed was right, we needed to finish the walk. I smiled at him and gently I said, "Thank you, this last twenty-four hours have been the best and happiest of my life." I felt self-conscious having said too much and looked away. Ed lifted my head by placing his hand under my chin and tilting it up. He bent his head down to meet mine and kissed me.

"Me too," he whispered, our faces still so close I felt the breath of the words on my lips.

Then he leapt to his feet, proffering a hand to help me up. We straightened up our clothes, giggling like teenagers as we did so and then, hand in hand, made our way home. My home, our home, my mind was ablaze with possibility.

Sitting outside in the garden surrounded by the heady scent of the flowers that fringed my garden, *I really should learn their names*, I thought.

When I had been creating the garden, transforming the muddy mess I had inherited from the previous owner, I had trawled garden centres every weekend buying plants that made me happy; colours and shapes that worked with what I had already planted. Pinks and purples and whites of every shade and hue that had its place, short at the front, tall at the back. At least I had taken the time to read the label to see how tall they would grow to. The colour scheme was designed to stand out against the greenery of the shrubs that would eventually grow to fill the borders. I felt so at peace, so happy, so blessed.

And so went on that special first weekend together. We were barely out of each other's arms. When we were it was because we had a need to, not just the obvious visits to the bathroom, but also to cook. But when we were eating we were touching, when we were walking we were touching, when we made love we touched in entirety. We melted into each other's being, becoming one and staying as one as often and for as long as our energy would allow.

The following afternoon, drinking tea, again on the loungers, soaking up the sunshine in the garden, my fears began to rise in my chest. I wanted the weekend to go on forever. But inevitably, as Sunday afternoon drew to a close, Ed turned serious on me.

"I have to go, I'm so sorry. I would like nothing more than to stay with you but I have work tomorrow and it's just too far to commute," he said with genuine regret.

"I know," I replied softly. "I had hoped this moment would never come, but I know you have to go."

I watched, solemnly, as Ed neatly folded and packed his clothes into his overnight bag. I walked, solemnly, as we made our way downstairs. I waited, solemnly, at the front door as he put on his coat and joined me. We kissed, savouring every last moment. I stayed in Ed's embrace, feeling his strong arms filling me with strength.

Eventually we eased apart, ruefully, solemnly.

"I'll call you when I get home," he promised as he walked out of the door.

"Drive safely," I called after him as he strode down the path. Now that we had to part there was no point in making it worse or prolonging it.

He paused as he closed the gate. He looked up, gave me a hearty smile and a wave that neither of us was really feeling. And then he was gone.

I lingered by the door. I don't know why, maybe somewhere deep inside I was hoping to see him come running back along the path and into my arms once more. But he didn't.

I found myself at a loss as to what to do with myself now. The house was different, oddly quiet, empty, lonely and cold, not something I had experienced before in my beautiful home. I felt ill at ease and knowing Ed wouldn't be calling for a couple of hours I decided to go for a walk into town to see if there was anything happening that might distract me from my thoughts.

It didn't work. The shops were long since shut and the town didn't really have much of an atmosphere on Sunday evening. It didn't fill me with joy as it usually did, apart from the people enjoying the evening sunshine on the Common – families having picnics, friends playing football, couples cosying up to each other despite the openness of the space. *No, this isn't helping*, I thought, and trudged back to the house.

As I sat in front of the TV, some programme lighting up the room, I was neither watching it nor taking in what was happening. Instead I was tuned in to my emotions. I was so excited and nervous. Naturally my fears grew as the hours passed and there was no news from Ed.

I'm not pessimistic by nature, I always try to see, or at least look for, the good in any situation. I'm a glass half full, not half empty type of person. But I had been here before both emotionally and relationship-wise. I knew these feelings and they scared me. Maybe if I had been luckier in matters of the heart before then I would be more relaxed and savour this moment, but I couldn't. My father used to say that I wore my heart on my sleeve, and now I was sitting, alone, on my sofa, reviewing everything I had said, and cringing at some of it, allowing myself to sink into pessimistic thoughts about the outcomes of those mistakes. In truth I had good reason to be like this.

I didn't want to think something bad had happened, but equally I didn't want to believe that he had changed his mind about calling me, even if briefly to let me know he got home safely. Eventually, and to my enormous relief, the phone rang.

"Hello, you," I purred as I answered.

"Hello, you," he said softly in reply. "I'm so sorry it's taken me so long to call you. It's okay, nothing happened on the journey back, that was remarkably quiet and straightforward. No, it's what happened when I got home that kept me from calling."

My heart was in my mouth, fearing the worst that he had been burgled or there had been bad news of some sort. But Ed's tone was light, as if he was smiling, so I reassured myself that it couldn't be anything terrible.

"Do tell me," I said. "The suspense is killing me."

"Well, as I walked through the door, phone in hand to call you…"

Good sign, I thought.

"The phone rang," he continued, "and it was my son, Dan, he sounded rather excited and asked if he could come around, so of course I said yes. I could have given you a quick call while I was waiting for Dan to arrive to let you know I was ok, but I really wanted to chat without rushing, I hope that was ok?"

"Of course," I assured him, the fact that he wanted to chat after spending the whole weekend with me filled me with joy.

Ed continued his story. Clearly some great and important news had been imparted during that visit, as his voice was bursting with pride and happiness.

"Dan arrived with Emma, his girlfriend. They were holding hands and beaming from ear to ear as they walked up to the front door where I was already waiting for them. As they passed me I happened to notice Emma's hand and was so thrilled to see a gleaming diamond ring on the third finger of her left hand. *Good news indeed*, I thought, but I didn't let on I knew, as I could tell they wanted to tell me themselves otherwise they would have told me over the phone.

"I offered them drinks which we took out into my courtyard garden. As we sat down Dan turned all serious so I tried to mirror his mood, but it was so hard, given I knew what he was about to say.

"'Dad', he said, 'we have just come from Emma's parents where I asked them if I could take their daughter's hand in marriage.' At this point all three of us gave up the pretence of being serious and beamed at each other. Dan continued, 'Luckily they both said yes, as you can see.' At that point Emma lifted her left hand with her fingers pointing down to show off the ring. I don't know much about rings, it's been a while since I bought one, but it looked pretty and modest, I would say.

"'So, Dad,' Dan said, getting all serious again, 'Emma and I wanted to check that you approve as well.' I have to confess that I felt very proud of my son. We've had our ups and downs as a family and yet here he was being very traditional and respectful. It almost moved me to tears."

Ed paused and I let out my breath, then gushingly responded, "What wonderful news, congratulations to you and to them of course, you must all be so, so happy."

"We are," he replied. "They told me they were going on to see my ex-wife, Dan's mother, Clare," he stumbled over the words, "after they told me, so I didn't want to keep them too long, just offering to support them in any way they needed, they only had to ask. There is no date set for the wedding, for now they are just happy to be engaged and are enjoying that.

"As they were leaving Emma asked me if I'd had a good weekend. She had rather a wicked twinkle in her eyes as she asked and I have to confess I rather let it all out of the bag, telling them how amazing a time I had had. I hope you don't mind?"

"Of course not." What else could I say? I felt a glow of happiness. Not only had he told me he'd had an amazing weekend but he also told his son and future daughter-in-law. *Wow*, I thought, the weekend had gone even better than I had dared to hope.

Ed continued, "Dan and Emma are both really excited about meeting you soon…" He trailed off, now sounding a little more uncertain, maybe that he had gone too far in making assumptions about the future and the direction of our relationship.

"I can't wait to meet them," I reassured him. I genuinely wanted to meet the people who meant the most to him.

"Wonderful," he said, the confidence returning to his voice. "We'll have to arrange it when I'm down this weekend. Oh, that is if you would like to see me?"

"Of course I would, in fact I would like nothing more than to see you this weekend." My whole body let out a metaphorical sigh as all my dreams started falling into place.

We chatted on for another half hour before realising the time and the need for sleep before work the next day.

This is going to be a very long week, I thought as I curled up, alone, in my king-size bed, pulling the pillow that smelt of Ed in close to my body for warmth and comfort. *Yes*, I thought as I was drifting off to sleep, *this is going to be a long week*.

six.

Not all relationships are created equal

Not all relationships start with such promise. There had certainly been those that satisfied the basic human need to be in a relationship but nothing more than that. Fred 3 had been such a relationship.

Looking back, with the gift of hindsight, it was a complete waste of time, emotion and, as it turned out, money. Why I ever started seeing him was anyone's guess. Mine would be that I was lonely. All my friends were in relationships and I felt increasingly left out as they did more and more couple socialising.

I was out for after-work drinks one Friday and Fred 3 was cracking on with my diminutive, beautiful, funny and flirty colleague. She was not interested. It was not the age difference; Fred 3 was ten years older than me so at least fifteen years older than my friend. The issue was that she was already in love and obviously not with Fred 3.

Having failed with my first friend he had moved on to the second, a beautiful, lithe blonde – an incredibly friendly, easy-going and insightful person. She had quickly got the measure of Fred 3 and made her excuses, plus she was also in a relationship with a man she had previously loved and lost and was determined not to make the same mistake again.

So that left me. Stupid, gullible, lonely me. And I fell for it. Not the charm, there really was none of that in evidence. Not the looks, they were pretty thin on the ground, as was his hair. He was of average height, slender, but with a rapidly developing beer-induced pot belly, his bald scalp accompanied by grade-one-cut greying hair covering the rest of his head. These in themselves wouldn't necessarily negate a relationship, I have never been driven by looks, but in this case Fred 3's personality didn't make up for the lack of attraction. So why, oh why did I waste so much time and effort on this hopeless case? Loneliness. Loneliness and the need to save people, not in a superhero type of way, but send me the lonely, the lost, the sad, the unconfident, the ones that put up a front to hide behind, the hurt – mentally and emotionally. All my life I had been attracting this type of man and they had always been my downfall. As soon as I had fixed one of them, they moved on. Within weeks or months of deciding I was not worth marrying they were engaged to someone else. Go figure.

Back to the waste of space that was Fred 3, or as my family named him 'the unmentionable'. Deep down I knew what he was, but chose not to see it, at first. Within weeks he had all but moved in. He just stopped going back to his flat. He was entertaining, I will give him that. But soon he 'lost his job' as he put it and seemed in no hurry to get a new one. I offered help with job applications, but he never seemed to get any interviews let alone offers. He occasionally took casual labour jobs, but even those didn't last. I paid for everything, even giving him money to go out with his mates just so I could get some peace and quiet.

Most people may consider this evidence of my gullibility, but the sequence of events didn't all happen at once. It snuck up on me in stages over a few months until I was trapped. He needed fixing, he had a lot of issues. Boy did he have his issues.

Some years later, I'm afraid to confess, I had finally had enough of his 'thinness' – thin in mind, thin in ambition, thin financially, thin physically and thin-spirited. Luckily for me Fred 3 aided my escape plan by pinning my friend up against a wall and trying to kiss her whilst her boyfriend and I were ahead of them walking into a pub.

A week later, over dinner, my friend confessed what had happened. She had told her boyfriend straight away and they had agreed I needed to know. They were right, although interestingly they waited until after we had finished eating the homemade lasagne, followed by the shop-bought lemon tart I had served up to everyone. I'm not sure, maybe the alcohol I had plied my guests with had loosened tongues as it so often does.

I kicked Fred 3 out of the house that night. Sobbing on the doorstep he had tried everything. "But I'll get a job", "But I will get counselling", "But I was going to ask you to marry me," he claimed. That was the last straw and I slammed the door on him.

If any of what he said had been true he would have done it before now. If it were true, he wouldn't have cheated on me. If it were true, he wouldn't have run up massive phone bills calling sex lines whilst I slept in the room above.

At the end of the day it didn't matter if it was true or not. It was over. I was done. The mockery of a relationship was finished. Until now I had not realised how angry I still was about all that. Let it go.

Back to the present

Thinking back on disastrous relationships was doing me no good. It might be passing the time but it was not good for my mood or for my mental state. *If Ed calls now*, I thought late on Tuesday evening, *I certainly will not be the best company*.

Luckily by the time he did call I was feeling much better, given I had been watching a comedy on the TV and wishing Ed was sitting on the sofa next to me and laughing at the programme, and also probably at me.

We spoke, Ed and I, every night that week, finding out more about each other, deepening our bond. Every day a rollercoaster of anticipating the call, the ecstasy of the call, the pit of emptiness after the call finished and the prospect of a lonely bed and another twenty-two hours before we spoke again. At least I managed to sleep that week, some much needed, blissful sleep, and for once work was a dull roar rather than all-out panic stations.

I'm an organised person. I like to plan out my work to ensure I hit deadlines and, as much as possible, even out the work flow so it's never feast or famine. But that never seemed to work out in this job. Despite planning out the week there was always some crisis that would come crashing down and throw everything into disarray. I had long since learnt to distinguish between hard (immoveable) and soft (moveable) deadlines.

This week seemed calmer than most. I'm not sure if that was due to Ed's influence, or because I was looking forward to the weekend so much that I was not letting anything distract me from the pleasure and anticipation of what was to come. I sailed through the week, completing tasks, being proactive, being busy and always smiling.

My colleagues were noticing that something had changed. By Thursday I could see they were getting close to interrogating me. Not that I'm usually miserable or unfriendly, I get on well with everyone, but they could see there was something I was not telling them and yet I felt ready to burst. I thought about skipping lunch, but I knew they would make time to find out what was going on if I didn't join them, so I did.

Lunch in the canteen was always a bit of a risk. Not because it made you ill, it was usually very tasty. It was more a case of pot luck. I liked to try to stick to a light lunch, so salad, but sometimes the prepared salad either had some strange protein like goat's cheese or it was full of carbs like potato or pasta. On those days I had to hope one of the hot options was low carb and I could pair it with vegetables. As long as I felt full I could make it through the afternoon. The temptation, if not, was always to break the diet and go for some terribly delicious and totally sinful cake mid-afternoon.

Lunch on that day was good – a healthy, hearty salad bowl topped with salami – and as the sun was out we took over a couple of the picnic tables on the grass outside.

There was a moment's silence as we picked up our knives and forks. Not a moment of silent prayer or contemplation of the food we were about to enjoy, more a girding of the loins before the interrogation began.

Sarah was the first to break the silence. "So, are you going to tell us what's changed this week or are we going to have to…?" she asked inquisitively, a forkful of jacket potato hovering near her mouth for dramatic effect, but now uncertain how to end this line of enquiry in this politically correct world, she popped the food in her mouth, cutting herself off.

My other colleagues gave each other furtive glances and then turned to me. "Well?" they all chimed, not quite in perfect harmony, but with friendly smiles illuminating their faces and their eyes.

I took my time finishing the mouthful of salad I was eating, building the tension. No one, I noticed, had eaten anything else. I suddenly felt like I was back at PGL camp, huddled in the middle of our tent in the Brecon Beacons telling ghost stories to pass the time, my fellow campers, and friends, huddled around me, spellbound by the eerie tales.

Yet here I was all these years later, at work, in the sunshine, about to embark on another tale. Whether they would be spellbound was yet to be determined.

I clinked my knife and fork down onto my plate for dramatic effect, making it clear I was preparing to start. As I did everyone else resumed eating. *Lucky mine's a salad*, I thought.

"What do you want to know?" I teased, and was met with raised eyebrows that told me they wouldn't be fobbed off, fooled or made to wait any longer.

"His name's Ed," I beamed, deciding to get right to the point given I would give up the information eventually and lunch was only an hour long. "He's a policeman, gorgeous, intelligent, funny and we've only just started seeing each other so it's early days but I'm very, very, very happy." I finished with a flourish and picked up my cutlery to resume eating my lunch.

"That we can see," Sarah said. "So how did you meet? I didn't even think you were in the market for someone new, not after the last one…" Again she trailed off. Everyone around the tables knew how that had ended – bitterly. Tears. Frustration. Anger. Despair. Betrayal. Another cheater, another one who let me save them only to abandon me when I needed support myself. But he was not going to ruin this moment like he had done so many others.

"I know, I know," I began slowly, still reeling from the memory Sarah had invoked, but picking up speed as we returned to Ed. "That's the strange thing, I wasn't looking and I certainly wasn't looking where I found him."

Everyone around the table looked confused.

I had finished eating and sat back a little on the bench, settling in to tell a synopsis of what had happened. These were work colleagues after all and some things were better not shared.

"We actually met many years ago in a club in Nottingham and then didn't see each other again until a couple of weeks ago when we bumped into each other whilst I was out on a walk. We've been on a couple of dates since then and it's amazing, he's amazing. He currently lives too far away for us to see each other during the week, but we talk every night and he'll be moving down here soon for a new job."

"When are you seeing him again?" Fiona asked.

"This weekend," I said, almost squirming with delight at the thought that he would be arriving on Friday evening and I was so ready for him. All of which I kept to myself. It didn't take a genius to work out that if he lived too far away to see him during the week then it was probably too far to travel up and down for each date, and therefore the question of where he would be staying would inevitably be on everyone's mind. Luckily they were all too polite to raise the issue or ask the question.

Mine, he's staying at mine, I yelled in my head, but no one heard it. *I may tell them in time, but for now some things are just for me and Ed.*

"We'll be expecting a full report on Monday," Jess said with a knowing smile. A couple of the team giggled nervously and then conversation broke out between smaller groups and continued until we had to return to our desks.

My conversation with Ed that night was animated. We were both clearly excited about seeing each other. There were no mind games, no playing it cool, just good, honest, open conversation. As I fell asleep that night it struck me that whilst technically I had only known Ed for a couple of weeks it felt so, so much longer.

Without wanting to enter cliché alley – and at that point it really was too early to tell if he would be my soul mate – right there, on that night, I couldn't imagine being without him, let alone being with anyone else. *Oh, I hope this lasts*, I thought as I turned over in bed, readying myself for sleep. *Just one more peep [sleep] to go, just one more.*

*

I have no idea how I got through Friday. It was a blur from the moment the alarm brought me starkly into the new day.

I kept myself busy at work. The only way to make time pass quickly is to work through it. I must have had lunch, talked to my colleagues, driven home, but I don't remember any of that. I just remember my focus: get home, get changed, get ready.

Ed had told me on the phone the night before that he would head down straight after his shift so was hoping to arrive about eight, have a quick shower, change and then out for a late dinner. I couldn't wait.

To my surprise, as I arrived home I saw a car just like Ed's, a silver convertible BMW, parked on the lane beside my house. My heart skipped a beat as I pulled up onto my drive and saw him sitting on my front doorstep with a massive bouquet of bright yellow and white flowers in hand. He was in his uniform, and what a sight he made.

I leapt from the car, barely remembering to put the handbrake on and lock it. As I ran over to him he eased himself up from the step. I flung myself into his embrace, drawn in by his powerful arms and large bouquet in a bear hug to end all bear hugs. Before a word was spoken we were locked in a passionate kiss. It was like we had been apart for months, not days. We kissed like our lives depended on it. We kissed like the other person's lips and tongue were the oxygen our bodies needed to survive. It took all of our willpower not to sink to the ground right then and there. However, eventually propriety and our proximity to the street, not to mention my neighbours, made us pull apart.

"There you are," he said, smiling down at me.

"And there you are," I replied, shaking with excitement. "I didn't think you were going to make it until later this evening."

Ed cupped my face in his hands and planted a single kiss on my lips. "I know, I changed my shift and started early so I could get here in time to meet you from work," he explained as I reached into my massive bag, now regretting its size and the difficulty in finding anything in it when I really needed to. All I wanted was the key to the front door, so we could fall inside, to hide from the outside world, to return to the safety of our cocoon.

I stopped scrabbling around inside, took a deep breath, focused, opened the bag wide and retrieved the key. As I stood in front of Ed, opening the front door, his body was so close I could feel the buttons on his uniform pressing into my back, the warmth of his body, the heat between us, his hot breath on the back of my neck.

I unlocked the door and as I stepped forward, over the threshold, he gently tapped my right bum cheek with his hand. I smiled to myself as I held the door open for him. *Yes this is going to be a very good weekend*, I thought.

*

Some considerable time later, we lay in each other's arms, sheets tossed and crumpled following the passion that only a short absence had created. We didn't speak, we were happy just to be in this heavenly embrace. Happy that we had found each other.

It was too late to go out for a meal now, but we needed to eat, so whilst Ed finally took that shower I busied myself in the kitchen rustling up a quick omelette with onion, bacon and cheese – not exactly healthy, but quick and filling.

Ed came downstairs wearing nothing but a towel

wrapped around his waist, pulled tight across his flat stomach. I regretted giving him a large bath towel. If I had known he would appear wearing it I would have selected a much smaller member of the towel family!

"I hope you don't mind," he said, wearing nothing but the towel and a mischievous grin, "but I've got dressed for dinner."

I laughed as he pulled me back into his arms and kissed my neck provocatively as he continued, "Besides, I don't think I'll be wearing it for long."

I draped my arms around his neck, bringing my flimsily covered body in close to his and whispered in his ear, "I think you might be right about that."

I kissed his cheek and reluctantly pulled myself out of his arms, taking a seat next to him at the breakfast bar, our thighs touching as we ravenously ate what turned out to be a much better meal than I had anticipated. Whilst I'm a great baker of cakes, biscuits and all things a diabetic on a low-carb lifestyle should avoid, I lacked the basic cooking skills for anything other than my trademark lasagne and from time to time a half-decent cottage pie.

After I had cleaned up the dishes we took a couple of glasses of wine – well, it was a Friday after all – and curled up on the sofa, facing each other, cupping the large glasses in our hands, mirroring each other's body language.

Even though we had talked about the proposal and of how proud Ed was of Dan and Emma, we talked about it again. Ed was clearly very excited and wanted to share it with me again, face to face. And sitting there watching him happy and animated made me happy. I only interjected at key moments with appropriate noises, affirmations or questions if required. When we had finished the wine and the story had run its course, Ed reached over and took my glass, putting both wine glasses gently on the large, solid oak coffee table before him.

He leant forward and we kissed, slowly at first, then with increasing vigour and passion and heat. He pulled me down the sofa, under him, and again we were lost in the moment. It felt like nothing else existed, there was just us and the moment and that was all that mattered.

*

The next morning we woke at 8am. I don't think either of us intended to wake so early after such an exhilarating and exhausting night, but the windows were open and at 8am one of the neighbours' children had clearly decided it was time for piano practice. Plink, plonk, plinkedy, plonk, plonkedy, plink – on and on it went, endlessly. I don't think either of us would have minded if it had been either in tune or even a tune, but it was neither. If I had been on my own I would probably have been annoyed at the selfishness of the intrusion and wondered why the parents had not seen fit to put a stop to it. Clearly they were neither conscious of other people's feelings nor cared about them. On and on it went.

Luckily I was not alone. We didn't move, lying there face to face, smiling, then giggling at the ridiculousness of the situation. We inched closer together and were once more transported to a world of ecstasy, a million miles away from the plink plonk of the piano.

When we were finally sated, glowing not just from the warmth of love-making but also the sweat glistening on our bodies, we laughed at the realisation that the piano had been replaced by equally bad violin playing.

"I think it's safe to say that is the end of our lie-in," Ed said, somewhat stating the obvious. "How about I go and brew some coffee?" he suggested, leaping from the bed and into a fresh pair of boxers, but not quick enough that I couldn't take an appreciative look at his toned and beautiful body.

I showered, threw on my makeup and dressed before joining Ed in the sunshine on the terrace. The delicious smell of a freshly made cafetière of coffee wafting through the house had drawn me downstairs.

At times like this, I thought, *I wish I'd invested in a swing seat. How nice it would be sitting together gently swaying back and forth whilst enjoying a strong, reviving coffee.* But it was not to be. Instead we were sitting in separate teak chairs, next to each other in front of the large garden table and still close enough to touch, and occasionally our fingertips found each other's and entwined, bringing smiles to our faces.

"So, what shall we do today?" Ed asked, turning towards me, giving me the chance to admire his handsome face and wonder again how I had been so lucky for someone like him to be in my life. I guess I had kissed enough frogs (indeed some toads) to eventually deserve a prince. Just to be sure, I thanked my lucky stars, the heavens, whatever celestial being had brought him to me.

For now, though, we needed to decide what to do. For a moment I had wicked thoughts about not straying too far from the bedroom, but Ed was right, it would be good to have a change of scene and as long as we were prepared we would never be too far from a bed, of sorts.

"How about a run out to the coast?" I suggested. "It's a lovely day and it's still early so we could be there in time for lunch."

"Sounds like a great idea," confirmed Ed. "I've not been to the beach in years."

"That's settled," I said. "Now, where did I leave the bucket and spade?" I joked.

We didn't need much and were soon in Ed's convertible, with the roof down – well, it would be rude not to on a day like this – and were soon speeding our way down the country lanes deciding to take the slightly longer, but much more fun, scenic route rather than bolting down the dual carriageway. For all its directness it was boring with its high embankments, trees or fences. This way we got to enjoy all the quaint villages, with their idyllic duck ponds, cafes bulging with customers enjoying the sunshine and some light refreshments.

Passing through villages and hamlets, avoiding towns wherever we could, we pointed out houses to each other that we would love to live in, both of us preferring the traditional farmhouse with outbuildings and away from anything modern, cramped and characterless.

I was musing to myself about how alike we were, how our tastes complemented each other and how even after such a short time I could already imagine myself living in one of these beautiful homes with Ed. Maybe not the husband, children and a four-by-four-on-the-drive-type lifestyle but a happy and carefree one nonetheless. These thoughts all wafted through my mind just as the breeze wafted through my hair as we dashed through the green and luscious countryside until the shimmering blue sea finally sprung into view.

I had always loved the seaside. I had even spent a year living on the Devon coast. I had rented a house on a hill above the town, looking down on the bay and from where, in the summer, I had the perfect viewing spot for the speedboat racing just below – the noise, the thrills.

Living on the coast was glorious, but as with so many coastal towns these days they have become a magnet for hen and stag dos, which could, on occasions, get a little trying when having a quiet night out with friends.

The job had not worked out for me in the end and a little over a year after arriving I moved back across the country to be closer to my family. Still, it had served its purpose. Moving to the opposite side of the country had enabled me to finally escape from Fred 3.

Leaving the coast had not diminished my love for it: the sounds of the gulls and ice cream vans competing for attention and often found in close proximity; the smell of the sea; the warmth of the sand as it squishes between your toes; and the cooling, refreshing, salty sea when paddling. However, it had been some years since I had swum in the sea.

As a child we used to have long family holidays on the coast. My parents, brother and I stayed in a large, Edwardian rented house on one of the grand, wide, tree-lined avenues leading away from the beach. Even more special we stayed there with some of my grandparents, aunt, uncle and cousins. The house came with its own beach hut, and we spent endless, carefree days playing on the beach, building sandcastles, swimming, sheltering from the wind and rain and drinking hot tea in the beach hut. There was so much love and laughter. Even now the memory makes me smile and long for those days to return. I turned to Ed, wondering, hoping, that they might be about to.

We had arrived in good time for lunch so decided to go for a stroll first. We walked hand in hand through the pretty seaside town, with its old fishermen's cottages hunkered down, built strong to withstand the winter weather that rolled in across the sea. They were painted a myriad of pastel shades, all different, all complementary. With quaint cottage gardens facing the sea, shuttered windows and white picket fences, it was all so serene.

We walked past the ancient lighthouse – not huge, but the land around the town was so flat that it could be seen from the sea for miles.

The pubs and cafes were starting to fill up – well, the gardens were – and we decided to lay claim to one of the remaining tables outside the front of a typical pub, long and narrow, stretching along the edge of the promenade with a commanding view of the sea. Somewhere out there, far out there, was another country, but you couldn't see it, not even on a clear day like this.

We both ordered a ploughman's with a pint of ice-cold sparkling water. When the food arrived I passed my bread roll to Ed and he exchanged it for his coleslaw.

We were surrounded by people, from babes in arms to doting grandparents, people alone, couples, whole families, friends. Every person, every type, from all over the country, was represented in the pub garden, but we took no notice of them, wrapped up in our own little bubble.

I forget now at what point during the afternoon it was or even who decided, but at some point we agreed to stay over. We had no clothes, wash stuff or makeup. Luckily I had my medication, and a quick chat with the landlord secured us a double room with en suite for the night. We strolled into town to purchase a few essentials and after depositing them in our room, which smelt of centuries of open wood fires, we resumed our conversation in the garden, soaking up the atmosphere and enjoying a glass or two of Prosecco.

It was only one night away, our first together, but it felt like we were a million miles away on a holiday and we intended to make the most of it.

In hindsight this was the best impromptu night away I had ever had. There had been a few over the years with less success. There was the night with Fred 3. We had been out for the day. I was driving, as always, and he wanted to have a few drinks, as always, before heading home. As the driver I couldn't drink, as always, but it was a warm Sunday afternoon and the thought of spending the evening watching the boats glide up and down the river was too much to walk away from, even if it was with Fred 3 and I would have to pay, as always. I had enjoyed the scenery if not the company, but the very early morning start to get home, get changed and get to work on time meant it was not the relaxing night away I had hoped for.

Then there was Rob. I had met Rob whilst living in Devon. He was tall, with average looks, but what he lacked in the attraction stakes he more than made up for in wit and the gift of the gab. He could charm the birds from the trees and the fish from the sea, and he probably had done at some stage.

The night we met I was out with a friend in a local pub, away from the baying stag and hen dos, for a couple of quiet drinks before moving on to the more touristy, busier and buzzier town pubs and clubs. We got chatting to a couple of lads – one local, married, the other his brother visiting him from out of town, and that was Rob.

We ended up spending all evening in the pub, never venturing any further, but enjoying the company of our new friends.

Rob was a gentleman. He made me feel special and he made me laugh. We kissed that night and it was not until later when we exchanged phone numbers that he dropped into the conversation that he was married with two young children – a girl and a boy. He was at pains to point out that the marriage was over, but they were staying together for now as the children were so young. That said he requested that I didn't phone him, he would call me when the coast was clear. I should have walked away right then and there, but I didn't. Stupid me. Another wounded animal for me to help. He wanted to talk, to tell me how bad his wife was, how hard done by he was, and I listened and I sympathised, I counselled and I consoled.

We met up when he came down to visit his brother and sister-in-law, a lovely lady, full of love and laughter. Or Rob and I would talk on the phone until late in the evening, assuming his wife was not at home.

There were other times when we would meet up halfway between our two homes, at country pubs with rooms. But I always paid because he couldn't have anything come up on his credit card bill. Even that didn't put me off, even though it struck the same chord as Fred 3 had done, only more charming and less abusive. The sex helped of course. The sex was amazing and made me feel wanted, very desirable – again something Fred 3 had spectacularly failed to make me feel.

Eventually, though, it was not the wife or the money that split us up, it was his selfishness. Having spent months listening to his woes, supporting, sympathising and helping him, the minute life took a rather stressful and upsetting turn for me he was nowhere to be found. He just cut contact and left me to deal with it myself. Finally showing his true colours. I did what I always did and survived, not because of a man but in spite of him. I have always been blessed with the most amazing family and friends, and it was them that gave me the strength to get through this particular episode.

Back to the present

Luckily, though, Ed had none of those traits. He had been honest from the outset and true to his word. Even though I tried to insist on always splitting the bill, on most occasions he picked it up with a smile and paid without any request for reimbursement. What a fantastic change of luck. Not that that was the reason why I was with him, but it had often been the reason why I had ended it with his predecessors.

After a delicious dinner of steak, salad and chips – Ed picking up my share as I didn't want to feel bloated when I wanted to feel lithe for the night ahead – we washed down our food with more wine, the candles on the table flickering in the slight salty breeze coming in off the sea; Ed's smiling face illuminated by the candles below; hands held across the table when our empty plates had been taken away and our compliments passed on to the chef.

Eventually we gave up trying to pretend that we wanted to be anywhere other than our room upstairs and the giant bed was calling. It was an old coaching inn, hence the smoke smell in the room, but the facilities were modern, including a lovely walk-in shower wet room and two armchairs tucked under the leaded windows that framed the view of the sea.

I'm not going to divulge the details of what happened after we closed the door or even when we woke the next day, but you can, as always, fill in the blanks.

We made use of the few toiletries we had bought the day before and indulged in a huge full English breakfast, washed down with lashings of strong coffee to replenish the energy we had expended during the night and revive the body and mind after the alcohol and lack of sleep.

We sat drinking coffee for some time before collecting our meagre belongings from our charming room. As we shut the door I took one last glance around the room, savouring the memories and knowing I would never forget this place.

We left the car in the car park and took a final stroll around the town and along the beach, turning our faces in to the cooling sea breeze and the glorious hot sun, absorbing every second, every sense, creating new and lasting memories. Neither of us wanting to break the spell or make moves towards home. We stood, leaning on the high sea wall, looking out to sea, holding hands, engulfed in happiness.

Eventually Ed squeezed my hand, bringing me back to my senses, to the here and now. I turned to face him.

"I don't want to go home either," he confessed, reading my mind, "but I will need to drop you home, pick up my bag and make my way north," he said softly. I snuggled into his warm body, burying my head into his chest as we hugged each other. "It's been amazing and we'll definitely do this more often. Maybe we'll even remember to bring our overnight bags next time," he said, laughing.

I pulled my head back from his chest and looked up at him. "Thank you, it's been glorious and you're right, we can do this again." I paused. "Soon."

We kissed, a mellow, loving, soft kiss. This was not the time to reignite our passion. We walked slowly back to the car, eking out every last second.

The drive home was more subdued than the journey just one day before. From time to time I glanced over at Ed. He stared ahead, focusing on the road. But he knew I was looking, as each time I did he smiled, reassuring me he was aware of my presence. What he couldn't see was the love emanating from me. I was glad he was unaware of it. I was not ready to share that with him, I didn't want to scare him off. I had realised I had fallen for him at some point in the early hours. We had made love just after dawn and Ed had fallen asleep shortly afterwards. It had taken me a little longer to find sleep again and in that time I had laid on my side, my hand under the side of my face, my other hand holding down the edge of the pillow so I could see his sleeping face. As I lay there, feeling this swelling of emotion and love, yes, I had fallen in love. It scared me slightly, not just the revelation but also the speed with which it had descended, unannounced, uninvited, upon me. I thought I was more cautious now, after all the disasters that had come before.

Sitting in the car I felt more confident now. I felt the warmth of love flowing through me. I would wait to see if Ed felt the same. For now, though, I would keep my feelings a secret. If I could. If my face didn't give it away. I had to try to keep it to myself and enjoy whatever this relationship was and where the journey would take us.

For now, though, we were heading towards my home much more rapidly than I would have liked.

It was another sad farewell as Ed continued his journey home. Sad, yet I felt less anxious than before, as I knew it wouldn't be long before we saw each other again, and even less time until we spoke, as we had agreed he would call to let me know he had reached home safely.

seven.

New begets new

That week was a reversal of fortunes. With the security established in my relationship with Ed it was now the turn of my job to cause stress and doubt.

Not long before I met, or re-met Ed, a new director had been employed and I would be reporting in to her. I made her feel welcome, I told her what I did and was helpful and polite. However, before long she started to show her true colours. To my face she listened, expressed an interest and contributed to the debate. Behind my back she portrayed a very different picture, either taking credit for my work or, having agreed on a particular course of action or position on an issue with me, she then presented the opposite view to the chief executive. As a result I would be hauled in front of them both to be told I had to go with the line manager's opinion, making out that I was being difficult and disruptive, even putting a question mark over my ability to do my job, leaving me feeling confused and betrayed.

That particular week everything became clear. My new

line manager wanted me out. She was making my work life increasingly hard, either micro-managing every element of what I did or undermining me. It was hard to take. I had been there for seven years and put my heart and soul into raising the profile of the organisation. But none of that mattered. I had to go. I was not foolish enough to think I could just hang on in there. Knowing what I knew, I could easily have played the game. But I knew I had lost the fight, and more importantly I didn't have the energy or desire to cling on.

So, that week, my days were spent doing my best to keep my head down and out of the firing line at work. Then in the evenings the longed-for chats with Ed, during which we discussed and agreed it was time to move on. I worked and reworked my CV.

One way or another it was time for both of us – the organisation and me – to have a new future.

CV ready I scoured the job sites, registered with a few recruitment agencies, contacted a headhunter I had worked with previously to let him know I was looking. Being proactive made me feel like I had taken back the control that I had lost when my new line manager started. Being busy also helped the week pass quickly before I would be reunited with Ed.

On Friday morning I was engulfed in an opinion piece that I was rushing to proof and send off to meet the publication deadline when my personal phone sprang into life. Looking at the screen I saw it was Ed. Both excited to hear from him and worried he might be about to cancel the weekend that had been the light at the end of this particularly long and dark tunnel, I answered nervously.

"Hello, you."

"Hello, you too," he said softly, sounding his usual self, no hint of a let-down or regret that I feared I would hear.

"Sorry to trouble you at work," he continued, "I know you're working to deadline, but Dan just called. He and Emma are really excited about a potential venue for their wedding and was hoping I would go and see it along with Clare and Emma's parents this weekend." He rushed on, not letting me interject, maybe sensing I was feeling despondent at what I thought was about to be a rain check on our weekend. "I told them I was seeing you, which, to cut a long story short, ended up with the conversation being diverted and off track for some time, but at the end of it they said they'd love you to come too, to look at the venue that is, and also, of course, to meet you. I'd love you to come, but do you think it would be too much, you know, to meet all of them in one go? We could meet Dan and Emma for lunch first and then the rest, to split it up a bit. Of course, if it's too much too soon just say and I'll make it over to the venue another time and come down to you this evening as promised..." Finally he trailed off, pausing for breath after his words had tumbled out at hastening speed.

I smiled. Ed couldn't see it, but I was so relieved that I would be seeing him and excited at how he wanted me to meet his family and to be part of the wedding planning. I didn't make Ed wait though, as I knew he was on tenterhooks. "I'd love to come with you. You'll need to send me your address so I can find your house, assuming you are happy for me to stay with you? Otherwise the address of a local hotel or pub would be fine. I'll need to go home and pack a bag and will get underway as soon as I can."

All I heard at first was a massive outflow of breath. Ed had obviously been holding it. "Yes, yes of course," he said, sounding mightily relieved. "I'll text you in a minute. I'm so pleased you want to come. Dan and Emma can't wait to meet you. I'll leave you to it now, but let me know when you set off so I know when to expect you."

I could not wait to get out of work that afternoon, not only because it had been a horrible week, but also because I really felt like my life was about to get a whole lot better.

I dashed home and threw clothes, makeup, wash stuff, medication and camera into a large, doctor-style, leather bag and almost jogged to the car, pausing only long enough to pick up a bottle of wine before securing the house and heading out to the car on the drive.

I sent Ed a simple text, 'I'm on my way', set the coordinates into my Sat Nav and set off.

The journey was straightforward enough, the sun was shining and the air con helped to keep me cool. I had packed two CDs – two 80s artists enjoying a revival, Rick Astley and Kylie – but I didn't need them as Radio 2 was playing some mighty fine tunes. With the windows up and alone in the car I allowed myself to sing out loud. I felt so happy, so light, so excited, that I couldn't stop myself.

Soon I was pulling up on the drive of a modern family detached house in a cul-de-sac of similar properties. I smiled as I saw the 'For Sale' sign on the perfectly manicured front garden. *It really is happening, he really is moving closer*, I thought as I grabbed my bag from the boot and approached the dark green front door.

Outwardly I hoped I looked calm; inside, however, I was skipping.

As I raised my right hand to ring the doorbell, I was stopped by the door being flung open wide. Ed took one step forward, enveloped me in his arms and kissed me, kissed me hard and passionately. I dropped the bag.

Finally, we pulled apart. Up until that point we had been completely oblivious to anyone passing by or prying eyes. Up until then we were in our own world.

Now we stepped back, Ed picked up my bag and my hand.

"I've missed you," he said, squeezing my hand as he led me into his home. "Come on in, let me show you around and then we can have a drink before heading out for dinner."

I said nothing as he led me through the door, shutting it behind us and leading me up to the bedroom. We didn't make it out to dinner, but we did have that drink and some nibbles (of the food variety!) in the garden some time later.

We were mesmerised by the flurry of cabbage white butterflies flitting from one flower to another and for a moment I was lost in the recollection that some people believe butterflies are the souls of people we have loved and lost. I think there may be some truth in that. The day of my mother's funeral, a cold but sunny Thursday in March, 350 people were crammed into a small Anglo-Saxon church. All the seats had been taken and there was little standing room left in the aisle at the back. As we all reminisced and cried, all but two of the congregation, my aunt (my mum's sister) and I being the two exceptions, saw two large white butterflies dancing in the sunbeams streaming in through the high, arched, stained-glass windows.

When my cousins told me about them later that day I thought, *Perhaps they were my mum and her brother letting everyone know they were okay.* Although sad to have been one of the very few mourners not to experience the spectacle, it brought some comfort nonetheless. Others, however, perhaps the more sceptical, suspected that the butterflies had been awoken by the heat being put on in the church two days before the funeral.

*

Saturday came with an air of anticipation and a touch of trepidation. What if Ed's family didn't like me? What if I said or did something wrong or stupid or foolish? No, I resolved, I would need to make sure I got it right: think before I speak, consider before I act, avoid alcohol if possible.

Sensing perhaps my concerns that morning, it was the first time since we had been together that we didn't make love. Instead we lay in bed, engulfed in each other's arms. Feeling safe, secure and comforted my confidence began to grow.

Eventually Ed stroked the hair from my face, breaking the spell. "Come on, you, time to get up. I'll go and get breakfast on. Help yourself to the shower if you like, there are spare towels in the cupboard in the bathroom." He bent down and kissed me before jumping out of bed and disappearing downstairs at a trot.

We were due to meet Dan and Emma at noon at the hotel they were hoping to be their wedding venue, choosing to have the wedding, reception and accommodation all in one place, which had always seemed like a sensible option to me.

Ed and I had time for a leisurely breakfast, but as I

grew quiet again, worrying about whether Emma and Dan would like me, Ed, observant as ever, came over and gave me a strength-inducing bear hug.

"It'll be okay, they'll love you like…" My eyes shot up to meet his but he trailed off before finishing the sentence. He looked at me with uncertainty. I smiled at him, willing him to finish what he was going to say. Clearly he was not ready to commit to it, or maybe the time was not right, either way it didn't stop the rising feeling of joy spreading through my body as I realised he felt the same way as I did, even if he didn't say it. I could wait until he was ready.

"Let's get this cleared up," I said, changing the subject, much to Ed's relief. "We don't want to be late."

*

It was a short, half-hour drive out of the city suburbs to the country hotel, situated at the end of a long, narrow drive, flanked by thick trees and shrubs that hid what lay no more than a few feet from the tarmacked road. The evil little speed bumps threw us around the car despite the modern suspension and the slow speed we were travelling at. Every few feet the lane widened to provide a passing place for guests coming and going, but we didn't need to make use of them on our journey down to the hotel.

Eventually we emerged from the canopy, back into the sunlight, the woods giving way to the rolling countryside. To our right the grass rose up to more trees at the top of the hill; to the left the lawn sloped away down to the valley floor below.

As we continued towards the hotel there was a new

block of suites on the right, and ahead of us was a stunning sandstone mansion. We approached from the side, the gravel crunching beneath the tyres as we slowed to a stop alongside a handful of other smart cars in the large parking area. Ed squeezed my hand and turned towards me. "They're already here," he said, indicating a smart, dark BMW a couple of cars to our right and not dissimilar to Ed's own car.

I took a deep breath, and as I was about to open my door it was opened for me and a hand appeared. I took it, allowing it to lift me gently from the car.

As I rose I came face to face with a younger version of Ed.

"You must be Dan," I said, smiling at this charming, young, self-assured man.

"And you must be Chloe," he responded, leaning down to kiss my right cheek and then the left.

"Hands off my girlfriend," commanded a beaming Ed as he joined us, "and you are spoken for. Speaking of which, where is my future daughter-in-law?"

"She is with the hotel manager. We saw you approaching so I thought I'd come and greet you. We're so excited to meet you, Chloe, and about this venue. Come on, come inside, we can't wait to show you around."

Dan led the way from the brilliance outside, through the cool shade of the portico and into the light interior of the grandiose entrance hall where the massive windows welcomed the sunshine in, casting beautiful beams across the large black and white chequered marble floor. A magnificent oak staircase adorned with a deep red runner, pulled in close to each step by a carefully polished brass rod, rose in front of us. At the bottom was a beautiful, petite, dark-haired young lady beaming from ear to ear. She rushed forward and kissed Ed on both cheeks.

"Hi, Dad-to-be," she said before turning to me, now hesitant as to how to address me, deciding to keep it formal with, "Hello, I'm Emma," and proffering her hand to be shaken.

"Hello, Emma, it's a pleasure to meet you, I'm Chloe. What a stunning location, I can't wait to see more of it," I said, smiling at her. I felt the glow of happiness, the warmth of a new friendship and the fact that it was nice to meet such an enthusiastic and lively young woman.

We half shook hands, half kissed cheeks, unsure of the etiquette. A hug might have worked just as well, but at that point we both felt a little awkward so went with what felt right.

"Mary, the wedding co-ordinator, will do the full tour later, but for now we've booked a table on the terrace for lunch." With that Emma turned, hooked her arm through mine and confidently led the way to the back of the manor house.

It truly was a stunning location. The terrace ran the entire length of the house, providing panoramic views of the valley below and the hill opposite. We were sitting next to the stone balustrade that marked the edge of the terrace. There were two sections to the balustrade; an expertly centred gap in the middle opened out to a wide, stone, well-worn staircase, dipping in the middle due to centuries of footsteps, leading gently and elegantly down to the manicured lawn below.

The sun was beating down, but we found shade below

the large umbrella extending out over the table. I love the sun but no one wants to sit and sweat during the first meeting with your boyfriend's son and his fiancée. The situation was stressful enough without adding that social *faux pas* into the mix.

Immediately it became clear that the table was set for four and not for Ed's ex-wife and her husband or for Emma's parents. I looked at Ed quizzically. He had clearly made the same observation and gave a slight shrug to indicate that he, too, was confused, as the invitation had been for all of us to meet and view the venue.

I was stunned into silence by the sheer elegance and splendour of the hotel. The attention to detail was second to none. As soon as we were seated waiters appeared to fill our glasses with ice-cold water whilst another lifted, flicked and delicately placed the crisp white linen napkins onto our laps. I turned this way and that to thank each waiter in turn, finishing with the third that was handing out the leather-bound menus. As we perused them in studious silence I avoided looking at the prices, all of which seemed rather excessive, so I decided to focus on what I wanted to eat rather than how much it would cost. It was not that I don't earn a decent wage, nor that I would skimp on such an occasion, but having spent much of my life watching the pennies, that avoidance of extravagance had remained with me.

In the end I decided to skip the starter and plumped for a Caesar salad, without anchovies. I had never understood why anyone would ruin a perfectly good salad by putting small salty fish on it. I was not having salad to make a point, but I just didn't want anything too heavy this early in the day.

Ed and Dan, like father, like son, had decided on steak, medium-rare, with chips and a nod to a side salad for good measure. Emma, maybe in consideration of the tight-fitting dress in the not-too-distant future, although looking at her I suspected it was her lunch of choice, also went for a salad, opting for a tuna niçoise – now, that is an example of where a fish in a salad is acceptable.

We were all on soft drinks, aware that we would need to drive home later. Despite the fabulous setting all our attention was focused on the conversation around the table, which, thankfully, was flowing largely between Dan and Ed who were catching up on jobs and life. Emma and I sat quietly, listening in as the men we loved waxed lyrical.

Eventually conversation turned to the wedding. Emma and I became more animated and involved in the discussion. Emma had already picked her bridesmaids – her best friend as maid of honour and two nieces as flower girls. Dan had picked his best man, an old childhood friend and son of Ed's best friend, which took the conversation off at a tangent whilst Dan and Ed again started down memory lane, updating each other on what their counterpart father and son were up to.

We were drawn back to the topic of the wedding by the appearance of an elegant and professional-looking young woman as we were drinking our assortment of coffee and tea. The new arrival was young, but with an air of maturity, of quiet confidence. She had long blonde hair drawn back into a very formal, neat, tightly controlled bun just above the nape of her neck. Her suit – black jacket and knee-length black skirt with buttoned-down crisp white blouse – made her smart and officious without being extravagant or showy. She appeared discreet, confident, perfectly mannered.

She smiled at the ensemble. "Good afternoon, everyone. Dan, Emma, it's great to see you again." She shook their hands before turning to us. "You must be Ed and Chloe, it's lovely to meet you." Her handshake was an affirmation of her physical appearance – strong and heartfelt. "I'm Mary. The wedding co-ordinator. I trust you enjoyed your lunch?" She smiled at us as we all murmured our agreement and our confidence in the venue being the perfect setting given the quality of the food, the attentiveness of the staff and the overall ambience.

"Is it alright if I join you now?" Mary asked, ever the consummate wedding planner. Again we agreed in unison. Mary carried a chair over from another table nearby and placed it at the short end of the table so she could maintain eye contact with all of us. We adjusted our chairs slightly to face her. She was in control and commanding the situation.

Laying the professional black leather portfolio on the table she opened it to reveal a collection of beautifully produced wedding brochures, a notepad and a beautiful antique-looking fountain pen. She took the lid off the pen, ready to make notes.

Mary turned to Dan and Emma. "Are we ready to plan the most important day of your life?" She smiled. A momentary flicker of doubt danced across Dan's face – gone as soon as it appeared, but there nonetheless. It hadn't been lost on Emma who had been staring at him the whole time. She gently lifted his hand in hers, squeezed it, smiled at him, and said, "Yes, we are," on behalf of them both.

It became clear in that instant that Emma was the strong

one in this relationship, in the emotional sense at least. Emboldened by Emma's support Dan looked up, smiled and confirmed, "Yes, we're ready." He squeezed Emma's hand and smiled at her.

"Well, the first place to start," Mary picked up, "is to say thank you for choosing Astley Manor. We are at your service and will be with you every step of the way to make sure it's the best day of your life." Clearly Dan's momentary lapse hadn't been lost on Mary either. In fact the only one who appeared to be oblivious was Ed, who had yet to take his eyes off the formally presented young woman before us.

"Secondly, and I say this to all my couples as it's so often forgotten or overlooked, this day is about you, for you. It's about celebrating your love and it should be the day you want. It's easy to feel you need to accommodate the requests of others." At this point Mary glanced at Ed. "But planning a wedding involves a lot of decisions which can become stressful. So focus on what you want, how you want it to happen, who you want to invite and it will help you to keep in mind what is important."

Ed nodded his agreement to the sentiment, which Dan, Emma and Mary appreciated. Ed had clearly received the message and was not going to interfere.

Mary continued, "At Astley Manor we only have one wedding per day to ensure we can focus on one couple and their guests. But as I'm sure you can imagine, it means we are booked up for every Saturday for the next eighteen months." Dan and Emma both looked crestfallen. Clearly they had hoped their nuptials would be sooner than that.

"However," Mary continued quickly, hoping to move the conversation back to a more happy note, "if you are flexible on the day of the week then we can find something sooner, for example Fridays are the second most popular days and Sundays are not far behind, but Mondays and mid-week are far more flexible, and if you have your heart set on a particular time of year I'm sure we can find something that would work."

Emma looked at Dan, still holding his hand. "I was hoping for a day in spring, it's always such a joyful time of year, especially when the blossom is out. Do you have any dates in April?" she asked hopefully.

Mary unzipped the pocket on the front of the leather document wallet and pulled out the slender iPad concealed within. A few swipes of the finger and she looked up smiling. "As luck would have it we have a few options in late April. We have a couple of Thursdays, otherwise it would be mid-week if that would work for you?"

Dan and Emma exchanged looks. Mary picked up on their reluctance, adding, "And of course mid-week is cheaper than weekends." The ever-present smile.

"Well," Emma began hesitantly, "all of our friends work and some of them will need to travel, so we were really hoping for a Friday, Saturday or Sunday. We can be more flexible on dates if that would help." Clearly the betrothed couple were prepared to be flexible and wait rather than risk friends being unable to attend.

Mary focused on the iPad again. She swiped and read, swiped and read, swiped and read for several minutes whilst four pairs of eyes were fixed upon her, wishing, hoping, fearful that we were disappearing into years from now rather than months.

A big smile began to spread across Mary's face, before

she slowly raised her head to face us. "Well, I have some good news for you," she said. "I was overseeing a wedding yesterday so I hadn't noticed that a wedding cancellation has been received by the Admin team. How does Friday 18 December…" she paused for dramatic effect, "this year sound to you?"

Dan and Emma leapt from their seats, leaning over to hug a rather shocked-looking Mary, who did, graciously, accept and return the hugs before continuing, "I'll take that as a yes then?" Dan, Emma and Ed all nodded their consent.

At this point another member of staff quietly appeared beside Mary. Mary acknowledged her presence and excused herself, taking a few steps away from our merry band of lunch-takers, for discretion.

When Mary returned to us she apologised and explained, "We have a wedding this afternoon and there has just been a delivery I need to take care of. My colleague Sarah," she indicated the young lady next to her, "will give you the tour if that is okay with you? Obviously we'll need to show you around before the wedding guests start to arrive. Sarah will arrange for some refreshments once you have finished and I can come and talk you through the packages available. But don't worry, the packages are simply starting points from which we tailor the plans to exactly what you would like." She took our smiles as agreement, turned on her polished, sturdy high-heeled shoes and was gone.

Sarah did a great job in Mary's absence, starting by leading us through a massive Victorian orangery, hot on a day like this and filled with aromatic plants and flowers, before she returned us to the airy, cool entrance hall, through the heavy oak doors which led into the former ballroom which is where the wedding would actually take place. It was a great opportunity to see the venue all set up ready for the wedding that afternoon. The chairs were lined up in perfect union, all expectant for the events soon to unfurl, the end of every other row adorned with sprays of white flowers. Sarah explained that whilst the guests had drinks and canapés in the adjoining room and the bride and groom had photos taken in the grounds, this room would be re-set for the wedding breakfast, the large circular tables set around the dance floor that would be revealed from under its carpeted hiding place after the meal. The DJ was already set up, discreetly hidden from the congregation behind an elegant screen that matched the decoration of the room.

Through another set of heavy, wide oak doors set halfway down the interior wall we were shown where the refreshments would be served. From there Sarah took us to see a selection of the bedrooms and suites available, although not, obviously, the honeymoon suite, as the bride was already in occupation.

As we took the tour, Emma and Dan hand in hand, mirrored by Ed and me, my mind wandered and a dark cloud crossed my mind as I remembered the only time in my life when I had been the bride-to-be, visiting different venues with my fiancé and family in tow. In our case we had decided on a marquee in my parents' garden, having failed to find a suitable hotel or venue nearby. Most were too commercial with several weddings each day, which made us feel anything but special, despite their reassurance that each wedding was kept separate and had its own team. It felt like a profit-making production line, the opposite of how Astley Manor was making us feel, even though we were not the betrothed. If Astley Manor had been an option I'm sure we would have jumped at the chance to be married in this paradise. Not that that would have made a difference to the outcome.

As it turned out all the arrangements – dresses, tiaras, church, catering, marquee, chairs, cars, luxury toilets, band, string quartet – all got cancelled, minus the cancellation fees, three months before the wedding when Fred 2 had changed his mind and decided he could not, or would not, go through with it.

It was ironic really. He had been the first to say 'I love you', catching me by surprise while we were out one night. He was the one that started calling me a pet name – my initials but the first letter of his surname rather than my own. He was the one that called my father while my parents were away on holiday and asked for my hand in marriage. He was the one that took me away for a romantic break and got down on one knee to propose. But none of that mattered in the end. I had been in London with my bridesmaids picking out shoes and when I couldn't get hold of Fred 2 on the phone, somehow, I just knew that something was wrong, very wrong, and headed home. He didn't come back that night. He didn't come back the next day. Finally, on the Monday morning he breezed in to shower and get ready for work, pausing only long enough to tell me it was over, and then he breezed back out as if he had just told me he didn't have time for a cup of tea before work.

Best diet I had ever been on. I lost a stone that first week. I fled back home to the bosom of my family. I didn't eat. I did cry. At the end of the week I was strong enough to face my future alone.

I called the flat and told Fred 2 to get out. I was on my way back and didn't want to find him there when I arrived. He was shocked. "Where am I to go?" he asked in disbelief.

"I don't know and I don't care," I replied honestly. "You've made your bed, now deal with it."

I returned to an empty flat.

The thought of Fred 2 was a stark reminder that love is a fickle and dangerous game and one that, suddenly, I was not sure I wanted to get entangled in again. The pain was too great.

Back to the present

I must have slowed down or tensed up. I stopped to find Ed looking at me, concerned. Sarah, Dan and Emma had walked on and stopped some way up the corridor, a discreet distance ahead and were quietly engaged in conversation.

"Are you okay?" Ed asked quietly, putting his hand on my cheek. "You've gone very pale."

"Sorry, my thoughts were elsewhere. I'm good now, let's catch up with the others." Clearly I didn't sound convincing. Ed moved his hand from my cheek to my arm to restrain me.

"You looked scared for a moment, is there anything you want to tell me?" He sounded very much the cop. I really didn't want to share my thoughts on what should be a happy day, and I was not up for being interrogated.

"No, no, honestly I'm fine," I said, mustering every ounce of happiness and confidence I could. "I'm sorry to have worried you. I really am okay." I smiled and bumped his arm with my shoulder in a reassuring gesture.

"Okay," Ed responded, clearly not convinced, but he removed his hand and we caught up with the others.

I'll have to tell him sometime. But today is definitely not the day, I mused as we made our way back outside.

The tour complete, Sarah returned us to our table on the sun-drenched terrace and went to arrange refreshments. Despite having only finished lunch less than an hour previously a waiter was soon unloading a large silver tray – a pot of tea, pot of coffee, milk, biscuits and petite cakes. We tucked into the drinks, and the boys popped a cake each, explaining it would be rude not to, and confirming they were delicious.

We were enthusiastically discussing how perfect the location was when Mary reappeared at the table, her arms folded around her leather case and two glossy brochures. One she handed to Dan and Emma, the other to Ed and me.

Ed and I politely flicked through the brochure and accompanying eye-watering price list. Luckily the bulk of the cost would be picked up by Emma's parents. I didn't know their financial situation, but given how relaxed Emma and Dan appeared to be as they were studying the details, I would say that it wouldn't be a problem.

Emma looked up. "Mary, this is all great. Dan and I have some ideas of what we are looking for but will need to discuss everything with my parents before we can confirm the details."

"Of course, of course," Mary said. "Well, how about I leave these with you? Here's my card, just give me a call when you're ready to make plans and I can provide an initial estimate. The date is confirmed." Mary handed over her card, thanked us for our time and returned to focus on that afternoon's wedding.

I looked at Dan and Emma. Watching this young couple so very much in love, I banished the ghosts that had haunted me earlier in the afternoon. I no longer had to pretend, I was back on cloud nine.

The afternoon was whiled away in the glorious setting. No dark clouds bothered the horizon, either in reality or metaphorically, and finally we needed to drag ourselves away from this paradise.

Originally the plan had been to go on and meet with Emma's family and Ed's ex, but Dan explained that Clare had had to cancel that morning so they were just going to take the brochures over to Emma's parents and talk about budgets. He didn't need to say it, we understood that would be a delicate conversation, one at which our presence was neither needed nor wanted.

Before they headed off, Ed pulled Dan to one side. He told me on our journey home that he had offered to pick up the bill for any of the extras. As his only child he wanted to ensure they were able to have everything they wanted, but didn't want to step on toes. He didn't want to offend Emma's parents so left it with Dan.

Having waved off the happy couple from the now packed car park, Ed turned in and kissed me passionately. I smiled at him. "Thank you," he said, much to my surprise.

"What for?" I asked.

"For today. They loved you, as I knew they would. I really appreciated having you by my side." He looked at me hesitantly and then continued, slowly and measured, "At some point we should talk about where you were when we were on the tour but now, I think, is not the time. You know you can trust me, you can tell me anything."

I assured him I knew and that one day we would talk about it. We climbed into the car and made our way back to his home.

eight.

One step forward, two back

"I have some good news and some bad news," Ed confessed over a leisurely breakfast the next day.

"Oh, I'm not sure I like the sound of that," I teased. "Give me the bad news first."

"Well, as you know I've seen you every weekend since we met, or re-met, and I should have been on shift for some of them, so I'm going to have to work the next three weekends. I could come down during the week if you are okay with me hanging around yours while you're at work?" he asked.

"I'd love that," I said eagerly, relieved I was not going to have to endure four weeks without seeing him, "if you're sure you don't mind?"

"No," he said. "I need to start thinking about where to live when I move down and it will give me a chance to set up appointments to view a few places."

I desperately wanted to shout, "No, no, live with me," but hindsight has taught me well and moving in too quickly could sound the death knell of even the strongest relationship. If Ed had been hoping I might make the offer he didn't let it show. Maybe relieved that I had not, he continued, "And would you like the good news?"

"Of course."

"Well, I think it's good news and I hope you do too," he said coyly. "I've got a week off next month. I'd already booked to go to the Le Mans Classic 24-Hour race with a group of friends and I was wondering if you'd like to join us? I'd only need to sort out a ferry ticket, the rest is already sorted. It's camping I'm afraid, I'm not sure how you feel about that, or if motor racing, or indeed classic cars, are your thing?"

I paused, it was a lot to take in, and in truth there was little I hated more than camping, especially in July, in France, which would be super-hot, trudging to a toilet across a dark, badly lit campsite, queueing for the shower, having to keep food cold in order to cook it. Hmm, I weighed up the options. A holiday with Ed, yes. A holiday with a group of people I didn't know, maybe. A camping holiday, preferably not. All that raced through my mind, but instead of saying any of this I heard myself say, "That sounds great, what are the dates? I'll need to check with work but I'd love to go."

Arrrggghhh, I screamed in my head. *What am I doing? The things we do for love. There, the 'L' word again. Focus on the conversation*, I told myself as I realised Ed was now talking animatedly about his previous trips and how legendary they were. I tuned back in at the important bit.

"I say camping, but it's more like glamping. We tried the general camping once and it was carnage so we go private camping now. They pre-erect the tent so we only need to take bedding and it saves on the hassle of putting up a tent in ninety-degree heat. The site is fenced off from the rest of the campsites and has a security team checking everyone that tries to enter. There is a marquee with a bar and restaurant, private showers and toilets which are cleaned round the clock and the best thing is it's right on the race track on the inside of the famous Porsche curves. Have you seen the race, the twenty-four-hour version?" Ed finally stopped to draw breath as I told him I knew of it and had caught parts of it from time to time, but was not that familiar with the race or the track.

Ed motored on, "Well, the classic race is like the twenty-four-hour one, but that runs every year and is one race that lasts for twenty-four hours. The classic runs every other year and is a series of races that run over twenty-four hours – the classic cars just couldn't last the distance, literally."

Ed clearly loved the race and I let him ramble on with his reminiscing, nodding at appropriate points, enjoying seeing him so excited, so animated and clearly thrilled that this year I would be joining him on the biennial pilgrimage to the classic.

"You'll love the guys," he said, at which point it occurred to me that there had been a lot of references to 'the guys', but not so much about 'the girls'.

"So," I asked, "how many wives, girlfriends, that is to say, women, are there in the group?"

Ed paused for a second, looking a little sheepish. "Girls," he repeated, "um, well, none, well, not usually, but the guys are all really up for you coming with us and are really looking forward to meeting you. I've told them all about you."

Whilst reassured and happy that Ed had told his friends of my existence I was still a little worried. "I'm not crashing a lads' holiday, am I?"

"No, not at all, we're too old for those sorts of holidays. Most of the partners aren't interested in cars, or racing, or camping, or any combination of the above, so we've just been lads on tour, but we'd all love you to join us. That won't be a problem for you, will it?"

"No, of course not, I just wanted to make sure I wasn't intruding."

"Of course not," he reassured me. "I wouldn't have invited you if I, well, all of us, didn't want you there."

Ed gave me a little more background on the race and famous drivers taking part that I might know. I didn't. However, I decided I had better do some homework ahead of the holiday. I really didn't want to let Ed down.

*

The weather had been glorious for weeks – warm sunshine and cooling breezes making for perfect weather – but the last few days had been unbearable. The winds had died and the temperature had built and built. Now it was oppressive, breathing became harder, movement became slower. It was like walking through cotton wool. There was no let-up and no escape bar the air conditioning in the car or large shops. Every day the news reported, "Hottest day since…" The old and the young were suffering, wild fires were breaking out across Europe and lives were being lost.

We all started praying for rain, blessed relieving, cooling rain, and that afternoon it came. It was like Armageddon.

The clouds had been rolling in for hours making the air yet more dense and stifling; the hot winds and menacing dark grey clouds tinged with orange where you could see the edges. Then it came, in a flash of lightning and booming, reverberating thunder that you could feel tremble through your body.

Ed and I were sitting in the garden. We had been watching it roll in, fascinated but terrified. We looked to the heavens as huge drops of water slowly, then with increasing fervour, fell hard onto the patio, the sound of the rain growing. It was exhilarating and awoke some carnal desire in us. We were holding each other huddled under the large umbrella, but our feet and legs were getting drenched. We were relieved that the storm would finally clear and clean the air.

The smell of the water reawakening the parched earth was a smack to the senses, the taste of iron in our mouths. The water, unable to sink into the tightly packed soil, now ran down onto the patio and pooled around our feet.

The rain became harder as the water was replaced by hail and at that point we decided we could no longer stay out, enjoying our childish reverie, and made the short dash to the protection of Ed's home. We stopped just inside the wide-open door and stared out at the mesmerising storm. Unable to take our eyes off it, partly worried that the garden would flood with the intensity of the deluge but excited by the very danger of it, we were fixed to the spot.

Twenty minutes later the storm eased up and we ventured outside to survey the damage. Chairs had been turned over but there was nothing too dramatic. Parts of the crisp, yellow grass were even showing signs of life, not yet green but a step away from death's door where they had been just half an hour earlier.

Looking up, the clouds were still moving at a considerable pace, with more menacing clouds flowing in behind.

"Well, it looks like it'll be wet weather games this afternoon." Ed gave me a cheeky smile and a wink, picked up my hand and led me back into the house.

We didn't emerge from the bedroom for some hours after that, having lain in bed listening to the storm rage around us, feeling cocooned and safe in the house, in each other's arms.

By early evening the storm had passed and the sun was out. Small, fluffy white clouds now dotted the sky and a blessed cooling breeze was keeping the temperature closer to the seasonal norm.

Glad to be out in the glorious evening air we pottered down to Ed's local pub. It would be a very early start for me on Monday morning to get down to work on time, but I was not ready to go home yet.

Ed's local was a small inn tucked between an optician and a dry cleaner and was more like someone's home than a pub. On the walk there the previous evening the streets had been dry and dusty. These had now been washed clean by the storm. There were stones and twigs gathered around metal drain covers where they had been washed down the street in the deluge before becoming lodged at the entrance to the sewer. We noticed some branches had been blown or snapped by the storm and lay abandoned on the path. Twice we had to move them out of the way to make the pavement clear and safe.

We found a table in the small courtyard garden at the back of the pub, surrounded by high walls which were adorned with hanging baskets overflowing with brightly coloured flowers. The scent was delicious and heady. We enjoyed a few glasses of wine and a light meal, then took the long way home to make the most of the breeze and the chance to be outside.

The next morning I had mixed emotions when I was rudely awoken by the shrill early alarm call, happy to be in the warmth of Ed's arms, but tinged with sadness that we wouldn't be able to have a lazy morning in each other's embrace today. But I had to work, and I knew Ed worked shifts when I met him and had, for all intents and purposes, signed up to this lifestyle, so I resolved that I had better get used to it.

When it was time to say goodbye we clung to each other, not wanting to let go, conscious this was silly given we would be together again sooner than usual but not for as long.

We kissed, deeply, slowly, not as passionately or as ferociously as it was at times. It was neither the time nor the place to give in to the desire.

The journey to work was long, not because the traffic was bad that Monday morning; it was long because it was sad. The journey north had been filled with joy, hope and excitement. The journey south was the polar opposite.

I sat in the car park outside work and dropped Ed a quick text to let him know I had arrived safely, then dragged my heavy and reluctant feet to my desk and plonked myself down to work.

*

As I unlocked my front door that night I was disappointed to realise that, for the first time since I bought the cottage, it didn't feel like home. As I worked this through in my mind I realised it was because Ed should have been there, and he wasn't.

Putting my weekend bag back in my cosy bedroom I sat on the edge of my empty bed. The duvet had been on the dresser for weeks due to the heat and the sheet I had been sleeping under was still screwed up in a bundle in the middle where I had left it on Friday morning. Now it just looked sad and empty.

I called Ed to let him know I was now back at home and to catch up on our days.

"What's wrong?" he asked. "You sound down."

"Sorry," I said, trying to put more effort and light into my tone, but with little success. "I'm a little tired after the early start. Sorry, that's not it, Ed. The reason is the house feels so empty, I feel so empty." I paused, and then said softly, "Without you." Fear struck me and I worried I had said too much as I always do, inevitably. The silence from the end of the phone was deafening and seemed to confirm I was right.

"I miss you too," he eventually whispered down the line. "I felt it the moment you left and I've been sitting in the garden brooding since then. I wasn't sure whether to say anything. I didn't want you to think I'm some sort of needy person. But I need you, I… I…" he stuttered and decided to let it go. "I can't wait to see you."

Having got our feelings out in the open we chatted a little longer before ending the call and heading to our respective, empty beds for lonely sleep.

*

Ed was working nights at the beginning of the week and due to get to mine on Thursday evening after I returned from work and he had managed to get some sleep.

Wednesday night I cleaned and tidied the house, and stocked the fridge. The preparation distracted me from the fact there was another night until I would see him.

Ed's shift patterns were all out of sync because he had been doing deals with various colleagues to keep the weekends free and so, inevitably, it had caught up with him. Although he was due to arrive with me on Thursday evening he would have to head back just twenty-four hours later. We would have to pack as much as we could into those magical few hours.

I had set my alarm even earlier than usual, aiming to be in work by 7.30am rather than the usual 8am in order to ensure I could cover all my work and be away at 5pm prompt. Nothing was going to keep me at work late that night.

I was beaming from ear to ear at the mere thought and anticipation of Ed's arrival that evening. As I was leaving the house to go to work, I opened the door, gasped and jumped backwards as I was greeted by an exhausted but smiling Ed, with his hand raised ready to knock on the door.

After a moment, while I grasped the situation, the shock and joy had tussled to be the dominant emotion. Finally I came to my senses and leapt into Ed's open arms. I flung my arms around his neck and kissed him with all my might, all my heart. Ed reciprocated. We stood, enveloped in each other's arms on the doorstep, even after the initial kiss had drawn slowly and reluctantly to an end.

"What are you doing here?" I asked.

"I can go if it's not convenient," he teased.

"No, no, come in, you can't go. It's just I thought you were coming down this afternoon." I stepped back, leaving the door wide open for Ed and his overnight bag to step through.

"I was, but I finished work and was too excited about coming down to try to sleep so I thought I would try to catch you before work and then have a sleep and shower. I hope that is okay? It looks like I only just caught you though. I never considered what I would do if you hadn't been home."

I leant in for another kiss. "I was going in early so I could be away on time. You really only just caught me, but I'm so, so glad you are here. How I'll get through a day at work I have no idea. Look, I had better go, make yourself at home, you know where everything is and the fridge is bursting to the seams," I said as I pulled myself away from him.

I was on my way out of the door when I remembered I had left my spare keys on the counter in the kitchen and dashed back inside to retrieve them for Ed. "There you are," I said as I handed them over to him. "So, you can come and go as you please," I explained, then more hesitantly, "You can keep hold of them if you like, that way if you had missed me you wouldn't have had to spend the day on the doorstep." I laughed as I said it to try to make light of what was quite a significant moment. I was still nervous.

"Thanks, that's a great idea." He clenched the keys in his hand and smiled down at me.

We stood there awkwardly, me knowing I needed to leave and Ed looking beyond ready for sleep. I stood up on my tiptoes, placed my hand on his bulging chest, feeling his body warmth and rapidly beating heart, and planted a kiss on his cheek.

"I'd better go," I said sadly. "I'll be back as soon as I can, I promise." I smiled, leant in for another quick kiss and left before things took their natural course.

"Later," I called back over my shoulder.

"Later," he replied, leaning on the open door with his right hand holding the top to steady it.

I didn't look back again, knowing if I did I would probably give in to the burning desire bubbling up inside me and then I would not be early in work, let alone late arriving, but in fact not in work at all.

*

The day flew by and soon I was home again. Running into my house, now magically a home again due to Ed's very presence, I stopped dead inside the door. I looked around and listened, the house was silent. No noise, bar a ticking clock. My heart sank. I wandered from room to room, looking. It didn't take long, the house was not that big, but each room, each empty room, stared back at me.

As I was coming down the stairs I heard a key in the lock and leapt down the last couple of steps, to meet Ed as he walked in with a large bouquet of yellow and white flowers in one arm and a bag of shopping in the other. I couldn't imagine what we needed that I hadn't already provided.

He hadn't noticed me as he pushed the door shut and put the key in his jeans pocket. Turning back he saw me standing in the middle of the room. He dropped everything, literally, took two strides towards me and swept me up into his arms. This time we kissed passionately, hot, urgent and long.

Finally pulling apart and retrieving the flowers, Ed handed them to me rather apologetically. "For you, mademoiselle. Sorry, I dropped them, they should be okay though," he said as he bowed, the perfect romantic gesture.

"They are beautiful," I said as I bent my head into the bouquet to breathe in the heavenly scent. "I'll pop them in a vase," I said, walking into the kitchen. Ed picked up the bag of shopping and followed me.

"And what's in there?" I asked as he put the bag on the counter next to the flowers.

"Ahh, I thought as we only really have tonight and a couple of hours tomorrow night, that I would cook for us. I don't feel like sharing you with anyone tonight," he said honestly, laying himself bare.

"Well, that might not be the case." I left it there as Ed looked at me a little perturbed, I guess feeling put out that I was going to share these precious few hours with other people.

Seeing his face I decided it best to put him out of his misery. "Don't worry," I said, stroking his arm, "I don't have any plans for tonight, but when I was at work, it occurred to me that given how I felt leaving you this morning, that it would be impossible leaving you again tomorrow. And, well, as I have a lot of holiday owing, I have booked tomorrow off work so I can come house hunting with you, if that is okay?"

Ed reached out and pulled me into his arms. We kissed and made our way upstairs.

nine.

A home is where the heart is

Ed had set up a number of property viewings, spread across a ten-mile radius emanating from the town where I lived. The properties were all different types, ages, sizes. We politely made appropriately positive noises as we were given the typical tours involving stating the obvious in each room – "This is the kitchen", "This is the bathroom" and so on, six times over. The only differences were whether there was parking, a garden and/or additional bedrooms.

It was, in fact, quite tiring and as we sat having dinner that night, ahead of his drive home, we considered the options, working our way through each one in turn, listing the positives – nice garden, decent-sized kitchen, refurbished bathroom – and the negatives – location, lack of parking, only one bedroom.

These were only properties to rent. Ed wanted to try out the area and of course his new job before committing to buying somewhere, which was, of course, sensible. However, the first day had been a whitewash. Ed was going to have to line up some more appointments. More appropriate, more suited to his needs.

The next day was strange. It was the first weekend without Ed and it felt odd. Unfortunately it gave me time to think, or more accurately, allowed my head to overanalyse the relationship and how it made me feel. Being with Ed made me feel amazing. I don't know how, but I felt slimmer. Of course all the new exercising we were indulging in was helping me to both lose weight and to tone in certain areas, which was, of course, inevitable in the 'honeymoon' phase of a new relationship. Somehow, though, this felt different. I just felt that I was slim. I felt confident and empowered and light. And I liked feeling this way.

It had not always been that way in relationships. Sometimes it started out okay, but over time I guess it's natural to stop making the effort. Some relationships became staid and stuck but worse than that, one relationship had made me a nervous wreck. I don't think he had set out to achieve this effect. After all, that was not who I was when we met, but that was where I ended up nonetheless.

In truth it was the shouting that really got to me and drove me in a new direction. At its worst I had to examine every action for how it might be perceived and the consequences it might generate. In the end I did everything I could to avoid being yelled at, avoiding situations and conversations that might lead to that conclusion, but the more I did that, the more I withdrew into myself, the less I engaged in conversation and life. As a result I was no longer attractive in my partner's eyes. Eventually it drove us apart, but it need not have if, when it first started, I had stood up to him and to what was tantamount to bullying.

But that was the past and if it had not ended then I would not be with Ed today. And that was a good place. A happy place. A place I wanted to stay.

Luckily the time between the self-assurance-sapping relationship and Ed had been long and healing. Being alone I had rebuilt my confidence: celebrating success, listing what I did well, remembering who I used to be, spending time with those that loved me and that I loved. Most of all staying away from confrontation and from shouty people who made me jumpy and nervous, not letting people belittle me. Even now, I still have moments of overthinking a situation but generally I'm okay. It would not take me long though, if Ed ever showed signs of similar traits, for me to walk away, however much I felt for him.

We talked on the phone when Ed was on his breaks, talking about something and nothing. Life was just a little duller without him around and on Saturday I barely left the house, feeling apathetic and unmoved to venture too far, which left me with little news to discuss with Ed. By Sunday, though, I was going stir crazy and decided to make the most of the cool morning, heading out on a long two-hour walk to clear the cobwebs and reinvigorate my soul. It was like old times and I revelled in the familiarity of the walk, the scenery, the wildlife. I counted squirrels, pheasants, even a small roe deer who was standing stock still in a sunlit glade in the woods I passed.

Inevitably my walk brought me back into town via a coffee shop and I sipped the large latte as I made the last few steps home. This, at least, gave us something to talk about that evening.

The rest of the week passed quickly as I focused on work and wished the time away.

As I returned home on Wednesday, I was exhilarated to see Ed's car parked outside my house and rushed in to find him preparing dinner.

I threw my arms around his neck and kissed him with all my might before we had even uttered a word. Finally, pulling apart we beamed at each other and whispered, "Hello, you," almost in unison.

Ed had made a simple but delicious dinner of chicken breast wrapped in bacon and a selection of salads. He was as keen on healthy eating as I was – a huge bonus not to have to prepare different foods. Just a few years before I allowed myself to succumb to temptation, without consideration of the consequences, which is why over the years living alone I had gained weight, allowing myself cream buns, ice cream, pasta, potatoes, bread – particularly the freshly baked white loaf variety, the smell was enough to make my mouth water – and all the other carb-heavy delights. Once I had adopted the low-carb lifestyle the weight had started to shed and now I didn't want to go back to where I had been, so I stuck with the theme, although I was not as strict as I had once been.

Ed had set up four more viewings for the Thursday and I was sad not to be able to join him, but having taken an unplanned day off the week before I could not keep taking off random days every week.

It was reassuring that Ed had wanted me to have an input to his future living arrangements, but I would have to leave that to him this time. No doubt I could view the particulars online and hear Ed's take on them.

I just hoped, as I sat at my desk that morning, staring into space, that he would find something close to me.

At dinner he reeled off the details of each property and again they were too far away, too big, too small or too grubby. I don't think it was that he was being too picky or too difficult. It was just that there was nothing suitable, nothing that met his needs. And weirdly that made me happy. It was not that I didn't want him to move down. In fact, I was desperate for him to be closer, I just didn't really want him living somewhere that didn't make him happy.

In fact it occurred to me that I didn't really want him living anywhere except with me.

Ed stopped talking, looking at me with concern on his face. "Is everything okay? You've gone very quiet."

"Ummm, well, it's just that…" I struggled with the words, finding the right ones to express my thoughts without scaring him off.

"Oh, I hope you don't take this the wrong way, but I don't want you living in any of those places. They sound dreadful. And as I was thinking about it, it occurred to me that actually, what I wanted, what I really wanted…" and at this point I avoided his stare and looked down at my almost empty plate of food. I felt nervous and unsure. What if he took this the wrong way? What if, what if? *You're overthinking again*, I chided myself, forcing myself to lift my gaze and look Ed in the eyes. He smiled an encouraging smile, giving me the confidence to continue. "What I really want…" I hesitated again.

I looked back at my hands resting on the table beside the plate before continuing. I took a deep breath. "In truth what I would really like is… What I'm trying to say, or ask, maybe, is that if you can't find anything you like, then maybe you could move in with me. That is to say until you find what you're looking for. No, what I wanted to say is that I'd like, I want, you to move in with me. I know we've not been together..." Ed stopped me by holding up his fingers to my lips. Now I realised, looking him in the face for the first time in a while, that he was beaming from ear to ear, and instantly my fear and nervousness vanished.

"I thought you'd never ask," he said, and in one swift move pulled me out of my chair and onto his lap. I wrapped my arms around his neck, smiling back at him.

"I did intend to find somewhere else to live," he went on, "but the more I looked, the more I came to the same conclusion as you. That really all I wanted to do was to be with you. Without sounding too much like a song lyric." He laughed, we kissed and went to bed to seal the deal.

*

Ed surprised me with a cup of coffee in bed just as my alarm shrieked into life. Sitting next to me on the bed he told me that he was going to cancel the viewings he had lined up and spend the time arranging removal vans and storage instead, as clearly all his belongings wouldn't squeeze into my cottage. He was back at work on Saturday morning but would still be at home after I finished work and would then drive north when the traffic calmed down.

And that is what happened.

The second weekend without Ed was easier. I spent the time researching the Le Mans 24-Hour and Classic races. I wanted to be prepared, not just so I could hold my own in a conversation, but also so I knew what I would need in the way of clothing, camping equipment and so on.

The twenty-four-hour race looked exciting but confusing to say the least, with so many cars, split into categories depending on the type of car and type of driver, all taking part in the same race. I was not sure how you were meant to know who was where in the race. I asked Ed when we spoke later that day.

"Well, it's easy to tell the first three cars in each category because they will have lights lit on the side of the car to show their position, so the first car has one light, the second has two, the third-placed car has three. Beyond that it's a little harder to know, which is where the race radio and TV coverage comes in handy. It's a long course and a longer race. Cars can be lots of laps down and then something happens to the car ahead and everything changes. It's not just about the race, it's about the camping, the holiday, the sights and sounds and smells. And of course the beer," Ed informed me.

Having read up on the race I spent Sunday buying the essentials – hot-weather clothes, sun tops and shorts, as well as wet-weather gear, just in case. Good trainers and socks – Ed had told me there was a lot of walking in excessive heat and I was renowned for getting blisters on a walk into town. Then there was the equipment. Ed had arranged for an erected tent and had an inflatable bed, bedding and fold-out chairs, but there were still things I needed. A good light so I could find the tent in the dark. A powerful torch if I needed to cross the campsite in the dark. Plastic wine glasses, tropical-strength bug spray, suntan lotion, after-sun, painkillers, first aid kit, to name but a few. It was little surprise then, whilst in France, the lads would nickname me 'Mum'.

Being busy, writing lists, getting organised had kept my mind off the ache I felt in not seeing Ed. It wouldn't be long.

It did occur to me that this would be a big test so early in our relationship, but we wouldn't know unless we gave it a go and it did sound like it would be a laugh, even if the only person I would know in the group was Ed. And of course, it was sort of a pre-runner to us living together. If we could manage to share a tent in excessive heat, then we could manage to share a cottage in middle England.

ten.

Racing to the race

The next few weeks flew by in a similar pattern of highs and lows as the excitement built towards the road trip to Le Mans.

Ed, true to his word, arrived early on the Wednesday morning, and after our usual method of greeting and a spell catching up I finished packing my bags and we loaded Ed's car ahead of the ridiculously early start the next morning.

That evening we were both sensible, avoiding alcohol and opting for an early night without the usual bedroom antics.

I had checked and rechecked my rucksack to make sure I had my medication and the all-important tickets, passport and money which Ed had handed over to me, as the passenger, for safe-keeping and so I could present them at the appropriate moments.

As I lay in bed listening to Ed's snoring, wishing I could drop off as easily as he did, I couldn't quite make out if I was nervous, excited or both. Luckily sleep fell upon me before I could overthink the situation and work myself into a sleepless night.

The alarm brought me back to the world at 5am. I was awake but could quite easily have turned over and gone back to sleep if it had not been for Ed's beaming face beside me. Clearly he could be awake as quickly as he could be asleep.

"Morning, gorgeous," he said. "You ready for an adventure?"

I snuggled into his warm, bare chest. "Yes," I whispered, "although it might take me a moment to wake up."

A couple of minutes later I stole myself out of my happiness cocoon and hit the shower, hoping it might revive my mind as well as my body and above all hoping it wouldn't be the last shower I had before returning home the following week.

After Ed had been through his ablutions I put all the wash stuff into the bag I had already prepared, with dry towels already rolled tight and secured inside.

We made our way to Ed's car in the early morning light. Makeup, wash stuff, handbag and us – the last additions to the car.

As Ed started up the engine he reached over and squeezed my knee. "Let's go!" he roared. He was like a little kid in a sweet shop. I hadn't seen him this excited before. I liked it. I liked it a lot.

We had arranged… well, I say 'we', really it was Ed who had made all the arrangements. I will start that again. Ed had arranged to meet the others in the car park at Eurotunnel. The rest of the group lived all over the south of England so it was the only sensible and logical choice.

We had a pleasant journey down, Radio 2 blaring out

some classic hits, Ed singing along, me mouthing the words to show I knew them, but without waking the living dead through my toneless warbling.

Every so often Ed squeezed my knee, making me jump and scream when I didn't see it coming, possibly guessing I would be nervous at meeting so many of his friends in one go. Maybe nervous himself at his friends meeting me and what they might make of me.

Oh dear, I thought, *I really didn't think this through. Why did I say yes? There are too many 'firsts' for our first trip: the first time I will meet his friends, my first time at a race, first uninterrupted week together.* I was staring out of the window and the car had grown quiet over the last few miles. The reassuring squeeze again.

"It'll be great," he said in the most reassuring tone he could muster. "They'll love you." He smiled over at me, I smiled back.

"I know it will," I said, resting my hand on his thigh. "I'm looking forward to meeting them. I just hope they like me."

"Of course they will." Ed was looking straight ahead focusing on the road. "They'll love you as much as I do." He glanced at me sideways then returned his gaze forwards. I didn't know how to respond. I felt the glow of happiness burn my face up.

What if he is now regretting letting that slip? I thought. But I need not have worried. The knee squeezes again. When I looked up at him he smiled. "I meant that, you know. That I love you."

My face nearly exploded with the pressure of my smile. "I love you too."

The gulf between us evaporated and seeped out the windows. He was smiling now.

"That was not really how I intended to tell you that," he admitted sheepishly. "I was hoping for a more romantic moment when I was holding you in my arms rather than as we sit next to each other, driving down a motorway, while I'm unable to look at you."

I turned in my seat so I could see him better. "That's okay. These things rarely happen how we hope or even plan they will, life or fate has a strange way of interfering in that."

"I don't suppose I can get you to forget I said it and then when a more appropriate time comes up I can spring it on you?" he asked in the same light-hearted manner.

"Not a chance. Well, you can tell me as often as you like, but I can't forget that you told me. If you like I can pretend I don't know and try to act all surprised. I'm no actress but I could throw my arms in the air for some dramatic expression of shock and wonder."

"That sounds ideal. Let's do that."

I felt a lot better about meeting Ed's friends now that I knew how he felt about me. I had the reassurance that if they didn't like me, I knew Ed was deep enough into the relationship to not let any negative comments sway him. At least so I hoped.

As we pulled into the Eurotunnel car park an entire hour ahead of our schedule, Ed's phone pinged.

"We've set up a WhatsApp group for the trip," he told me. "A couple of the guys are already here and parked at the far side, near the exit, so we can all park together." Ed reversed out of the space he had pulled into and we quickly found the other early arrivals.

"They must have gone into the terminal for breakfast. Let's join them, I'm starving," Ed suggested, getting out of the car and waiting for me to join him at the boot.

"Yes, me too," I confirmed as we made our way across rows and rows of waiting travellers. I was unsure whether the pains in my stomach were hunger pangs or indeed nerves, but either way it would be good to meet the lads in smaller numbers. If nothing else it might help me to remember names. I was, and am, notoriously bad at that, finding creative ways around actually having to mention someone's name.

Well, I thought, *here goes everything. Yes, 'everything' is right, I have too much to lose now.*

Apparently there were to be ten cars in total, each with two people, a driver and a navigator, although in this day and age, with the help of Sat Navs the passengers were almost redundant.

The first four arrivals, two brothers and two friends, were already tucking into huge full English breakfasts when we closed in on their table. They were all chatting animatedly, obviously just as excited as Ed. As we approached, one of them spotted us and leapt to his feet, followed by the others in quick succession, their breakfasts forgotten temporarily.

They all half shook hands, half hugged Ed and then turned to me for introductions and the usual pleasantries.

That wasn't so hard, I thought as we lined up to order some food. I desperately needed caffeine. We decided against the full English, instead opting for a more continental coffee and pastries. I had already told myself that carbs were okay for the next week. With all the walking and the limited food options it would be hard to avoid them, so I might as well make the most of it and embrace them.

We found a spot next to each other at the end of the table and the, 'So what do you do?' followed. There was a headhunter (not literally, but in the recruitment field), a car salesman, an architect and an engineer. They all came across as intelligent, successful men, but right now they were just excited boys. Let loose from work and their families they clearly intended to make the most of their week away.

Our table grew bigger as more and more arrived. In the end, just as our train was called to embark, there were twenty of us, taking up half the tables in the cafe. When I say twenty, I should be more specific at this point. That is, there were nineteen men and me. This certainly was going to be an interesting few days.

I had been in the Eurotunnel just once before, but that was many, many years ago in another lifetime and in very different circumstances.

The first time, there had been just four of us in the group, all in one car: my fiancé, my soon-to-be mother- and father-in-law, and of course me.

My fiancé, Fred 2, was never to be my husband, but on that day we were very much in love and heading to France for a celebratory engagement lunch. The day had been glorious. We had eaten in the garden of a rustic restaurant in a small town in northern France and on the journey home picked up champagne and wine from a *supermarché* near the terminal. I had no idea at that point what a whirlwind and how tumultuous the next year would be.

Back to the present

I was equally excited, but for very different reasons as all twenty of us got back in our respective cars, and one by one lined up behind each other as we left the car park. We managed to stick together as we filed onto the train, the barriers between the compartments breaking up the convoy, but we went through the heavy airlock doors and met in the middle carriage. It was hot, but as we leant against the side of the train with the cars positioned between us, we joked and laughed and I finally began to relax.

It was a quick journey and soon the train was speeding out into the bright French sunshine. High fencing surrounded the track marking where the refugee camp, The Jungle as it was called, had once stood and where so many had tried to access transport to carry them under or over the sea to safety. Now disbanded and the refugees moved on, it was still a stark reminder of the desperate and dangerous measures refugees will take in order to find sanctuary. Somewhere peaceful. Somewhere where they could be safe, find work or for the young, unaccompanied children to engage in education. Lord only knows what those young, impressionable eyes, ears and minds had seen or been subjected to on their journey to, and in, this place.

The train slowed down as it approached the terminal so we made our way back to the correct compartments and climbed into our respective cars. The heavy compartment doors swung back and rolled up out of the way. Soon we were rolling off the train and into the brilliant French sunshine.

While we had been on the train the organiser had given

us all instructions. We were heading straight down to Le Mans, the quickest way possible, which meant toll roads and motorways. The plan was to try to stay in convoy and pull off the road somewhere near Rouen for lunch.

"It shouldn't be too hard to stick together on the motorway, as long as no one decides to floor it and leave the others behind. Each driver should keep an eye on the car behind and if he slows, you slow and we all stay together." These simple instructions, should, in theory, work, but with nineteen men in ten cars on their way to a race it didn't sound very likely to me.

We had programmed the Sat Nav. I was glad to realise that the likelihood of our arriving at the destination was not solely down to my map-reading skills. My degree in Geography would stand me in good stead for the task, but my knowledge of, or ability to, measure distance and my limited French were distinct disadvantages. I was not sure our young relationship could have stood that particular test so early on.

We nearly lost half the convoy at the first roundabout. Luckily they caught us up soon after we joined the motorway and were soon trundling through the French countryside. Signs for familiar places like Le Havre and Dieppe sped by but we never actually saw any of them, as the motorway skirted them all. The exception, as with every rule, was Rouen, where the motorway slowly descended down into the heart of the town. A succession of junctions and traffic lights played havoc with the convoy and soon we were one of two cars. The organiser clearly knew this would happen and had arranged for us to stop for lunch just the other side of the city, giving us the opportunity to regroup.

It was a peaceful, sleepy French town, at least it was until ten British cars came roaring into the main street. Parking up on either side of the road, we perused a few of the menus displayed on the outside of the cafes and restaurants. In the end, the availability of a lot of tables in the shade along the outside of the cafe nearest to our cars swung our decision. After the early start, I'm not sure anyone had the energy or enthusiasm to explore much further.

I have only rudimentary French, enough to order a couple of beers, coffee, ask for the bill, secure a room for the night and of course say please and thank you. To my relief one of our travelling companions was an accomplished and fluent speaker, and soon we were pulling tables together, drinking ice-cold beer and water, and trying to find something I understood on the menu. I decided on a ham omelette, foregoing the *frites*.

The food took some time to appear and when it did it came two plates at a time. Clearly the kitchen was not used to such a large group but it was entertaining as a Julie Walters-type Mrs Overall from Acorn Antiques brought out the plates, walking slowly, purposefully and carefully placing one foot in front of the other, bent at the middle in a semi-permanent bow. However, after slowly laying each plate in front of the hungry recipient she spun on her heels, and as she walked away she straightened up to her full height and sped back to the kitchen.

By the time the last plates were delivered the first two or three had already been finished. We were in no rush. We were over halfway to our destination and were making good time. Plus it enabled us to relax, get to know each other and enjoy our surroundings.

The buildings around us were fairly modern, and not of any architectural style or note, but nearby was a tall, simple building named 'Fromage'. My French was good enough to know that it meant 'cheese'. However, it generated a debate as to whether it housed a cheese market, the local cheese producers' association, was just the name of the building which provided a central meeting place for the townsfolk, or a combination of the above. Who knew, and to be honest, none of us cared enough to wander over and make enquiries, it was just a means to keep us entertained whilst the last of the lunch plates were polished off.

I was glad of the air conditioning in the car when we clambered back into the hot leather seats which had been baking in the sun for the last couple of hours. The air was hot and thick, the heat of the seat quickly penetrating our thin summer clothes and turning my legs and back to a sweaty mess. The car quickly cooled and the seats became bearable as we made our way back to the motorway and on to Le Mans.

*

It was early evening when we arrived at our destination. Despite it having been dry all the way down, there had clearly been rain in the town, as the roads were wet and the air felt clearer than it had all day. As we drove along a wide boulevard, Ed excitedly exclaimed, "We are on the race track, we're actually driving along the race track." He went on to explain that the majority of the track is in fact everyday streets and they are just closed off on practice and race days. There is only a short section of dedicated race track centred around the grandstands and pit lane.

Arriving early, as we were, the roads were open and it was quite exciting to think we were travelling on the very tarmac that would soon by subjected to the roar of hundreds of engines, whilst tyres squealed their way round the track in hot pursuit of their nearest competitor.

We had to go through some tight security to get into the general camping area, in which our private site was located. I was not entirely sure what they were searching for but they had a good root through our belongings before releasing us.

There were numerous sites dotted around the track, all with their own benefits and detriments. Our site was the other side of a general camping area. My heart sank as we started driving through the site, tents, cars, caravans all pitched in disarray wherever the camper had seen fit. It looked hot, dusty and not particularly hygienic as we passed through. There were some hastily erected, ramshackle eating places near the track we passed along, and despite arriving early for the race there were already queues for what I assumed were showers and loo.

I felt trepidation rising in me. How on earth was I going to survive this, more to the point was there any way I could get out of it? I worked through the scenario in my head: how to tell Ed, how to find my way home, not even really knowing where I was in France and without sufficient French to get me home even if I knew how to get there.

Ed must have seen my expression but chose to keep quiet. Not even the reassuring knee squeeze to alleviate the fears. This was terrible.

Through another gate and across a field of chaos and

there in front of us was a high metal fence with orderly pitches marked out on the grass behind. I looked at Ed optimistically. If this was us it looked a lot better organised and if that was how they had arranged tents then surely there would be better facilities as well.

Reading my mind Ed confirmed, "This is us." Then reminded me that "It's private camping so only paying customers can get in. There is a bar and restaurant next to the track, private loos and showers and a courtesy bus that will take us up to the pits. We have stayed in other sites before but these guys are the best. They are also on the inside of the Porsche curve so a great position for watching the race, but noisy, obviously." He was so excited it was infectious, and my momentary escape plans were put aside as we rolled up to the gates and showed our tickets to the security team.

The organisers had pitched us together – five pitches, backing on to five more, so we had room to create a central meeting space between our cars and tents.

The rain had helped to cool the air but the sun was out now and the temperature was rising, despite it being early evening. *Thank goodness we don't have to erect tents in this heat*, I thought, grateful Ed had decided to spend the extra money to have a pre-erected tent. We unloaded our bedding, blew up the mattress and made the bed, putting our bags in the entrance area and hooking open the 'door' to let some air in.

Even that was hot work and I made my excuses to go and find somewhere I could splash some cold water on my face before I melted in a pool of sweat – not a good look, trust me. To my surprise and delight, the facilities were just as good as Ed had promised. They were spotless and even better they were both labelled as either 'male' or 'female', so no sharing (not literally) required. And better still, there were no queues.

Having cooled down I took a quick look around the rest of the site. Again to my relief there was a large bar and restaurant in a sturdy marquee. Clearly the catering was going to be good, looking at the large menu boards suspended from the walls. This was going to be a lot better than I had feared.

I went to the bar and ordered five large jugs of ice-cold lager and twenty plastic glasses. Having paid I realised there was no way I was going to be able to carry all of this back to the group. Luckily one of the barmen could see my dilemma and offered to help.

I was met with a cheer as I arrived, laden down with the nectar of the gods. The tables and chairs along with a sound system and speakers had been set up under a gazebo in the middle of our pitches, and we laid out the drinks. The barman returned to his duties, and we all sat down to enjoy the lager as I passed around the sun lotion and mosquito spray for everyone to make use of. I realised that I had both proven myself a good addition to the group but I was also in danger of being seen as a parent. Ed dispelled that by leaning over and passionately kissing me to cries of 'oi-oi' from the lads.

It was a hot evening and we descended on the restaurant for a two-course meal and a lot of lager, all of which we enjoyed in the 'beer garden' – numerous tables, chairs and umbrellas that filled the space between the marquee and the race track where a practice session had got underway.

Whilst the facilities had been much better than anticipated, the noise emanating from the track just feet away was far worse. It was not just the volume, it was also that it reverberated throughout my body. This was going to be another sleepless night with Ed but for very different reasons. Clearly in a tent, surrounded by friends and only a very thin piece of material between us, nothing like that was going to happen. Apart from the lack of privacy, the heat and the blow-up mattress also acted as a barrier to any joyous unions.

That said it was still hard to curb the passion. But, given the circumstances, a long passionate kiss had to suffice and we reluctantly pulled apart and, after a long and tiring day, fell into a deep sleep.

I woke in the night in need of the loo, but it was still dark outside and I was worried about walking across the site in the dark and whether I would be able to find my way back to the tent.

I tossed and turned for a while hoping I could hold on until dawn.

Ed must have sensed how uncomfortable I was and put his hand out to touch me, asking, "Are you okay?"

"Sorry, I didn't mean to wake you. I, well, to be honest I need the loo and I'm worried I won't find my way back," I confessed sheepishly.

"That's okay," he said, reaching up to turn on the camping light. "I'll come with you."

We picked up a torch and left the light on in the tent. We held hands as we picked our way along the temporary track between the rows of dark tents. The ground was damp from dew and dawn was starting to creep over the horizon.

All around us the dark structures and sounds of snoring created an eerie atmosphere as we headed towards the lights in the main complex.

We were not the only ones in need of the facilities. We nodded and said hushed 'hellos' to our fellow campers as we passed.

The long weekend may not be the most physical of our relationship but it was already turning into one of the most romantic.

Later that day, after showers and a hearty breakfast, the group split up, deciding on different activities for the day. Having arranged to meet later at the bar, Ed and I headed up to the pits. It was a long, hot walk. We had foregone the free transfer in the campsite minibus. Having spent the day before sitting in the car we both felt the need to stretch our legs.

Sensibly I had brought a large-brimmed hat to protect my head from the intense sun, but beneath it I was sweating horribly. I dreaded the moment I would have to remove it, but for now it was serving its purpose.

We walked among the crowded pits, often little more than canvas tents strewn with car parts, tools and fold-up chairs. Some of the better prepared 'garages' included fridges and coffee machines. There was a hub of noise and excitement as mechanics, drivers and fans mingled together in the cramped space.

Ed would periodically stop at a tent and point out a car, telling me about famous drivers it had carried or races it had won. There were cars of every shape, make, colour and age spanning the motoring eras.

On several occasions we were hustled out of one of the

pits as cars thundered into life and made their way out to the circuit for practice or qualifying. Then we were hurled together in the cramped space between fans and temporary buildings. Whilst others moaned, barged and swore, Ed and I took a moment to enjoy our close proximity.

By midday I was starting to flag. Neither of us felt hungry due to the large breakfast and the heat, but a cold drink was definitely in order.

We made our way up to the main avenue of shops – Porsche, Aston Martin, Ferrari, designer labels, all tapping into this captive market, selling their branded products to the enthusiastic fans.

We found a bar and I ordered two lagers in my pidgin French – "*Deux bières, s'il vous plait.*" My accent was terrible but it was enough to get us what we needed. To my delight the drinks were served in sturdy plastic, branded pint glasses.

"Souvenirs," I said to Ed as we took over occupation of a couple of simple metal chairs and table under the shade of a tree as the previous customers gathered up their belongings, revived and ready to move on.

The heat, the lager, the noise, the smells, the sights… For a moment my head swam and I had to hold onto the edge of the table to steady myself, even though I was sitting.

We treated ourselves to another cool lager before gearing ourselves up to make our way up to the top of the circuit and the Dunlop Bridge. It was quite a climb, with high steps to get over it, but once on the other side there was plenty of room to stand or sit, if you didn't mind the dust and dirt, and watch the racing.

We were there some time, watching the session and

those around us of course, before the heat, the lagers and the walking made us feel increasingly sleepy. We headed back to camp, again declining to take the bus, ending up back at base a hot and sweaty representation of my former self. Luckily Ed had not fared much better.

We took our fold-up chairs to the gazebo and put them up in the shade. There were already a couple of the lads under the awning. We slumped down in our chairs and before long were knocking out zzzz's like the rest of them.

I woke before the others. Our numbers had swollen whilst I had been asleep and I was hopeful they hadn't heard me snore. Judging by the noises emanating from the sleeping giants around me I would have been in good company if they had.

There was a slight, but warm breeze wafting through the gazebo and I risked removing my hat before everyone awoke. I shook out my damp, lifeless hair, hoping the heat would work its magic. *I must look a state*, I thought, doing my best without makeup, hairbrush or a mirror to make myself look at least halfway decent.

I jumped and let out a small yelp as a hand tugged at my arm. Ed was still slumped in his chair, but his eyes were open and his hand rested on my arm.

"You look beautiful," he smiled, clearly aware of my vain attempts to make myself look less like the messy monster that I felt.

I smiled back. "And you look handsome," I said as I leant in to give him a kiss, nearly toppling over our flimsy canvas chairs. We laughed and in the process woke some of our sleeping companions who were slowly coming to.

As more woke up we started chatting about what we

had been up to, sharing good things to see, like the pits, and where was best to watch the action.

As we chatted, more of the group returned in dribs and drabs, all hot but enthusiastic about their experiences that day. At some point after the sun crossed the yard arm the music system was cranked into life and lagers arrived from the bar to quench our thirsty, dry throats.

We were having so much fun that we almost forgot to have dinner. At the last minute someone pointed out that food might be a good idea and we all piled into the marquee for a slap-up two-course meal washed down by the inevitable jugs of lager.

After eating we took a healthy supply of jugs back to our central gazebo, turned up the volume on the music and sat around talking and laughing. There were some incredibly entertaining people in the group and conversation never waned or got boring, it bounced around, jokes were made, not least at each other's expense. I contributed little to the banter, but I soaked up the atmosphere and enjoyed the company.

It occurred to me that I couldn't remember the last time I'd had so much fun. The last time I had got completely and utterly captivated by the moment. The last time I hadn't thought about removing myself from life.

I didn't dwell on any of that at the time. I was having too great a time and I didn't think about it when we were dancing and a few other people from across the site crashed our free party. I didn't think about it as Ed and I stumbled back to our tent some hours later. And I didn't think about it as I crashed out on the mattress fully dressed.

It was in fact in the middle of the dark, still night that

the thoughts started crashing into my brain, which woke me and prevented me from falling back into a peaceful sleep.

For a number of years before I met Ed I had been depressed. Not that I had been diagnosed, or treated, or even recognised it at the time, let alone talked to anyone about it, but I knew I had dark thoughts from time to time. Thoughts about not wanting to wake up the next day. It was not one thing that had led me to that point. It had been a series of somethings, sometimes big, sometimes small, events that each took their turn in sapping my strength. I started drinking more and more, not as a way to cope but as a way to forget. I didn't drink every day and I didn't always drink heavily, but I found excuses to drink – I had a good day, I had a bad day, it was the weekend and so on.

If I was not drinking too much then I was overindulging in food. I was trying to fill a hole, a cavernous, gaping emptiness.

The eating and drinking excesses didn't affect my work, but slowly I realised that I had a problem. It was not until Ed came bounding into my life, a rejuvenating breath of fresh air, that the thoughts and then the drinking had subsided.

Yes, I was drinking a lot on this holiday and I still enjoyed a tipple, but I no longer needed it to black out the hurt. Now I just drank with company and for company but no longer without company.

Back in the dark days, when the abyss took over, I had wanted my life to end, but I never intended to do anything about it. I just hoped I wouldn't wake up. I did realise that was a selfish desire. That millions of people wanted nothing more than to be well, to be alive, and here I was wishing for the opposite. In recognition I prayed to anyone who might be listening to take my life and spare theirs. I couldn't see the point in life. I was single, never married, no children. I just worked to pay my bills. There was no hope, no joy, no future and I struggled with that. How little I knew. Then I felt destiny was against me. But now, in that small, hot tent somewhere in western France, I prayed again, this time in thankful gratitude that my previous prayers had gone unanswered. I said thanks for whoever, or whatever, brought this amazing man into my life and for the joy and happiness he brought with him.

I lay on my side, smiling, staring at my miracle snoring in front of me. Slowly I let the peace overtake me and I fell back into a deep sleep.

Saturday was much like Friday. Ed and I had walked up to the pits again to see the bits we had missed the day before. We had been passing the Porsche shop and were surprised at the queue, so stopped a moment to see if there was a driver signing autographs or some special event taking place. When we realised they were handing out free Porsche flags we joined the throng to claim our prize.

The twenty-four hours of racing started at 1pm and we had found ourselves a good vantage point just below the Dunlop Bridge from where we could watch the madness get underway. Armed with our flags and a rapidly warming bottle of water we watched the first of the many races whilst the sun beat down on us.

During the brief lull between races we made our way back to camp – firstly on the free mini train that ran up and down the complex behind the pits and then transferred to the courtesy bus which took us right into the heart of our campsite, having decided to duck out of the heat rather than walk through it.

Despite the heat we avoided lager during the afternoon, not wanting to overdo it too early. We had taken some of the cafe's plastic chairs to the fence on the edge of the site which was right next to the race track and watched the cars speeding past. Oblivious to who was winning, not really supporting any particular car or team, it was just thrilling to be so close to these magnificent machines.

Early evening we made our way back to our tent and changed. The gazebo was starting to fill up and conversation and music flowed.

Again the dancing went on until the early hours. Fireworks were being discharged from various campsites around the circuit and our music was competing with the roar of the races going on around us. No one cared though, we were having way too much fun.

People periodically wandered off to watch the night racing, mesmerised by the headlights growing larger as they approached and then after sharp braking for the corner, their red lights disappearing off into the night. It was electric, it was thrilling – the smell, the vibration, the sights all assaulting and invigorating all the senses. Under any other circumstances it could have been the forerunner to a truly passionate moment, but we were surrounded by hundreds of campers and so settled for holding hands and stolen kisses instead.

Saturday night was another sleepless night, not because of passion or haunting memories, but because of the noise. The only trouble with twenty-four hours of racing is that there is very little let-up in the action other than when the race finishes and the next grid lines up to race.

I woke as the sun rose and the heat in the tent started to rise to uncomfortable levels. *Time for a shower*, I thought and turned to tell Ed – only his side of the bed was empty.

He was not back when I returned from the shower, nor was he back once I was dressed and made-up.

I wandered over to the marquee feeling in need of a lot of coffee and some breakfast but he was not there either. I eventually found him asleep in a fold-out chair right next to the track, a couple of the others around him. Clearly they had decided to watch some of the night racing and fallen asleep. How they could sleep in the full sun and next to the track was anyone's guess but here they were.

I bent over and kissed Ed on the forehead, wanting to speak to him, but at the same time feeling a little guilty at waking him. I hovered, no reaction, I waited some more. As I was about to turn and leave, Ed's arm caught hold of me and he pulled me back down for a proper kiss. If it hadn't been such an uncomfortable position I would have gladly stayed lost in his embrace, but as it was, it was hurting my back and I had to stand up.

I looked down at his sleepy face. "Good morning," I mouthed, not wanting to wake the sleeping beauties around him.

"Good morning," he said as he slowly stood to his full height and then pushed his arms hard and high above his head in order to stretch out his aching limbs. Clearly the chair had not been a comfortable place to sleep.

I was, by now, leaning on the metal fence that separated the campsite from the racetrack. Ed put an arm either side of me, pinning me to the fence. We smiled at each other momentarily while I put my arms around the back of his neck and then we simultaneously pulled each other in close and kissed passionately, only pulling apart when a voice shouted, "Oi, get a tent," followed by laughter.

We pulled apart and turned sheepishly to find most of the group laughing at us. We joined in.

After breakfast we packed our bags, deflated the mattress, re-bagged that and the bedding and loaded it all into the car. Apart from a couple of plastic beer glasses and two flags we were going home with what we came with, but it seemed to have grown over the weekend and the car was laden down.

It had been hot work but with the cars all packed we had time to watch some more racing. We knew we'd have some distance to travel through congested streets before we were back on the open road, so had decided to set off just before the racing ended to avoid the worst of the traffic.

As we pulled up to the gate, our convoy reassembled, we thanked the staff, all of whom had been amazing and who really made us feel so welcome and so well looked after. I felt a little sad as we headed out onto the dusty track, back towards the tarmac roads that would lead us home. I had made some great new friends on this trip, and despite the heat and the camping our relationship had stood the test. If anything we were even stronger for it. Now, on top of everything else, we had this amazing shared experience too.

We had been given the postcode of where we were staying that night – a château, we were led to believe, a bed and en suite. I couldn't wait. It was in a small town roughly halfway between Le Mans and Calais, all back roads, which meant the convoy had no chance of sticking together as it soon turned out. Before we even got to the limits of Le Mans we had split and split again at every junction and every roundabout and now there were just two cars.

We drove at pace along the quiet roads, through rolling countryside bathed in sunshine, through beautiful medieval town centres with Communist-Bloc-type apartments on the outskirts, through dark woods and farmland. Ed and I had the radio on but it made no sense to us and we were not listening anyway, recounting, as we were, the last few days, laughing at the jokes, regaling tall stories and antics and of course the racing itself.

Ed looked several times in the rear-view mirror as we were leaving a hamlet, nothing more than a row of houses on either side of a short stretch of road.

"Is everything okay?" I asked.

"I hope so," Ed replied, "but Jon in the car behind is flashing his lights."

A short distance further we pulled onto the dried, dusty earth at the side of the road. I stayed in the car whilst Ed went to find out what was wrong.

After a few moments he returned.

"It's okay, they suggested we find somewhere for lunch, which seems like a good plan, so keep your eyes peeled for somewhere suitable," he instructed me.

Twenty minutes later, as we were driving through a wood, we could see up ahead a clearing, and a building with a number of cars parked out front.

"There on the right," I pointed with my hand as Ed followed its direction, indicated and slowed as we approached.

"Great, that'll do," Ed confirmed and a few minutes later pulled in to a packed car park. To our surprise and delight we recognised a couple of the cars. Four of the group had stopped ahead of us and were just finishing their lunch as we joined them.

They gave us instructions on how it worked and then got back in their cars and roared off up the road.

The four of us remaining entered the slightly strange cafe. It may well have been a petrol station at some point, the shop converted into a counter displaying cold drinks but with little information on what food was available. The tiled floors and walls seemed clean, though the toilets left a little to be desired. One was out of order, the other strewn with loo roll, but in these circumstances, beggars cannot be choosers.

We ordered four ham and cheese baguettes and a combination of soft drinks then found a spot outside the front of the cafe where we could keep an eye on the cars and waited for our lunch to appear. That took some time, but it was good to be out of the car for a while at least.

Fed and watered we climbed back into our baking hot cars and got the last leg of that day's journey underway.

As we approached our destination we saw the four guys from lunch now quaffing lager outside a bar and noted its location.

The 'château', it turned out, was more of a large house than the typical romantic view of a castle with turrets and moats, but what do you expect in the middle of a town? Of more concern was that it appeared to be very much shut. The large wooden arched doors that gave way into an inner courtyard were locked and no one answered the door. It didn't bode well, so we decided to make our way through the bustling town centre to find the guys who had set up a forward command at the pub.

We pulled some tables and chairs together and ordered more lager from a passing waitress, again my basic French achieving the desired outcome. It was quite a spot that the guys had found. We were bathed in sunshine, sitting on a bridge that spanned a pretty river. Although there was no evidence of waterfowl or fish, the steep walls down to the sparkling and fast-flowing river were adorned with flowers.

"So, what's up with the château?" Ed asked once our drinks had arrived and we were tucking into the thirst-quenching amber nectar.

"Not sure," one of the guys confessed. "There was no sign of the person we made the booking with and the two boys who answered the door didn't seem to know anything about us. Their English was about as good as our French so it was hard to be sure, but I don't think they were expecting us and none of the rooms are ready. They said it will take them an hour or so to get them ready so we thought we'd wait here."

"Good plan," we all agreed and sat back to enjoy the atmosphere, people-watching, relaxing and waiting, not just for our rooms but also for the rest of the convoy to catch us up. The spot was ideal for the last of those, as all cars would pass over the bridge to get to the destination, giving us the chance to shout directions and then wait for their return.

The later arrivals had found the gates open and their rooms ready, they told us after taking longer than expected to arrive back, having opted to decamp and have a shower before joining us. Once this was confirmed we dashed back to move our cars into the safe sanctity of the inner courtyard and were directed to rooms by the young boys who were now standing on guard at the main entrance. The inside of the house was dark and foreboding, with strange net curtains transecting the hallways and a collection of pianos arranged around the bottom of the dark oak staircase which became more spindly and twisted the higher we climbed.

The only rooms left by this point were at the top of the house, but it had all we needed: an en suite bathroom and a large double bed. Having dumped our bags, we forewent the showers. The lagers and the sunshine were too much to resist and we retraced our steps back to the bridge.

We whiled away a few hours, reminiscing about how great the trip had been and the escapades the various parts of the convoy had got up to since we saw them last. Eventually we realised that the bar owner had been discreetly packing up all the tables, chairs and umbrellas around us, shutting the bi-fold doors to the street and the open windows on the side of the building that faced the river. Now he was less than subtly looking at us, sitting in our island of furniture and half-finished drinks on an otherwise deserted bridge.

Deciding it was time for dinner, it was slightly disappointing to discover that the town pretty much closed on a Sunday evening and the only place open and able to accommodate us was a Chinese restaurant a short walk from the bar.

Our group took up over half of the small dining area, but our hostess was most accommodating. Between our French speakers we managed to order a feast, washed down by red wine and laughter. Every part of the trip was turning into a story to be recounted many more times over the coming months.

Full of food and happiness we wended our way back to the 'château', which we had, during the course of the evening, renamed the 'murder château', convinced as we were of some terrible goings-on within its old and crumbling walls.

No one was ready for sleep despite the late hour and no one was ready to stop drinking despite the amount we had already consumed. So the party atmosphere continued around a large wooden table on the first-floor terrace.

Ed and I had bought a box of wine before we left the UK and fetched it from the car. Others had purchased wine at a supermarket in Le Mans and that was also brought to the table. Someone found the kitchen and produced glasses of every shape and size but none that matched, not that it mattered.

Mobile phones were produced and we took it in turns to play songs loud enough for those of us on the terrace to hear but not so loud as to disturb the two strange boys or any of their neighbours.

I finally crashed at 1am and made my way to bed alone, leaving Ed and the others to continue the revelry. It was the first time since we had been together that we had not gone to bed together, but as that would be the last time he would see some of his friends for a while I didn't mind.

I woke the next morning to the sounds of car doors slamming and shouts between members of our group. Ed was still out cold beside me, so I sat in the open window watching the others pack up and carefully reverse out of the courtyard, clearly now desperate to get back to their homes and their families.

Ed and I were with our family, each other, and had no need to rush. I climbed back into bed and snuggled up behind him. We were no longer in a tent and there were very few of our party left in the house. *Now*, I thought, *will be the first time we make love on our holiday*, and I made sure we made the most of the opportunity.

We set off a couple of hours after everyone else, for the first time alone and not in even the tiniest of convoys. We made our way to the motorway and headed to the Eurotunnel. We were booked on an evening train, but arriving at lunchtime we decided to pay the extra money to get the next train with space for us rather than waste the afternoon in the terminal.

As we were being loaded onto the train Ed's phone began to ping. He read the message and laughed. "You'll never guess what," he said, "the others have stopped for lunch. We must have overtaken them somewhere along the road. It looks like we'll be the first back to Blighty, not the last."

The rest of the journey passed too quickly. I was glad to be home, in my own bed, with a shower and toilet just steps away and a kitchen nearby, but I had felt so close to Ed during the last few days and couldn't stand the thought that soon it would come to an end, even if that was only temporarily whilst he served the last of his notice period and then moved in with me.

Luckily neither of us were back to work straight away. Knowing we would be camping by a race track we had anticipated the exhaustion we would feel on returning home and had booked two extra days off. Two extra, blissful days, where we hardly left each other's arms, let alone the house.

I have to confess there were tears after Ed left me to complete the last leg of his journey home. Of course I didn't let him see them, but as I shut the door behind him I sank to the floor and cried silent, sad and tired tears. I had held them back not only because I didn't want him to think me foolish, but also because I didn't want him driving all that way worrying about me and distracting him from the road ahead.

The tears, I realised, were not just because we would be apart or the fact that it would be over a week until I saw him again. It might have been partly due to the exhaustion I still felt from the trip and the comedown from the exhilaration. The truth was I felt empty, truly hollow. I almost felt despair, ridiculous given that it wouldn't be for long, but after so much intimacy, in that moment it felt like a lifetime. I sank further into the dark, allowing the moroseness to take hold.

I waited up until Ed's text assured me he was home safe and I had acknowledged it. Then I crashed into bed for a night of fitful sleep.

eleven.
History often repeats itself

It was a good working week. Being only a couple of days, it gave me time to catch up on what I had missed, respond to urgent queries and plan out my next week.

I returned home on Friday night exhausted despite the short week.

That evening the rain came, giant drops of cold rain thundering down on the roof just a few feet above my head. The room lit up as lightning flashed and I lay in bed counting the miles before the thunder rumbled overhead, reverberating around the room. The weather mirrored my mood. I knew I would feel lonely. Due to Ed's shifts I would only be getting a few texts here and there, a strange contrast to the closeness we'd just had. There was something else though. I couldn't work out what but something was not right. I was afraid but I didn't know what of, what about or why.

The next week I was run ragged at work, preparing for the next launch event and all that entailed. The calls and texts from Ed became less frequent but I hadn't noticed, as I was working long hours and returning home exhausted, falling into bed after a quick supper. I fell asleep quickly but woke every night between 3am and 4am, tossing and turning, unable to get back to sleep as ideas and thoughts crashed and tumbled through my mind, stressing about work and how much I needed to achieve in an unrealistically short time. I had been turning the issues over, repeating and recycling them, trying to ensure I didn't forget any of it, which resulted in sleepless nights. On a couple of nights I ended up turning on the bedside light and dragging my tired body upright, reaching for a pen and paper waiting in anticipation on the table next to the bed and writing down all that occupied my conscious mind.

Soon the weekend was upon me and I climbed into bed after a few glasses of wine, ready for sleep and a chance to rest my weary mind. Physically fit but mentally exhausted I slept long and well.

The next morning I woke with a jump and a sudden realisation that when we had parted the week before Ed and I had not specified when we would be together again, and I had just assumed we would talk and make arrangements. I had hoped that I would see him again that weekend. After that thought there was to be no more sleep as the doubts crept into my mind. The fact that we had barely spoken all week, the texts had dried up. I had not paid much attention to it as I was so busy and had dismissed it as being the shifts that had kept him so quiet. But now it was the weekend and I finally had plenty of time to overthink the situation.

The shower refreshed my body but not my mind, other than a decision to send a text. Maybe he was working on another shift, but that was no excuse not to let me know what was going on. I'd had uncommunicative boyfriends before who just vanished, leaving me unsure of whether to plan my own day and do my own thing or wait for them to return. Those relationships had damaged my self-confidence. Somehow a lack of communication played havoc with my trust, always wondering where they were, what they were up to, who they were with and I was damned if I was going to let that happen again.

I felt those old familiar palpitations spread across my chest and reverberate around my tense body. I would send a text and see what happened. And that is what I did. I sent a light-hearted, noncommittal message, not that I felt that way. 'Hey you. I hope you're ok? Would be great to chat if you get a break. Miss you. Xx'

I deliberated over the kisses, but if I hadn't been worried I would have put kisses, so in the end I decided to keep them. I held my breath. Pressed send. I put my phone back to sleep and laid it on the table, only seconds later picking it back up, returning to the text and checking its status which had been updated to 'delivered'. *Well, at least I know he's received it even if he hasn't read it yet*, I thought.

Deciding to keep myself busy I walked into town after running around the house getting my chores done: clothes washed and hung out to dry on the racks in my spare room; kitchen, bathroom and living room cleaned and tidied; and finally putting the dishwasher on before leaving the house.

It was overcast, but humid, the worst of both worlds in my opinion. I walked the short distance into town, past the new build on what used to be the local police station before it was moved into the council offices, carefully crossing the small roundabout and past the takeaway shops that had for some reason all positioned themselves in a row – a pizza chain, independent pizza shop, Indonesian and Chinese.

I didn't need to get anything, but I needed a change of scenery. I had decided I would go for a walk first, a large loop around the town like I had done on the day I bumped into Ed. But now I realised that would give me far too much thinking space and I didn't want to dwell on the situation. For all I knew everything was fine and as always I was making a mountain out of a molehill. I pulled my phone out of my bag and for the tenth time checked the status of the text. 'Read' came the glaring, heart-stopping revelation.

'Read'. I stopped walking, staring at the phone. 'Read', yes it definitely said 'Read' and yet no reply, no pulsing dots to show he was typing a reply, just a cold, emotionless 'Read'.

My blood ran cold. *This is not good*, I thought. This was more than just me being paranoid, he would never just 'Read' and not reply, even to say he was tied up and would be in touch soon. No, just 'Read'.

I closed the text and my phone and zipped up my bag, my hand across it, hoping to feel the buzz of a new text or the vibration of a ringing phone. But nothing came.

I was on the way to nowhere, unsure where I was going or what I was doing. I felt empty. I saw nothing, heard nothing. I drifted onwards.

I passed the bike cafe, a small independent bike shop and cafe combo, on the route of the Tour de France when it passed through the town centre a few years before. Lined up outside were racks for bicycles, and small red metal fold-up chairs and tables.

I glanced at the customers enjoying refreshments

outside the cafe, and as I refocused on the path ahead I jumped as a hand reached out and touched my arm. Suddenly brought back to the present, for a moment my heart soared as I turned, expecting, hoping, to come face to face with Ed. Instead I turned to find Jon, one of the Le Mans crew.

"Hello," he said as he rose from his seat. "You looked like you were a million miles away."

"Sorry, I was. I was deep in thought. How are you?" I asked as I pushed myself up onto tiptoes. Even so, he still had to lean down so we could exchange the socially accepted greeting of a delicate kiss to both (note, not one) cheeks.

"I'm good. Finally caught up on sleep after the trip. How about you?"

"Much the same as you. I didn't know you were from around here," I replied, uncertain as to why this never came up whilst we were away.

"I'm not, actually I live about ten miles away but I bring my bike here to get it repaired and was just having a coffee while I wait. Would you like to join me?"

"That would be lovely," I confessed, relieved to have some company and to engage in conversation to take my mind off Ed and away from the dark thoughts.

Jon went into the cafe and reappeared a few minutes later with a large, strong, white coffee in a bowl-sized, solid white cup that snuggled into my grateful hands. I thanked him and we settled back in our seats. We reminisced about our exploits in France, whilst sipping the hot coffee and watching the world go by.

"And how is Ed? Is he down this weekend?" Jon asked innocently.

"Umm no," I said rather hesitantly, my hand again going to my bag to check if he had responded before stopping myself. It would have been rude to look at my phone, but I was looking to delay having to respond to the question. This was one of Ed's friends, how would I respond to such a question?

I smiled at Jon. "Actually I haven't heard from him much. I'm not sure if he's working or still catching up on sleep…" My voice trailed off as I was not sure how to complete the sentence. It didn't look good and Jon was starting to shift awkwardly in his seat as the silence between us grew.

"Have you spoken to him recently?" I asked, immediately regretting it despite my attempt at a light-hearted question, as it put Jon in the awkward position. I smiled, hoping that might get us back to where we were a few moments before. Our drinks were too hot to drink quickly and we would be stuck with each other for some uncomfortable minutes if we were not careful.

Jon looked down at his coffee, like something amazing was happening in the froth that he couldn't drag his eyes away from. "Actually yes," he said quietly without looking at me. "I spoke to him yesterday. He said, well, maybe I shouldn't tell you, but he said he wasn't working this weekend which is why I assumed he'd be here, with you. You were so…" His eyes now met mine, but his voice trailed off, clearly nervous about saying any more.

"Oh," was all I could muster as my heart sank to the pit of my stomach. I felt the prick of tears in the corners of my eyes. They bubbled over and ran down my cheeks, starting as drops, escalating to a flow. I lifted my hastily drawn tissue to catch them as they fell from my cheeks. These were heartbreak tears. I couldn't look at Jon. My mind was woefully running down the facts. *Ed isn't working, he hasn't come down, he hasn't called, he hasn't replied to my text. He is no longer my Ed*, I concluded.

I stared at my coffee, hoping it would magically cool sufficiently for me to drink and escape this impossible situation. All those years of making mountains out of molehills had put me in good stead for this moment. I pulled myself harshly and suddenly to my senses.

"Sorry," I said, with a slight attempt at a laugh whilst pulling myself up straight, and a quick, sharp shake of my head to make myself feel stronger. "No, I didn't know that, but that's okay, it's been pretty full-on of late and he probably needs a little space. I'm sure I'll hear from him soon." I smiled a hollow smile which convinced no one.

"I'm sure you're right," he said, tapping the back of my hand like an awkward adult trying to reassure a child they do not know well.

"Thank you," I said with sincerity. At least Jon had been honest with me.

We sat in silence for a while, taking as many hot sips of coffee as our mouths could endure. Eventually small talk resumed until one of the engineers from the bike shop came to tell a relieved Jon that his bike was ready.

"Thank you for the coffee, Jon, it was great to see you again." We exchanged kisses again.

"It was great to see you too, maybe we'll bump into each other again soon," he offered and then, after he had walked away a couple of steps and while I was deciding where to go next, I saw Jon stop, pause, then turn slowly.

"I'm sure he'll be in touch soon. We could all see how

much in love the two of you were in France. I'm sure there is a perfectly reasonable explanation for all of this. He's a good bloke, you know," he said in way of condolence.

"Thank you," I mouthed, unable to control the tears flowing down my face again. "I hope you're right," I mustered.

Clearly he wanted to escape, this was beyond socially awkward. He leant his bike up against the wall and stepped back towards me, intent on giving me a reassuring hug. But I put my hand out to stop him. "Thank you, but please don't. If you hug me right now it'll open a floodgate that I won't be able to shut, but thank you, I'll be okay."

I dabbed my face with the tissue as he walked away, not looking back this time. Who knows what the other patrons of the cafe must have thought. It didn't matter and I didn't care. I turned and walked away in the opposite direction. Somehow it felt like I was walking away from more than just one of Ed's friends.

I considered a visit to some of my favourite shops, but my heart wasn't in it. I didn't need anything. I didn't want anything. One of my usual emotional crutches – shopping – was not going to fill the empty void inside. My head swam with thoughts. I wanted Ed to text, or to call. I wanted to call him, but I knew I could not. Whatever was going on, he needed to come to me. The ball was firmly in his court.

I trudged home with a heavy heart. As I did my bag vibrated under my hand. I stopped suddenly, causing the middle-class couple behind me to puff at me as they sidestepped me. Normally I would have apologised for my inconsiderate behaviour, but all my attention, my very being, was focused on retrieving the phone, but my fumbling, shaking hands were more of a hindrance than a help. I stopped, eyes closed, deep breath in, deep breath out. Try again. This time I was successful.

I put my thumb on the button and the screen sprung to life.

It was a text.

From Ed.

I felt happy, then nervous, I wanted to read it, but I didn't. I was confused. I wanted good news, reassurance. I was fearful it would be bad news. Opening the text was not going to change the content, but it may delay me finding out the truth. It could be okay though, couldn't it?

I stood on the pavement, fixed to the spot, halfway between town and home.

Finally I made up my mind. If there were going to be more tears then best to do that in the comfort, security and solitude of my own home, away from prying eyes. No one wants to watch a woman crying in the street.

I rushed home, phone still clutched in my hand. I had the keys out ready whilst still five houses away. What had just a few days before been exhilaration at seeing a text from Ed had turned seamlessly into trepidation.

I slammed the door shut behind me, throwing myself, my bag and my phone onto the sofa. I pressed my thumb against the unlock button again. As I held my breath I read the simple, short, devastating text. 'Sorry. Something's come up. I need time to think. Will be in touch. Ed.'

No 'Hello you'. No warmth. No explanation. No timeline. No kisses.

It was like time stopped. I could hear myself breathe. But nothing moved. I was inside my own head. Then the swirling started. Tears, heavy, sobbing breaths. I coughed. Thoughts tumbling into and over each other in ferocious succession.

Is it over?

What has come up?

Who has come up?

In touch, but when?

How long will purgatory last?

Should I acknowledge the message to let him know I have received it? To let him know I am there when he is ready to talk?

At least I knew the answer to the last one. No. He could see from the text status it had been delivered and read. It was clear he wanted time. I wouldn't interfere with that. No, it was just a matter of time. A waiting game.

The thoughts whirled on.

Do I even know him?

How have we gone from loved-up and moving in together to needing time to think, in the space of a week? And think about what? What has happened in the short time we have been apart?

I could feel my face getting hot, the room spinning. I held onto the sofa, trying to focus my eyes on one point. My breathing was rapid, tears and sweat mingling together. Then nothing. Darkness.

*

I came around slumped on my side on the sofa, my phone lying forlorn on the floor where it must have dropped from my unconscious hand.

I pushed myself back upright and checked my phone. It took me a while to be able to focus but I was reassured to see that I had only been out for a couple of minutes at most. I realised that I must have fainted. It had all been too much to take and my emotions had overtaken me. I did a blood test to check there was nothing amiss with my diabetes. Thankfully the monitor showed everything was normal, in range. *At least something is*, I thought to myself.

I put the TV on for noise and distraction whilst I tried to make sense of it all.

I stared at the screen. I didn't hear or see anything that was being broadcast. I was in a stupor.

Okay, I eventually decided, *he's asked for space and that is what I'm going to give him.* I gave myself a mental slap round the face. *I've been here before. Better he quits now, rather than after he moves in, or when we have become even more entangled and in love. Good*, I concluded.

I hadn't been looking for love, love had found me. I had decided I was not going to be fooled again and here I was, back at the sink or swim moment as I had been so many times before. I would do what I always did, swim. Always a fighter, a survivor, I would get back on an even keel and carry on.

I had been a bad friend of late, doing what so many women do and seeing less and less of my friends as the relationship took hold. Now I reached out to my friends. They had every right to tell me to go to hell. But they didn't. They rallied round like we all had for each other at one time or another. Often at times like this. We arranged to meet in the pub in a couple of hours.

My relationship with Ed might be dead, but I was not. I

was not going to put my life on hold. I didn't need thinking time. I needed friend time. I needed to laugh. I needed to live. Above all, I needed wine.

I drank too much that evening, drowning my sorrows, some might say. I had shared my tale early in the evening to get it out of the way. I had not shared the full story. Somehow I was clinging, somewhere at the back of my brain, to the faint chance that it might not be over. I didn't want to taint my friends' opinion of him in case things made a turn for the better. We discussed possible reasons why this might have happened. There were lots of plausible reasons. None of them palatable. We loved him, we hated him, we didn't understand him, or any men for that matter.

We drank.

Then we laughed.

We danced where there was no dance floor in the middle of the busy bar.

My friends kindly escorted me home some hours later. I was understandably unsteady on my feet, the booze having worked its magic, particularly as I had forgotten to eat before we met.

I tried several times to get the key in the door, laughing each time as I focused with all my might, but the key skidded off across the brass plate as it missed its target. Eventually Kate patiently took the key from my hand and successfully opened the door.

They left me on my sofa with a strong coffee and a promise from me to be in touch the next day to let them know I was ok.

I woke the next morning curled up on the sofa where they had left me. I was cold – physically and mentally.

I tried to sit up, pushing myself up with my left arm. Something was wrong. Something was very, very wrong. I tried again, but I couldn't right myself. I tried to stand but fell back onto the sofa. I couldn't move. My left arm and left leg had no strength. They had no feeling. My left-hand side was numb.

I was terrified.

I didn't know what was happening. I wondered if I had had a stroke. I had never been troubled by hangovers, but I knew the symptoms and this certainly was not any of those. Certainly not something I had ever heard of.

I reached for my phone. My first reaction was to call Ed and ask for help. He had a key but was too far away and far more importantly he didn't want to hear from me.

I didn't want to worry my friends and anyway what could they do.

I did the only thing left that I could, I called an ambulance, tears again traversing my face, panicked. The operator tried to calm me as I waited for the tell-tale sounds of an ambulance getting louder and louder until it was ear-splittingly close.

I eased myself onto the floor and dragged myself across the carpet to the door. Using all the power and strength I had on my right side to reach up and open the door, I then sunk back down to the floor, out of breath, exhausted, terrified.

The crew arrived with a stretcher and I explained my symptoms, adding my diabetes and allergies for good measure. They didn't think it was my long-term illness but did a blood test just to check. It was normal.

They picked up my bag with my medication and took

me the twenty miles to our nearest hospital. Luckily at that time of the morning there was not too much of a wait in A&E, even so, by the time a doctor got to me I was already starting to regain strength in my defunct side. Blood was taken, my neck was scanned and my eyes examined, not that any of that revealed anything. The doctor brought in a colleague for a second opinion and the questioning and prodding resumed.

Two hours later I walked out of the hospital barefoot, as there had been no need to put shoes on when I was stretchered out of the house.

In the end a neurologist had been called and had, after further tests, concluded that it was a rare form of migraine brought on by extreme stress, which resulted in half-body paralysis rather than the usual debilitating headache.

"My weird body strikes again," I had told the doctor to his bemusement, as I explained I couldn't whistle, click my fingers, or wink, my eyes don't change quickly in response to changes in light and I have no reflexes in my knees or ankles.

I sent a text to my friends to reassure them I was okay, not mentioning what had happened for fear of worrying them.

I took a taxi home and put myself to bed. This was not a day for doing anything.

After a restful sleep I lay in bed for some time, not awake, not asleep. Not wanting to face what was left of Sunday, but unable to sleep further.

Nervously I got up. I feared a return of the paralysis, but I stood up unimpaired and went to have an overdue, refreshing shower to wake me from this day.

It was mid-afternoon and I had no plan to go out so I put on clean PJs and ignored my makeup box, deciding there was no point making an effort for my empty front room.

I felt so alone. I stared at my phone, willing it to ring, to hear Ed's smooth, reassuring voice. I wanted to tell him what had happened and for him to dash to my side (working or not). I wanted to feel loved, and safe, and comforted as I had just one week previously.

As I sank back into the black abyss I turned on the TV and went to the fridge to open some wine. Pouring a large glass I glanced at the food in the fridge, realising I hadn't eaten all day, but I was not interested in food or in eating at all. I closed the door and trudged back to the sofa – my familiar, consistent, reliable sofa.

I sipped my refreshing, medicinal wine and found myself staring at the Orkney chair next to the TV rather than the programme airing at the time.

A traditional chair from the islands that lie between the north of Scotland and Shetland, it was made to sit near the fire and protect against the howling winds of winter. The chairs come in different shapes and sizes but generally the base and arms are made of wood, with woven straw sides and back that rise around and above the occupant.

The chair had belonged to my mum, that is until cancer had cruelly stolen her from us some years before. I missed my mum, I missed sharing all the good as well as the bad things that happened. She always knew what to say and always provided me with sound advice. I was slipping further and further into the abyss and I was losing my way back.

I put the glass down. It was not helping. I was not going to find the answer in there.

I flicked through the channels until I found a familiar film. I curled up on the sofa, hugging a large cushion for comfort, and I let the tears flow across my face and into the soft furnishings.

As I reminisce, the pain I felt that weekend is still so clear and vivid in my heart and my head. And, truth be known, I have shed more tears in remembrance.

As the credits rolled at the end of the film I dragged myself off the sofa. I trudged upstairs. I curled up under my duvet, glad of the cooler night despite it being late June. Tonight I needed to feel comforted and somehow it's hard to feel that in excessive heat.

The alarm woke me as it always does on a work day at 6.30am. I tried to roll over to switch it off, only to find my left side paralysed again. During the night the paralysis, induced by the hemiplegic migraine, had stealthily snuck back into my body as I slept. That morning there was no panic as there had been the day before, as I now knew the cause and that it wouldn't last. True to form, within an hour the numbness started to ebb away.

As soon as I was strong enough to sit up, or at least prop myself up, I sent a text to my colleague at work to explain I would be late in, but that I would be on my way as soon as possible. It was another half an hour though before I had the strength to stand and make my way gingerly to the bathroom.

As soon as I was in the office I headed to my boss to apologise for my tardiness and to explain the reasoning. She was sympathetic if a little unsure, as I could not give any guarantees that it wouldn't happen again.

Luckily it didn't return that week, or the week after. Then again I didn't hear anything from Ed at the same time. By the Friday of the second week I had come to terms with his decision and having barely eaten anything during this period of purgatory I had lost almost a stone in weight. No bad thing. If not the healthy way to lose weight, heartbreak is definitely an effective diet.

On Saturday as I was leaving the house I told myself, *It's time to get a grip of yourself, stop dwelling on what might have been, time to start afresh*, although I had no intention of any new starts in the love arena. I had firmly closed, locked and thrown away the key to that particular door. *Never again*, I promised myself.

The first steps on this road to recovery were to make me feel better about myself. First stop was a haircut, followed up with a manicure. For the first time in a fortnight I fully accepted that Ed and I were over. I was not doing this for Ed, or any future suitor, I was doing this for me, because I deserved it and because I could. I wanted to feel good about myself for me and for no one but me.

The appointments didn't take long. My fair hair does not take much to cut but I had booked in for the full service: shampoo, conditioner, head massage, cut and blow dry followed by a manicure including a French polish.

An hour later I walked out of the salon looking at my white-tipped nails, knowing they wouldn't remain chip free for long. I was far too clumsy to make them last, but I enjoyed them while I could.

Obviously I couldn't fill all the emptiness with trivial acts of self-indulgence, but it helped.

I took my new hairdo and nails to Starbucks for my

usual and stopped on the Common to watch the world go by. I lost track of time watching groups of friends chatting, sprawled out on the grass, couples huddled in secretive discussions making my heart twinge as I looked on, jealous of their happiness.

The Common was busy this sunny Saturday afternoon. A new path had been laid across the bottom of the large green, flanked by elaborate wrought iron lights.

The new children's playground was filled with excited youngsters swinging, climbing and sliding whilst their parents engaged in animated conversations with each other, half an eye on their children, watching for potential danger.

Being in the sun, surrounded by people having fun, helped to lift my spirits. Life was not all bad, just a little lonely at times. It was with a lighter heart that I weaved my way through the groups, dropping my empty coffee cup in the bin by the exit, and made my way home.

twelve.

When changes are changed

I stopped short at my gate.

I held my breath.

I looked left and right to check I was not mistaken. But every time I looked back there he was. Sitting on my doorstep. Looking at his shoes.

He hadn't seen me and for a moment I thought about turning and running back up the street.

He looked up and caught my eye.

"Ed?" I said in little more than a whisper, as much a question as a statement.

I was glued to the spot unable to move. I put my hand out to steady myself on the wall.

Ed looked sheepish as he slowly rose and stepped to one side as if to allow me room to unlock my door, but I still couldn't move.

His expression changed to one of concern. "Are you okay?"

"Umm, no I don't think I am," I confessed. My brain was a mess, my thoughts a washing machine in its final spin. I couldn't grasp onto any of them. I couldn't focus. I felt dizzy. I held on to the wall as if my life depended on it. I didn't want to black out on the street.

Too late. I felt my knees buckle beneath me, unconscious before my body settled on the dry, dusty pavement beneath me.

I came to with Ed leaning over me, staring at me, talking into his phone. "She just collapsed." A pause as he listened intently. "I don't know what happened. She's diabetic."

I reached up and touched his hand. "I'm okay. I just fainted again. No need for an ambulance," I said, putting two and two together on who he was speaking to.

He was still holding the phone to his ear but was no longer talking.

"Give me a hand and I'll get up," I suggested, concerned I was making quite a spectacle in the street.

Ed stood and held a hand out for me then a disembodied voice asked what was happening. He returned his attention to the call. "Sorry, she's awake. She says she is okay, that she just fainted." He responded to a few questions and nodded to whatever instructions he was being given. He promised he would follow up with 111 once I was inside, then signed off with, "Sorry to have troubled you."

Ed helped me stand.

"I'm okay," I said, wrenching myself from the arm that was supporting me, patting off the dust from my clothes. I may have sounded rather harsher than was necessary, as he was only helping, and he looked hurt. *Well, good*, I thought. *It's the least you deserve.*

I walked through the gate which Ed had left open in his rush to my side.

Now it was my turn to stand by my front door as Ed lingered by the gate looking awkward.

"Well, are you coming?" Again my tone harsh, protecting myself by making it clear to him that I was hurt and I was not going to let that continue.

For the first time since we had met he had lost the spring from his step as he returned to my front door. Following me in, slowly and pausing, he softly closed the door behind him.

He looked small, no longer the strapping, trustworthy member of the community. He was diminutive in my eyes now. Now he needed me to make it easier for him. I would of course, but not too quickly. First he had to feel my pain, even if it was only a fraction of it.

I stared at him, my eyes boring into his. I felt incredulous. Why was he here now?

Eventually I sat down on the sofa and indicated for him to sit in the Orkney chair in front of me. He slowly did as I suggested, still barely able to look me in the eye.

"Well?" I asked, cold as ice. Somehow I had managed to completely switch off my emotions. I don't know how I managed it but something hard and alien took over me, perhaps a survival technique or some hidden strength I didn't know I had, but luckily it came from somewhere just when I needed it most.

"So I guess this is the point when you tell me what the hell's going on," I chided. Ed suddenly looked up at me, shock etched on his face. He hadn't seen me like this and I guessed it surprised him. To be honest I didn't care if he liked it or not, I was, finally, in control.

The sheepish look returned. "I... well, you know how

I felt... feel... sorry, feel about you..." He paused, clearly unsure of how to say whatever it was he had come to say.

"Freudian slip?" I enquired.

"What?"

"Felt, you said felt."

"No, I didn't mean it like that. I'm just trying to get the words right. I thought I had it straight in my head but now I don't know where to start and I'm getting this all wrong," he said woefully, each word pushed out slowly and deliberately.

"Well, why don't you do what everyone does at this point and start at the beginning. Maybe start with when you left here all loved up a couple of weeks ago and go from there," I suggested, the anger still brutally evident in my tone as I looked at his sheepish face.

"Oh heck," he sighed, looking at his hands and feet. Finally looking at me he began, "Okay. After I got home Clare called. She was in floods of tears and asked to come over. It was late but I said it was okay, as I had never heard her so upset. Well, not since we split up. I sent you a quick text to let you know I was home safe while I waited. I had every intention of calling you in a day or two."

He stopped to cough, his throat dry.

I stood up in silence and fetched a glass of water from the kitchen, placing it in front of him on the low table. I said nothing.

"Thank you," he acknowledged as I returned to my spot on the sofa, and he sipped the tap water, grateful for a break in his story, gathering his nerve for what was to come. My mind had already started to connect the dots and I thought I knew where it was going, but I hoped I had it wrong.

Hope, does it not spring eternal? Whether I was right or wrong, I needed to hear it from him.

"So Clare came over and we talked. She was in floods of tears. She had had a terrible fight with Steve and things had been said. I won't give you the details, that wouldn't be right, but trust me when I say it was a mean, dirty fight which ended in Clare walking out with just her handbag and nothing else. She was confused and didn't know what to do. She still loves Steve but couldn't see a way back from the fight and wasn't even sure if she wanted to.

"We talked late into the night. I was genuinely trying to help and support her. I know Steve, almost as well as I know Clare, so I played devil's advocate, but Clare still couldn't decide what to do. She was too scared to go home and it was too late for her to check into a hotel so I said she could stay with me.

"I showed her to her room." Ed sighed, at this point clearly preparing himself for the maelstrom he anticipated erupting from me in the not-too-distant future. "I sorted out towels and an old spare T-shirt for her to sleep in." He was providing far too much detail in a vain attempt to put off the inevitable, but as sure as night follows day, he was going to have to get the truth out at some point.

I sat patiently, not interrupting, not saying or doing anything to stop the flow. Ed might have been hoping that I would, that somehow I was going to make this easier for him. Clearly he didn't know me as well as he thought.

I stared at him, my facial expression never changing from hostile.

"When it came to saying goodnight we hugged as we have often done before. I realised in that moment how vulnerable she was and how I wanted to protect and care for her. We have a history together and a son," he said, trying to justify whatever it was that he had done.

Ed shifted awkwardly in his hard chair and continued, "Nothing happened." He looked up and stared at me. "I swear, nothing happened, neither Clare nor I wanted anything to happen and we went our separate ways."

He paused. Summoning the strength to get to the point. I was uncertain now, I had been convinced he was about to admit that they had kissed or worse still, but either way, it would have been cheating. He claimed nothing happened. Did I believe him? Maybe the story was not over, maybe that was still to come. I leant forward, eager to get this out of the way.

He stuttered and then continued, focusing on his hands, wrapped together in his lap, nervously picking at a button on his shirt.

"I couldn't sleep. I kept tossing and turning. Thinking about Clare." He glanced up to gauge my reaction. I was not surprised, she was all he had talked about since he had arrived. Still, I was hurt that I was no longer part of his thought process or consideration.

"I hadn't expected to feel this way. Seeing her so upset had awakened old feelings, feelings I thought were long past and buried. I realised I love her, I still love her. I promise you though, nothing has happened between us." He stopped talking like he had completed the account. Clearly, as far as I was concerned, he had not.

I sat in silence for a while, gathering my thoughts. My head spun and I struggled to stay focused. Ed seemed to think the point here was that nothing had happened. I was grateful for that of course, but the glaringly obvious elephant in the room were the words 'I still love her'.

If he still felt that way it would explain why he hadn't been in touch, but it didn't explain why he was here now. Maybe, this was the 'closure' part of this episode of my life. At least he had thought enough of me to have the decency to tell me himself, face to face, I had to give him some credit for that. Was my recently turned-to-stone heart beginning to melt? Not quite yet.

I stirred in my seat. Now the tables were reversed and it was my time to talk and Ed looked at me expectantly, lost, hoping for a lifeline.

I hadn't been looking for love, I was content with my life. He had barged into that, he had made me love him and now he wanted me to rescue him. I felt sick. I felt the anger begin to bubble inside me, churning in my stomach. Heat flashed to my face.

"Well, thank you, Ed," I said in a dead, ice-cold tone, "that's quite a confession. But you seem to have missed the ending." I paused. He looked at me confused. I allowed time for him to retrace his steps through what he had said but he continued to look at me blankly.

I sighed, deliberately, loud and deep.

"You just told me that you are still in love with your ex-wife. So what does that mean?"

"What do you mean?" he asked clumsily.

"I don't think it's my job to spell this out." I tried to control my voice. The tears were beginning to form, to spike the corners of my eyes as I felt the well of emotion take over me.

"Oh, I see. Yes. No. I don't know. This is what I've been

trying to work out. That's why I went into radio silence. I needed time to think, to decide."

"Time to decide? Time to decide who to be with?" I yelled at a shocked Ed, as I was no longer able to control my anger. "I'm not a commodity on a comparison website and neither is Clare." I could not believe I was standing up for her.

"And anyway," I continued, "how does she feel about you?"

Why am I asking that? How will asking it help me or this situation? I thought.

"I don't know," he mumbled, his head in his hands. "I've not spoken to her since the morning after. We had breakfast. We were both exhausted from lack of sleep, but she had made a decision."

Unlike you, I thought.

"She told me that she would go home and try to build bridges with Steve. I haven't heard from her since so I'm guessing things worked out okay. I was just…"

The phone in his pocket rudely interrupted his flow and he pulled the phone out, glancing at the screen, then at me, then back to the screen, unsure of what to do next.

"Take it if you need to," I said with a steely tone as I stood and went to the kitchen to get a cold drink and try to steady my nerves.

I could not hear what Ed was saying as he spoke quietly and calmly into the receiver, obviously trying to hide both the identity of the caller and the content of the conversation.

After a couple of minutes I heard the sound of the phone being placed on the table and made my way back to the sitting room.

"All done?" I asked a crestfallen, sad-looking Ed.

"Yes, that was Clare," he confessed. "She's back with Steve, they've made up and she just rang to thank me for listening to her and putting up with her moaning and tears."

He looked upset at what he had heard. *So he cares about her tears, but not mine*, it struck me and I realised his true feelings at that moment. We were over. The minute Clare turned to him for support there was nothing left between us except, perhaps, one day, friendship. I softened my tone.

"Did you tell her you love her?" I asked.

"No," he said, shooting me a look. "Well, yes, but only as we always sign off calls with love to you and the family, but no I didn't tell her about my feelings. She's happy. She has her life. I don't need to mess that up. Not that she would feel the same way anyway..." He trailed off, clearly upset, perhaps taking stock of what he had said and coming to the true realisation of his feelings, as had I.

"I'm going to be honest with you, Ed." He looked up, hopeful. "I don't know the purpose of your visit, whether you're here to finish with me, or explain your absence, or just be honest about your feelings." I paused, unable to gauge his feelings, no facial giveaways as I spoke so I continued, "I have to think of myself and protect myself."

The tears began to flow silently down my cheeks as I continued, "I can see that you still love Clare and clearly you can't love us both. It wouldn't be fair on me if you stay with me whilst in love with another woman. So," I said slowly, rising to my feet, "I'll make the decision for you." Deep breath. "We're over. You are free to do what you need to do. You no longer have a place in my life," I said as firmly and decisively as I could muster as I moved towards the front door. I opened it, making it clear our conversation was over.

Ed took the hint. He stood, put his hand in his pocket and silently withdrew a key, the spare key to my home, and placed it gently and somewhat reluctantly on the coffee table. *At least he had the respect not to use that when he arrived and discovered I was not at home* I thought.

Ed followed me to the door. He squeezed my arm as he passed. I guess it was an understanding.

How different to the bittersweet departure the last time, now it was just bitter. This was goodbye.

The tears became more urgent and pressing. I pushed the door closed but not quick enough, as Ed saw my tear-stained face as he turned to close the gate.

I leant against the closed door, sinking to the floor and letting the darkness take over. I sat there howling with hurt until I was exhausted and crawled to the sofa, wrapping myself in the blanket that ran across the back and fell into an exhausted sleep.

*

I woke in a dark room, disorientated for a few minutes, unsure of where I was. It scared me, I felt lost and afraid. It took a couple of minutes for everything to come back into focus and for me to remember the pain, and more importantly, where I was.

I stumbled across my living room in the dark and felt the wall, hands circling across the cool surface until I found what I was looking for. I switched on the light and stood for a moment before I closed the curtains, locked the door and checked the clock. Almost 10pm. I had been asleep for a few hours, but it had neither refreshed me, nor given me any peace.

I didn't feel hungry, no not that, I didn't even think about food. It was not that I avoided it, it just was not part of my consciousness.

Drink, though, that was part of my consciousness and I helped myself to a large glass of ice-cold (like my heart) Pinot Grigio and returned to the sofa where I wrapped myself up in the blanket once more and turned on the TV, hoping for some mindless film to distance me from my thoughts.

I didn't get a call from Ed to say he was home, not that I expected one. I didn't know what to expect, but as much as I wanted him to tell me it was all a mistake and he loved me, I actually needed him to stay away so that I could mourn the death of the relationship, allow me time to heal and rebuild my life and then, hopefully, find a new equilibrium. I doubt Ed even gave me, or my needs, let alone my heart, any thought. He stayed away. Maybe he did, at least, give my feelings some thought.

thirteen.

Time to dust myself off

As summer turned to autumn and the nights began to draw in I was finally starting to rebuild my life. I had revitalised old friendships and was planning a meet-up every weekend to keep me active. Being with friends was good for my mental state. That, and music, made me happy.

I kept myself busy, finding new energy and drive. I started sewing again, making a mountain of cushions, cafetière warmers, tea cosies and wine gift bags. I had no idea what I was going to do with them all but it was therapeutic. Being creative soothed my soul and my spare room slowly filled up with fabrics and finished products.

Despite all the good intentions and efforts to stay positive the autumnal weather was starting to reflect my mood, or vice versa.

As I drove to work on those cold mornings, the mist hung over the harvested fields as the sun slowly rose above the horizon and I felt a cold mist creep into me.

I was working hard, as I always did – early starts,

stressful days, late evenings. I was struggling to sleep, often waking in a cold sweat with work on my mind. I would switch on the bedside light and write a list of the things occupying my head in the hope that once they were committed to paper I would be able to sleep. Even with that accomplished I struggled to find peace, either returning to my pen and paper to add more to the list or tossing and turning, trying all sorts of ways to distract me from myself and my thoughts. 'And sleep', 'And sleep', 'And sleep' became my monotonous mantra to stop my mind wandering, but it didn't work.

My drinking, during those days, became exponentially heavy. I have to confess that I was aware of it and it concerned me, but I found it helped me get to sleep, even if it didn't help me to stay asleep.

Looking back now I can see this was a dark time in my life. This was not a revelation. I knew at the time that I was rapidly sinking to a place I didn't want to be in.

Some nights as I lay in bed waiting for blessed sleep to fall upon me I thought about taking my life. I couldn't see a way out of my misery. Work was eating at my mental state but I had to work. I had to pay the mortgage, bills, food all of which cost money. Whilst the luxuries like clothes and gifts could be reduced, the monthly essentials didn't go away.

Lying there one night it did occur to me that I had an easy way to take my life. The truth was, I didn't want to die. I just wanted life to be better, to be more fun, worth living, less hard.

I admonished myself as I lay there feeling sorry for myself. Here I lay in a peaceful town, in my own home, surrounded by friends and family. What right did I have to feel sorry for myself?

Friends, good, honest, young people, with families had cancer. Such a cruel and debilitating disease that sucked the breath out of the diagnosed. It had taken my beautiful mother. Even in her darkest, most painful hours, she didn't give in to self-pity. It broke my heart to see family and friends fighting it both mentally and physically. Even those who had been given the blessed 'all clear', the ones who got to ring the bell on the cancer ward to signify the end of their treatment, were never truly free of its grip with ongoing, crucial check-ups, always fearful it may return.

I had helped with my mother's care, taking her to hospital for appointments with the consultant, for chemo and/or for blood transfusions. I was grateful to be able to give something back after all she had done for me and the times she had sat by my bedside as a child.

I was grateful because I got some precious time in the last year of her life. Not that we knew that at the time. Mum slept a lot during her treatments, but when she was awake we talked and talked.

After a year of treatment we were given the devastating news that it was no longer working and the only treatment left on offer was palliative care. The blood transfusions and platelets would continue but the chemo would stop.

When the end came it was sudden, but not unexpected. I was lucky, I guess, as I was able to spend her last few days with her. My boss allowed me to work from my parents' house so I could help with medication. On the Wednesday mum had a terrible headache which she could not shake, but when I left to go home on Thursday she was feeling a bit brighter, was sitting up in bed and was even trying to eat some supper.

By Friday she could not eat or drink and was fading fast.

I called my brother and told him to come to our parents' home as soon as possible, and my father called my mum's sister in Orkney and told her the news.

My brother had arrived in time to speak to mum and say his farewell, promising to bring his sons, her three grandchildren, who she cherished, to see her the next day. That was about the last time my mum spoke.

Apart from half an hour when my aunt (dad's sister) took over, I was awake all night, by mum's side, dabbing her dry, cracked lips with water, checking her oxygen saturation levels and applying oxygen when needed, keeping a vigil. Late into the night, or possibly early the next day, she started moving her head away and mumbling, refusing the help.

The wider family – aunts, uncles, cousins and their children – were told, giving them the opportunity to say goodbye. Every member of the family who could get there in time descended on the house. Nurses and doctors came and went that Saturday, but the family stayed. All taking their turn to tell mum how much they loved her, recalling stories from their lives where she had played a part in creating the lasting memory.

It was a warm, early March day and the windows in the bedroom were open, letting in fresh air and the sounds of the youngest generation running around and playing in the garden below, their beautiful innocence unaware of what was transpiring in the room above.

We kept telling mum that her sister was en route. She

had landed at Heathrow. She was on the M25. She was getting ever closer. Mum clung on with all her might.

When my aunt arrived that afternoon she collapsed onto the bed next to her beloved little sister who was, by now, gasping for breath, her face sallow and pallid. In the tenderest of moments my aunt kissed mum's cheek and told her how much she loved her.

My father, brother, sister-in-law, aunt and I surrounded the bed, repeating our love whilst two nurses watched from the back of the room.

Mum tried to acknowledge her sister and the words of love pouring from all of us, but no words came, just the flutter of her eyelids and voiceless movements of her mouth and then she was still. Relieved of the pain that had possessed her body, free from the exhaustion and the fear. But filled with the love of the family that surrounded her. She was at peace.

Later a neighbour told me that she thought there had been a party at the house that day, given all the cars parked along the street outside. In a way she was right. It was a celebration of my mother's amazing life, a celebration of who she was and how many lives she had touched, how many lives she had improved.

Back to the present

Thinking back to how mum had clung to life in those last two days made me realise that I had to fight for my own life. Lying there in the pitch black of my bedroom, reliving her last few days, my pillow sodden with the tears that flowed every time I thought (and even now think) about her, I knew how disappointed she would be in me having thoughts of ending my life when she had fought so hard to keep hers.

She was right, as always.

No, I realised, this was a cry for help. I needed to change the things in my life that were creating this state. All I had to do was work out what and how to achieve that. First I needed to rest, I was exhausted.

*

And so my life trudged on and autumn started to take a grip. The solid black stove, the heart of my sitting room, was lit as soon as I got home and I sat watching the mesmerising glow of the red and orange flames as they flickered across the glass. The warmth filled my tiny home with the comfort that was missing from my life.

The drives to and from work were getting darker – a metaphor and a reality.

Arriving home one Friday night I entered my dimly lit front room. With the curtains open the orange street lights were providing enough light for me to see the post on the doormat. I reached down to pick it up. I was pleasantly surprised, letters were so rare these days. Most companies used emails or online accounts and friends used social media. I rued the days when friends wrote actual, physical letters which were posted; the joy of finding a long letter, curling up on the sofa and discovering what a friend had been up to, then writing long letters back. Even on birthdays and Christmas these days the mail bag was lighter than it used to be in the good old days, not that I had lost touch with people, but because people just stopped sending cards, which in my mind was a sad development and not progress.

It was not my birthday and it was not Christmas. Yet there in my hand, amongst the pamphlets and brochures, was a white envelope with beautiful calligraphed black ink inscription of my name and address. I felt excited for the first time in ages.

I threw the card – it was definitely a card as I could feel the firmness between my fingers – onto the sofa and fetched a glass of wine from the kitchen. The intention was to curl up on the sofa and enjoy whatever news this unexpected card held in store for me.

I took the time to light the stove and ensure it was well underway first. I didn't want to be disturbed.

I was putting it off of course, like the lottery. Whenever I received an email to say there was news about my ticket, whilst I was certain that it would only be the bare minimum payout, as long as I didn't actually look at it, it kept the hopes and suspense alive. Maybe, just maybe, on this occasion it really 'could be me'.

The same was true for the card, lying waiting on the sofa. It was probably some clever marketing ploy, trying to sell me something I didn't want, or need, but I was enjoying the anticipation.

Time to do this, I thought, curling my feet up under me as I opened the thick, top quality envelope and pulled out the silky-smooth card and accompanying folded sheets from within. It was a wedding invitation. I stared at the card. *A wedding invitation, but I don't know anyone getting married*, I thought. Turning it over in my hand, nervous now, I slowly opened the card to see who was inviting me to their nuptials.

I held my breath. *Surely Ed wouldn't be so cruel as to invite me to his wedding to Clare*, I thought. I had never truly believed that nothing physical had happened between them. For all I knew, after all the time that had passed since we had last spoken Clare might have left her husband, realising, as Ed had done, her true feelings. But no, they wouldn't stab me in the heart like that. Surely.

As I finally gathered my nerve and fully opened the card a piece of paper slowly fluttered down into my lap. I glanced at it momentarily, deciding to face what was in the card before turning my attention to the additional sheets.

It read, 'Mr and Mrs Finley,' I couldn't place the name so read on, 'Invite you to the wedding of their daughter Emma to Mr Dan Wiseman'. The penny dropped and it hit me like a ton of bricks. *This can't be right. Dan and Emma have invited me to their wedding. Surely this is some sort of horrible mistake*. I was confused. The only logical explanation I could come up with was that they had forgotten to take me off the list. *What is the etiquette for turning down an invitation that was never intended for you?*

I liked Dan and Emma. I liked them a lot. They had made me feel part of the family and part of their wedding, but they couldn't want me at it, not now, not after everything that had happened.

It was not just that Ed and I were no longer together, but both Ed and Clare would be at the wedding and that would be hellishly awkward for everyone. And, to be honest, I didn't want to see Ed again, I still wasn't ready, so this would need to be a polite, but firm, refusal.

I continued staring at the invitation racked by confusion and curiosity. We were all too old for games, and what sort of sick person would play a game like this, especially as it could go horribly wrong and I could accept the invitation and ruin their big day by starting a fight with some of their guests?

No, I thought, *this has to be a mistake. I'll have to choose the wording of my reply with care so as not to offend anyone.*

Then I remembered the note lying ignored in my lap. I picked it up, opening it quickly, hoping for a clue or insight into what this was really all about.

It was the wedding list. 'Emma and Dan do not expect any gifts, just your company on their day of celebration. However, should you wish to buy a gift then please view the list at…'

I was surprised to feel disappointed. I don't really know what I was expecting, but of course it was instructions on wedding lists. The next sheet had the details and directions to the wedding and local hotels for those who couldn't afford to stay at the venue.

I turned to the last sheet expecting some more instructions or formality with regard to the wedding. I couldn't have been more wrong. This final sheet was a typed page, the font and layout different to the rest of the pack, no pictures, and instantly I knew this sheet was no round robin. This sheet was for my eyes only.

It read:

> *Dear Chloe*
>
> *Yet again I find myself unsure of the words, so I will take your advice and start at the beginning.*
>
> *I'm sorry. I'm truly sorry for the way I treated you and for the way I made you feel. If it is any consolation*

I have been racked by guilt ever since.

You were right to kick me out. I was an idiot and an imbecile. You were nothing but honest and loving towards me and I trashed that and your trust and I'm sure you will never forgive me, but I won't forgive myself if I don't try.

I was honest about my confusion and I was telling the truth when I said nothing physical happened. I now realise that I never really wanted anything to happen with Clare. I was confused by seeing her in that way and I was afraid of the feelings I had for you. I was afraid of things not working out, of things falling apart as they had with Clare and I took the coward's way out, opting to sabotage the relationship before it went any further.

I realised as soon as I left you what my true feelings were, but you quite rightly didn't want to know or to speak to me. I understand that you cut me off to save yourself.

I want you back, Chloe. I love you. I miss you. I want to be in your life and you to be in mine. I want to beg you for another chance.

I know this is a little strange, to send this in an invitation to my son's wedding, but I talked to Dan and Emma and explained everything. They were shocked and I have to confess, rightly, called me some choice names. But they really like you and wanted to help me.

We thought, and I hope we have not got this wrong, that if we all showed you how much you mean to us then that might open a door for us to talk, to find some way to start again. Nothing says family more than a wedding and so, in case you are wondering, this invitation is genuine. I know we have a long way to go until you can commit to attending, if you ever will.

I, we, will understand if you don't want to know. If we do not hear from you I will understand and will accept your decision, but in my heart I know we could be fantastic together, again. If you could find it in your heart to let me back in I promise I won't break it again. I will hold it tight and protect it, forever.

Please, please, please, give me a chance.

All my love

Ed xx

By the time I finished the letter I was in floods of tears, the paper in my hand speckled with damp teardrops. I found a tissue and wiped my eyes, leaving wet, black smudges of makeup on the tissue and streaks across my face.

I didn't know what was going to happen or if there really was a way back from this. I didn't know if I could trust him again. I didn't know if we could get back to the heavenly place we had been before.

I knew I had never stopped loving him, however much I had tried. And I knew that this was the break I had been looking for. This was the hope I had longed for. This was the joy I had been missing.

I pulled my phone from my bag and through tears of happiness I typed, 'Hello you,' and pressed send before I could change my mind.

fourteen.

And start all over again

I had barely put the phone down when it buzzed and the screen lit up.

'Hello, you too,' it read, 'I'm so glad you texted. I assume you got my letter? I know this will take time & I have to prove myself & I will.'

I read and re-read it. I don't know what I expected. There were no kisses, no suggestion to meet or speak or next steps or even a request for the answer to the invitation. I could see he was being true to his word and letting me set the pace. But I was disappointed that yet again it was left to me to make the next move, even though I didn't yet know what move I wanted to make. This was an unexpected situation to find myself in.

I was confused but also surprised to find myself feeling excited. Why, why was I excited? I had been cheated on before. I knew Ed claimed he had not cheated but he had broken my heart, and trust, nonetheless.

Several boyfriends had been unfaithful. The first time I

had been a teenager. My first proper boyfriend had passed me a note during harvest festival supper saying I was pretty. I was so shocked. No one had ever said that before and at first I was convinced either the note was meant for someone else, or that he was pulling my leg and if I responded positively he and his friends would laugh at me. But it turned out to be real and we started hanging out together. Back then there was nothing more intimate than kisses, but he was a bit of a rebel and often got me in trouble.

Some months later a friend told me he was seeing two other girls and I dumped him. He may have been cute and cheeky, but I was not going to lower myself to that level.

Many years later through the power of social media we reconnected, only electronically. He was married, with children and living on the other side of the world. The first question he asked was what perfume I used to wear, as he had often tried to find it and could not. I could not remember, so suggested a couple of possibilities, neither of which was right. His second question was why had I dumped him? That one I could answer and did. He had replied, 'that sounds like me'. I was, however, rather disappointed he didn't remember.

The second time I was cheated on was some years later. It hadn't been the greatest of relationships. He was tall and thin, and I was short and, well, you know the rest. The problem was I could never get rid of that image from my mind.

We had met in a nightclub. He recognised me from work and made his approach. I have to confess that despite his height I hadn't seen him before. It turned out we worked in the same building, just one floor apart.

We had fun and dated for several months. I got to know his friends and his life.

One weekend I was at a friend's hen do while he attended the company summer party. When I went to see him on my return he told me the relationship was over. He had got together with someone else at work.

Apparently this very dour strait-laced lady had targeted him. It didn't surprise me, she had been curt with me, I would even go further and say she was rude, after she had found out we were dating. Clearly adultery was not part of her beliefs. She had decided I was not good enough for him but she was, and set out to snare him.

I was not that bothered, in truth, our relationship was not going anywhere. He was the first person I had dated after a long relationship and it helped me get back on the bicycle, so to speak. That was cheat number two.

Number three was altogether much worse, although it did give me the opportunity to end yet another disastrous relationship.

Thinking about it now, maybe that is my thing. Maybe I'm cheated on when I have disconnected from the relationship and, being the type of person who wears my heart on my sleeve, my boyfriends are left in no doubt that I'm no longer engaged in the relationship and decide to jump before they are pushed. Or maybe it's deeper than that. I seem to attract the waifs and strays, the hard-done-by, the damaged. I patiently invest my time, money and love to heal them, restore them. And when my work is done, they fly away and some new lady gets the benefit of my dedication. That seems more like it, having been the waif and stray myself when I was born. My birth mother was unable to raise me and so my parents adopted me and gave me the love, the nurturing and the life to make me strong. Maybe rescuing others was my way to pay back karma for saving me.

Of course I am no angel. I cheated once. That relationship had been good, but we had grown apart, not just emotionally but also physically, as he had taken a job a couple of hundred miles away and our visits became less frequent.

I wanted out but couldn't work out how to do it. Immaturity, I guess. I should have just told him. Hindsight is a wonderful thing. However, in the end I had got drunk and thrown myself at a male friend on a night out. He had rejected me but I was told in no uncertain terms that either I told my boyfriend or he would.

So I fessed up.

Many years later I met him again at the wedding of mutual friends and he admitted that if I hadn't ended it he would have, so there were no hard feelings. To everyone's delight there were no arguments but instead a lot of laughter and dancing.

Back to the present

What I learnt from all of these events was that once the trust has gone, it has gone. Then all you do is waste time trying to get it back, to recapture it, to move on, but in the end it never fully returns and you question every late arrival, unexpected change of plans, sly glances at the phone, calls taken in different rooms. All possibly innocent, but never perceived that way once the trust has gone.

Ed and I were too old to waste time. I was not looking for another relationship so I didn't need him back in my life. And yet, I sighed deeply, clearly I was not going to resolve the situation that night.

I finished my wine, threw my phone in my bag and wearily climbed the stairs to bed.

Sleep didn't come easily. I tossed and turned in bed, my mind in as much turmoil as my body.

With all the stress I was experiencing at work I really didn't have the energy for this.

My final thought as I lost consciousness was that I was going to tell Ed that this would never work out, so better to knock it on the head sooner rather than later.

I lay in bed the next morning, not ready to get up, or ready to face the day, feeling exhausted despite only just waking. I needed to get up and do something positive, but I didn't want to drag my warm body from under the snuggly duvet and out into the cold day.

I stuck my foot out from under the duvet and briskly pulled it back into the warmth. I pulled the duvet up round my neck, savouring the comfort for a few minutes more. I needed more sleep, but now I was awake my mind wouldn't rest.

The situation with Ed kept turning over in my mind and despite having made the decision just a few hours before to end the misery, now I was questioning it. I had strong feelings for Ed despite what had happened. I didn't want to be alone again. I had my routine, my equilibrium, and now all of that had gone. I was no longer content to go back to that way of life. But neither could I trust Ed. I couldn't see a way back.

I needed fresh air. I needed to clear my head.

I had a shower, enjoying the warm water starting to wake me up, and as I stood there the tears began to tumble down my face. I sobbed big, painful tears, obscured by the water. The only indication that they were present were my heaving shoulders. I put my hand out to the tiled wall to steady myself and bring myself back under control. I felt even more drained by the time I stepped out and wrapped myself in a huge, fluffy bath towel. I reprimanded myself as I dried. I had to sort my head out.

I skipped breakfast and even forewent a coffee, desperate to be out in the autumnal air.

I headed out of town along the main road, past the supermarket, and then started to climb the hill.

The path separated from the road and climbed above it through the arch of trees and bushes that had interwoven above the path to create a secret tunnel sheltered from the weather and the noise of the road. At that time of year it was a riot of autumnal colours, the leaves an array of shades and hues of green, yellow, orange and red, clinging to the trees and strewn across the path where they had lost their fight in the first heavy rain and wind of the season.

It was tranquil. It made me feel cocooned, protected and safe, the beauty of the surroundings occupying me. I slowed my pace, wanting this to last forever. I drank in the atmosphere. I stopped and breathed deeply. Luckily this was not a popular route and I was not disturbed in my reflectiveness.

I drank in the damp autumn air and steadied my nerves. I knew the facts, the emotions, and finally I knew my decision, for definite this time.

Feeling at peace I decided to continue my walk. I was enjoying being out and the exercise was good for me.

An hour later I arrived home, having picked up the obligatory coffee to stay my caffeine craving, and I had thrown caution to the wind and thrown in a freshly baked croissant, having been unable to resist the smell from the bakery as I passed, the smell of hot butter and pastry drawing me in to make the purchase.

After breakfast I cleaned the house, giving it an extra thorough going-over as it delayed the moment when I would need to contact Ed.

I had been gearing myself up to call him, working and reworking the words, keen to get it exactly right. I should have stopped and written it down rather than overthinking it, but I had nothing else to occupy my mind whilst monotonously pushing the hoover back and forth, moving furniture out and back into place as I went.

Despite the weather outside it was warm in the house and I was sweating by the time I finished. As I was putting the hoover back in the understairs cupboard there was a loud knock at the door.

I was annoyed by the intrusion, as I was ready for 'the talk', but instead I was making my way towards the front door. I looked a mess and more than that I was not expecting any visitors. Hopefully it was just someone canvassing or delivering a package to a neighbour who was out. Either way I was not in the mood to be interrupted.

I pulled the door open, trying to indicate to the caller that I was in no mood to be delayed from my intended actions. As I did so I came face to face with an exhausted, bedraggled face. It took me a second and then my heart leapt into my mouth.

"Ed!" I said with surprise. "Are you okay?" I was still standing holding the door open.

He looked me in the eyes. His sad, tired eyes bore into me, into my heart and soul. I stepped forward and threw my arms around him, drawing him into a heartfelt hug.

He didn't say a word, he just succumbed to the hug. He held me close and I could feel his hot breath on my neck. Just a few weeks before, this would have been the start of something animal-like and sexual but there was no hint of that passion in this embrace. This was two people clinging to each other for strength and support, for comfort, out of need not desire. We stood there holding each other like that was the only thing stopping us from collapsing, the only thing keeping us alive.

He sighed, a deep, guttural sigh, and I felt him loosen his grip. I followed his lead and we moved apart. His hands ran down the outside of my arms until they reached my hands which he held onto, and looked at me, still looking so forlorn.

I released the grip of one hand and turned, still holding his other hand, and led him into my home, closing the door behind us. He still hadn't spoken.

I led him to the sofa and we sat down in unison. I was unsure what to say. I had asked a question which he hadn't replied to. Maybe it was a daft question given his appearance, but I didn't know why he was here. I was surprised at how good it had felt to be in his arms again and how much I still felt for him. Perhaps it was my need to rescue the lost or maybe it was my maternal instincts, not that I really had any. But something was stirred inside me that Saturday afternoon.

I sat quietly looking at him. He looked like he had shrunken in on himself, like a heavy weight was pressing in on him from all sides. Clearly he needed help and unlike the last time we had sat here, I felt no anger or animosity towards him. I reached out and lightly touched his hand. He slowly raised his eyes to mine like there were lead weights in his eyelids.

"I'm so sorry," he said slowly, quietly, shaking his head in an equally pained and weary way. "I'm so, so sorry. I never wanted to cause you pain. I thought I was doing the right thing in telling you, in being honest with you, but it had the opposite effect and I have regretted that ever since and I have missed you so, so much."

"Ed, your honesty was not the problem. I'm glad you are that type of person. If you're not honest there can be no trust. Don't for a minute think you did the wrong thing by telling me," I said slowly and calmly, constantly looking at his fallen face. "I was upset because I had come to accept a single life and then you appeared out of the blue and made me think I might not have to be alone. Then I fell in love with you. I saw our future, living together, happy. Then suddenly it came to an end. The hurt in my life came flooding out and I just couldn't cope – mentally or physically."

Ed was staring at me through pained eyes. I had been so focused on my own hurt it had never occurred to me that he could be suffering too.

I changed tack. Clearly he was still in a bad place, a place I had dragged myself out of recently.

I picked up his hand and rubbed my thumb over the back of his hand as he had done to me in our happier days together.

"I'm sorry too," I said, to both our surprise. "I hadn't realised how hard this has been for you too. I was so wrapped up in my own pain I didn't stop to think about your feelings."

He smiled weakly at me, then said, "After your text I couldn't sleep. I just wanted to hold you, to be with you, but then I couldn't see how we could get back to where we were. I couldn't sleep. I got up and went for a walk. I walked and walked through the night. I didn't know where I was going. I fell into a couple of ditches in the dark, but I couldn't get away from my thoughts. Eventually I found myself here. I've been walking around the block for the last hour. I didn't know what to do, whether to wait until you called or to come and see you. But I'm exhausted and I needed so much to see you and here I am."

I was dumbfounded. No wonder he looked so bad, but there was no way he could have walked all the way here, it would have taken longer than one night. Ed read my mind.

"I moved down last week," he confessed. "I'm in one of the police houses until I can find somewhere more permanent to rent or buy," he said in a flat, exhausted tone.

I realised that this was not just about our relationship, he had also moved down for his new job. I hadn't given it any thought. If I had I would have wondered if he had changed his mind and stayed closer to his family. Although on the other hand he was here for the interview the day we met again. It was a career advancement, so maybe I was just the icing on the cake rather than the cake itself.

"You must be exhausted, and if you don't mind me saying, you don't smell too good either. So I'm not going to beat about the bush or make you wait, I am going to be totally honest with you. I want to be with you."

His face lifted, as did his whole demeanour. There was life back in his dark eyes and relief on his face.

"But," I said firmly, "it's not going to be easy. You will need to work hard to regain my trust. We go back to dating and take each day at a time and see where we end up."

"Thank you, thank you, thank you," he implored.

I shushed him and made a suggestion. "Why don't you go and have a shower and have a sleep, you know where the towels are. When you're rested we will talk some more."

"Thank you. That sounds like a good idea and I'm sorry to have turned up in this state." He waved his hands over his body to make the point.

"I'm not looking too hot myself," I confessed, for the first time realising how sweaty I had been when he arrived.

He leant forward and kissed me on the cheek.

"You always look beautiful to me," he said with his winning cheeky smile.

He rose and made his way up the old familiar stairs.

As I heard the shower spring into life I picked up my bag and let myself out of the house. I had very little food in the fridge and I didn't know what time Ed would wake, so I popped to the shop to get a mix of easy and quick-to-prepare food, some wine and some milk.

When I got home the house was in silence, as it had been for so many days and weeks recently.

For a moment I held my breath, fearing he had changed his mind again and had disappeared.

As I hovered at the bottom of the stairs I was relieved to hear the soft snores emanating from my bedroom.

I crept up the stairs. In the stillness I heard every creak and crack of the stairs. *Why does the house make so much noise when all I want is for it to be quiet?* I thought as I peered in through the door, smiling, so happy to see Ed sleeping peacefully, if noisily, in my bed, where he belonged.

I stood there for a while, watching him breathe in and out. I knew I had made the right decision, but I was going to protect myself if I could.

I crept back downstairs and unpacked my canvas bags of shopping.

I lit the stove, creating a warm glow as the flames licked the sides of the fire bricks that lined the inside of the black stove. Once the fire was underway and I had loaded a couple of logs to sustain it, I picked up my book and curled up on the sofa, grateful for the distraction, to be taken to another world of Elizabethan England.

As the light drained from the sky I lifted myself from the sofa, added more logs to the fire, drew the curtains and turned on the lights. As I resumed my position on the sofa I heard the stairs creak and turned to see Ed making his way downstairs, sleep still in his eyes.

"How are you feeling?" I asked gently.

He sat down next to me before answering. "I feel a lot better than I did, thank you. And thank you for putting me out of my misery before I went up. I don't think I could have slept without that chat. Thank you."

"It's okay, I have been thinking about you non-stop since last night and had already come to a decision. I had been planning to call you this afternoon but I'm glad you came, it was much better to talk face to face. It will take time. I'm not open to having my heart broken again, so you will need to prove yourself." He looked down. "But I know I want you in my life, I know I want this to work and I'm prepared to put in as much effort as you to make this work." I smiled at him, wanting to convey certainty when in fact all I felt was doubt, but he had suffered enough for now.

I stood up. "How about I put some supper on? I'm guessing you've not had anything to eat since yesterday."

He nodded.

"Come on then, you can pour some wine while I get the food on." I led him into the kitchen, reassured by how easily we were slipping back into old ways without it feeling awkward or difficult.

We made small talk as we eased back into the familiar.

"So have you started your new job?" I asked.

"No, I start on Monday. I moved down last week and have been unpacking and settling in," he said and then continued in a more serious tone, "I don't want you to think that I've made contact because I've moved down. I would have moved anyway and I would have stayed away if you had asked me to."

"I thought about it. I needed time and I'm really glad you gave it to me." I didn't want to talk about this anymore, it was still raw and I didn't want to go backwards. I decided to change the subject.

"So how are the family?"

Ed shot me a look, clearly aware that I was changing tack, but even if he had wanted to discuss the situation further he respected my unspoken wishes and sat up on the stool, glass in hand and replied.

"They're good. As you will have seen the plans for the wedding have continued to move forward."

There was a question, a big, burning, elephant-in-the-room-sized question hanging in the air. 'Would I go to the wedding?' We both shifted awkwardly. I was standing by the oven and turned back to stir the pot.

Quietly, but determinedly I said, "I'm not ready to make a decision on that yet. Can we put that to one side until we've been together a little while?"

"I totally understand and respect that," he said, his tone mirroring mine. "Dan and Emma are holding a place just in case, but there is no pressure either way."

I finished cooking and took the piping hot plates of food to the dining table. Ed followed me with a bottle of wine tucked under his arm and the two glasses in his hands.

We sat opposite each other, in our usual spots, slipping seamlessly back into familiarity. It felt good and worrying at the same time.

We kept conversation light, skirting any difficult topics or anything related to our relationship.

I'm not sure if it was the wine, the conversation, or the company. Maybe it was a dizzy combination of all three but I found myself relaxing, smiling, giggling and flirting until late into the evening.

As I began to yawn, I knew that awkward moment was upon us.

"I'm sorry, Ed, but I need to head to bed," I said, touching his arm gently.

"I can call a taxi and let myself out," he said, ever the gentleman, but there was a slight hint of disappointment in his voice.

"Thank you," I said, grateful he had solved the problem before it became awkward. I had loved the evening and I didn't want it ruined. It was too early, too soon, to rekindle the passion we had revelled in before.

We stood there for a moment. I rested my hands on his chest, feeling his warmth through my fingertips. I leant in and kissed Ed gently on the cheek, lingering a moment longer than was necessary.

"Call me tomorrow?" I asked, wanting to make the point that I wanted to move the relationship forward.

I turned and made my way to the bottom of the stairs and turned back to Ed. Smiling at him, I said, "Until tomorrow."

"Until then," he said, smiling back at me as he lifted his phone and started scrolling through his contacts to find a taxi number. I was quietly impressed he had only been living here for a week and had already programmed his phone with all the necessary numbers.

How very boy scouts, I thought, *or policeman*, I reprimanded myself.

I climbed the stairs slowly, undressed, cleaned my teeth and got into bed. It felt strange being in bed, alone, while Ed was downstairs. For a moment, a brief, pleasurable moment, I considered running downstairs, throwing myself into his strong arms, staring into his handsome face and kissing him with every ounce of energy and pent-up passion.

But I didn't. I reminded myself of the importance of re-establishing our relationship and of the fact that, when starting a new relationship I would never jump into bed with a potential new boyfriend on the first date, and even though this was the second first date, or possibly even third, the same rules and benefits applied.

Plus it wouldn't do Ed any harm to wait and to know he still had work to do to get us back to where we were.

I heard the door open and be pulled closed quietly as

Ed left my home. The place had seen both happiness and laughter as well as devastation and tears of pain and anguish.

I hugged the duvet close to me, smelling Ed on the cover. I drifted off to sleep with a smile on my face and a feeling of contentment that I hadn't felt for some time.

fifteen.

One step at a time

The next morning I was making breakfast, the sun streaming in through the open window, bringing warmth with it, when my phone rang.

I almost dropped the coffee pot, my heart thumping. It was Ed. Having rushed to get to the phone, I paused before answering. I didn't want to appear too keen.

"Morning, you," I purred into the phone, unable to hide my delight at Ed calling so early, and desperately hoping I would see him.

"Hey, you," he said, sounding very perky and more like the Ed I had known before.

"Did you have a good night's sleep?" I asked.

"Yeah, I wasn't sure I'd get any after sleeping most of the afternoon, but somehow I was out like a light half an hour after I got home. How about you?"

"Same, thank you, I drifted off not long after you left and I have had a very lazy morning so far. I'm just making breakfast." I glanced down at my watch and was embarrassed to see that it was 10.30am and I had just confessed to only now having breakfast. I coughed nervously.

"Me too," I was relieved to hear Ed say. "Hey, I was wondering if you fancy going for a walk then a late lunch. I'm starting my new job tomorrow so I will need to be sensible and have an early night."

"I'd like that," I said a little too eagerly.

"Great, I'll be over in an hour or so to pick you up."

"Fab, see you soon."

As soon as we hung up I changed my mind about breakfast and went into a panic trying to decide what to wear. I wanted to look amazing but in an effortless 'oh, this old thing, I just threw it on' kind of a way. I tried on three outfits before settling on the staple jeans, the bottom of each leg turned up, not so much a fashion statement as a practical solution to being short. I teamed them with a floaty top that cut low to reveal my cleavage.

The sun was out, but there was a chill wind and it was cold in the shade so I put on thick socks and my ankle boots and planned to throw on a coat when we left.

I always struggle with coats – either going too warm or not warm enough. At least I would have Ed if I ended up with the latter.

As the clock clicked closer towards midday I paced the room, filled with nervous energy. Realising this wouldn't be a good image to greet Ed, I made my way to the kitchen and perched on the stool, drinking the cold coffee I had abandoned over an hour earlier. Luckily I like cold coffee.

Just after 12 noon there was a loud knock at the door.

Calm down, I told myself. I stood, straightened my top

and pulled up my jeans. Head held high I walked sedately to the door.

"Hey, you!" I said as I opened the door to greet a beaming Ed with a beautiful bouquet of white roses, intersected with delicate dots of white gypsophila and a scattering of eucalyptus.

It should have been a wonderful gesture. However, a previous boyfriend had put me off flowers, as whenever he saw someone carrying a bunch he would ask, "I wonder what he/she is guilty of?" It was how he managed to get away with never buying me any, not even for my birthday, our anniversary or heaven forbid Valentine's Day. That mantra had stuck with me.

But Ed was trying very hard and it really was a beautiful display. This was a good start and I rewarded him for it by smiling, stepping back to let him in and planting a kiss on his cheek as he passed.

I closed the door behind him.

"Are those for me?" I asked coyly.

He handed them to me. "Yes, sorry," he paused, "sorry, I have to be honest I'm feeling nervous, I don't know why, it's silly really," he said slowly, shaking his head, not quite looking me in the eye.

I took the flowers and placed them delicately in the sink, breathing in the sweet aroma as I did so.

I returned to an awkward Ed and without saying a word I gave him a massive hug. He reacted immediately by wrapping his arms around me and pulling me in even closer.

As he released his grip slightly I turned my face up towards his and smiled.

Ed bent down and we kissed, a deep, passionate, heart-thumping kiss. It was like we had never been apart.

We stayed locked in the embrace for some time. Finally coming up for breath we loosened our grip on each other, suddenly aware that we had been clinging to each other with energy-sapping strength.

It was evident to see the reaction the embrace had had on Ed and I smiled while he looked awkward.

"Well," I said, "I hope you're not still feeling nervous?"

He laughed. "No, I feel much more relaxed, thank you." He pulled me back into his arms and kissed me again, this time more gently, with less urgency. We knew we had time and stepped back from the intensity.

When Ed had recovered his decorum I picked up my coat and we drove the half-hour to my nearest National Trust property.

We strolled slowly hand in hand along the well-trodden path, chatting about nothing, pointing out little flashes of colour on the leaf-strewn ground.

We laughed at the rude nude statues that were placed next to the path or inside almost complete circles of bushes, which created private places for contemplation or stolen kisses.

The path meandered through a beautiful collection of white poplars, planted regimentally in triangles. They were breathtaking.

Further on we walked through an ancient arched doorway, the heavy wooden oak door with sturdy ring of iron for a handle pushed back against a flint wall, never to be closed again.

Onwards and we came to the old watermill with white

boarded walls and rickety stairs leading up to the cobwebbed rafters. Amazingly it still worked and the flour they milled was sold in the shop by the entrance.

We walked along the swollen river that fed the mill. Two beautiful swans elegantly glided past us.

Some of the gardens had been closed off. The gardeners were busy removing the plants that had died back and were preparing the beds for the next season.

Large areas of grass were roped off to ensure they were not churned up by eager walkers and playing children. But it didn't detract from the walk. We were happy on the path and this was more about rekindling our relationship than about the walk in itself.

After an hour we made our way back to the car, avoiding the crowded restaurant and instead heading to a pub in a village on the way home.

We had a relaxed lunch, sitting close at a small table near the large open fire.

We opted for a selection of tapas dishes, which we shared with gusto. It was not until we had sat down that I realised how hungry I was, driven by the lack of breakfast and the long walk.

I soaked up the moment, not wanting to have to part, knowing we were fantastic together and things only went wrong when we were apart. But knowing Ed had a huge and important week ahead of him I had to let him go and prepare.

Reluctantly we left the warmth of the pub and we drove home in silence, both deep in thought, but content.

We walked silently to my front door, hand in hand.

We paused at the front door. I was desperate to invite

him in, to eke out the day some more, but I knew he would find it hard to refuse the invitation and I didn't want to put him in that place, given how far we had come in just a couple of days.

He was doing so well at making up for things. He had paid for lunch and refused my offers to contribute and I knew he would pick me over work, but I was not going to make him choose.

I gently put my hand on his chest to indicate I was putting a stop on anything happening.

I leant forward and kissed him gently on the lips.

"I will keep everything crossed for you tomorrow," I said. "I know you will be great." I smiled a smile I didn't feel inside as I struggled to keep my resolve.

"Thank you," he whispered as he leant in, drawing me close and kissing me hard and passionately.

"Wow," I said involuntarily when we eventually pulled apart, looking around to check no one was watching. "That was, well, wow."

"I'll call you tomorrow evening and let you know how it went," he promised.

He slowly pulled away from me, still holding onto my hand as he stepped away, until we could no longer hold on and our fingertips separated.

He turned at the gate and smiled at me, and as he got into his car he gave a hearty wave and was gone.

I trudged into the house. It was cold and the light was fading from the sky. I felt desperately alone. I flopped into the sofa, realising how quickly I had fallen head over heels back in love with Ed. *No, that's not right*, I thought, *I never stopped loving him. I was just telling myself I had.* "Oh dear," I sighed.

I shut my eyes, I felt palpitations take over, I felt sweat break out on my forehead and neck. I sat still, waiting for the feeling to pass, calming myself.

A minute or two later I stood up and put my coat on the rack by the door and was surprised when there was a tentative knock.

I opened the door to see Ed standing on the doorstep. He took me in his arms and half carried, half pushed me back into the room, slamming the door behind him as we passed.

We kissed. A hot, all-engulfing kiss. Nothing else existed. Nothing else mattered. There was just here and now and us, this moment. We were locked together in this loving and heavenly embrace for ages.

"Sorry," he said quietly as we separated, our faces flushed, still touching. "I couldn't leave without coming back to tell you something. I know you might not want to hear this, but I have to say it." The words were tumbling out of his lips, I could feel the heat of his breath on my cheek. I held my breath. "I love you," he said quietly, nervously.

"I love you too," I replied more confidently, relieved that we had both declared our feelings. "But you need to go, or I won't be held responsible for what happens next."

He laughed. "I know, I know, you're right."

He bent down and gently kissed my forehead, then held my face in his hands. "I love you," he said louder, more confidently as he looked deep into my eyes.

"Go!" I said reluctantly, and in no way convincingly, as I tapped him gently on his perfectly formed behind as he turned and left. This time he didn't return.

I emptied the ash from the bottom of the stove, laid

paper and kindling above the grate, opened the vents and lit the paper. I sat on the floor watching the fire spring to life. Once there was a glowing bed of ember I put a couple of logs in and closed the door.

I stared at the fire, mesmerised by the flames. It was good not to think. I stayed there until it was too hot to remain and I moved to the sofa.

Apart from making some dinner, putting on the lights and closing the curtains when the light disappeared from the sky, I stayed on the sofa watching whatever was on the TV that distracted me from thinking about Ed, or our future. I no longer doubted that we had a future I was pleased to realise.

sixteen.

Déjà vu

As always I was the first in the office the next day and got straight down to preparing the media monitoring report for the team. It was something I did every week, reviewing all the press articles that were relevant to our work. It was routine and I enjoyed it, and of course it kept my mind occupied.

The minute my colleagues arrived and we did the traditional, "How was your weekend?", my face must have given the game away.

"Okay," they said, "what happened?"

I felt nervous telling them about Ed. After all they had been the ones who had listened to my tales of woe, who had mopped up the tears and fed me with cake. How would they react if I told them we were back together?

I decided to keep the story simple, just saying he was back in my life and we were taking it slow and seeing how it goes.

They looked dubious but they accepted it was my decision.

Despite being busy, the day still dragged. I kept finding myself staring at the page I was meant to be reviewing, aware that I hadn't taken in one word of what was in the report as my thoughts kept turning to Ed. I was hoping his first day was going well and daydreaming about how we might celebrate the following weekend if it had been a success.

Normally I enjoyed my one-mile walk back to the car, but that afternoon I practically ran back, my mind racing, desperate to get home and to talk to Ed.

I was sitting by the phone forty-five minutes later when I heard steps approaching my front door and leapt to my feet, opening the door just as Ed lifted his arm, fist clenched, ready to announce his arrival.

"Come in, come in," I implored him, swinging the door open wide to let him pass.

"Sorry," Ed said as he stepped inside and I closed the door behind him, "I was going to call but I really wanted to see you. Sorry, I should have called first rather than just turning up unexpected."

"Nonsense, don't be silly," I reassured him as I sat down and patted the empty seat beside me. "Sit down and tell me how it went. I've been desperate to hear all about it."

Ed's shoulders relaxed and he smiled as he sat down, then the smile spread across his face, reaching his eyes. "Really good," he started.

It was great to hear his enthusiasm. He told me about the work, his colleagues. He talked on and on with passion and joy, and I sat and I listened and I nodded, not wanting to interrupt his flow.

Obviously he couldn't tell me any details, but I was

fascinated in his insights and something that struck me was when he said, "When you look at someone, how can you really know what is going on inside their head? They can appear confident or shy, honest or deceitful, happy or sad, but what's real and what's the impression they are trying to convey? Obviously if they are in front of me, accused of something, then it's likely they have something to hide, but are they trying to hide an unpaid parking ticket or a speeding fine or have they got murderous intent? It's hard, you know, to know."

I could not imagine how hard that must be, but I was grateful to be given an insight into his world.

"You're never in danger though, are you?" I asked some time later when he finished telling his tale.

"Um," he said cautiously, obviously giving himself time to answer, "yes, I can be, but we undergo thorough training and practise certain scenarios so we are prepared for most eventualities, plus we have protective clothing if needed."

I leant over and took his face in my hands. Staring into his eyes, I said honestly, "Well, you had better promise me that you'll do whatever you can to stay safe. I'm not going to lose you again." Then leant in and kissed him long and hard. He scooped me up in his arms and returned the passion and emotion of the embrace.

It was late when we finally went to the kitchen to prepare dinner and to be honest by that time I was no longer very hungry, so we made tea and toast and curled up on the sofa to enjoy the snack in front of the TV.

He didn't stay the night. We didn't talk about it but we both knew it was going to be an exhausting week without adding physical exhaustion to the mix, and of course it was still too early to be opening that door. Each day we were edging closer to getting back to where we were but there was no need to rush, it would happen, and we knew it would.

The week dragged. I was living for the evenings when Ed and I would spend hours on the phone chatting. The days and work were things to endure. And each day was one closer to the weekend and we had arranged that Ed would come to me straight from work.

I had driven all the way in to work on Friday, not wanting to waste time walking back to the car at the end of the working day. I just wanted to get home. I arrived at work early and I left early.

Running up to my bedroom, I changed into something sexier than my usual drab work clothes: a long, layered, floaty skirt and low-cut black top, a dab of perfume and a refresh of the makeup.

I was excited, so excited. The air of anticipation lay thick in the air.

There was no way I was going to be able to get away with cool that evening, let alone be aloof. I had made him prove himself again and he had passed with flying colours.

I was hovering by the window when I saw him open the gate, a huge bunch of flowers in his hand. I was at the door beaming at him as he climbed the step.

No words were needed.

He handed me the flowers.

I shut the door.

The flowers were abandoned on the small table by the door where I would leave my various bags on entering the house.

Ed's coat was thrown over the sofa as he passed.

We ran up the stairs, laughing as we went.

We stopped by the bed and the passion was released as we kissed hard and desperately. There was no denying where this was going.

We slowly undressed each other, taking our time, savouring the moment and letting the lust take over. We fell onto the bed already entwined.

Finally when we were sated and lying in each other's arms, Ed said, laughing, "Well, that dinner date didn't exactly go to plan!"

"Just as well we weren't out for dinner, I think we would have been banned from the restaurant, not to mention upsetting our fellow diners and terrifying the children," I replied with a twinkle in my eyes.

We lay there a moment longer, snuggled in the warm, crumpled bed.

Eventually dragging ourselves out, we helped each other dress, finding our clothes scattered around the room. We giggled at the situation.

It was too late to go out for dinner so again we made a light snack, but this time we married it with a deep, velvety glass of red wine and sat on the sofa talking into the early hours. When we returned to my bedroom we resumed where we had left off a couple of hours earlier.

When I woke the next morning I lay in the quiet for a few moments. Feeling confused I reached out my hand and was relieved to feel the warmth of Ed's body behind me. For a moment, when I had woken, I feared he had gone, but he was there.

"Morning, gorgeous," he said. He had obviously woken before me and was waiting for me to follow suit.

"Morning, you," I replied as I wiggled my body back into his.

He wrapped his arms around me and leant over. I could feel his hot breath on my ear, which he started to nibble. I felt the tingle surge through my body.

I turned around and kissed Ed like my life depended on it. Ed slipped back on top of me as he had done so many times in the last few hours and we were absorbed by our passion once more.

In those heady first few days of our rekindled love we spent a lot of time in bed or stealing moments in and outside the house. It was exciting and joyous and I felt truly alive, that life was worth living. I would do anything and everything to fight for this relationship, to keep these endorphins raging through my very being.

Now that Ed was nearby it meant the shifts were not a problem, we would meet when our schedules allowed rather than being limited by distance.

Even days when we couldn't meet we spoke on the phone. Every day, day or night we spoke or met. There were dinners and rainy afternoons watching old films curled up on the sofa. When the weather permitted there were autumnal walks, soaking up the colours, being surprised by the vibrant purple of the Michaelmas daisies, a sign that the wedding of Dan and Emma was drawing ever closer.

One evening over dinner at a local pub, Ed asked nervously, "I'm sorry to ask, I did say I'd leave it to you to let me know your decision, but I know Emma and Dan would love you to come to their wedding and in fact for you to be involved in some of the planning if you would like to, and I would love you to come with me. Dan has invited me up this weekend to talk about some of the arrangements and I'm hoping you might come too." He trailed off, going quiet now that he had finally got this off his chest.

"Yes," I said simply, toying with him slightly. I had in fact decided some time before that I would go. Nothing could stop me from going. I had just been waiting for the right moment to tell Ed.

He looked at me quizzically. "Yes to which part?" he asked.

"Yes to all of it," I said, beaming at him.

Clearly Ed needed more concrete affirmation. I thought 'yes' was as clear as I could be, but Ed was staring at me.

I took a deep breath. "Yes to coming with you this weekend, yes to being involved in the wedding plans and yes to attending the wedding with you."

Ed's smile erupted across his face. He jumped to his feet, knocking his chair over in the sudden force of energy. The wooden chair clanged onto the dark grey tiled floor to the shock and surprise of the other diners. But Ed didn't seem to notice.

He stepped around the small table. I had stood up in anticipation of the impending hug.

Ed swept me up into his arms and gave me the most amazing bear hug, reminding me as he did of my father and how safe and warm and loved I felt when wrapped in his arms as a child, the smell of stale pipe smoke on his breath as he held me close. As I had grown, for some reason, still unknown to me now, I changed from being a father's girl to a mother's girl. Sometimes I had longed to return to the days of innocence when it was pure joy to be in that place, but somehow it had gone and was replaced with distance.

But now I was wrapped in the arms of my love and I could have stayed there forever.

Eventually Ed pulled back and, holding my shoulders in his strong hands, he beamed at me. "Thank you," he said, sounding both happy and relieved.

We both knew the significance of me saying 'yes'. It meant the hurt from earlier in the year had been forgiven – if not forgotten. It shouted that I was ready and happy to move on and fully commit not only to him but also to his family.

"I'll let you into a little secret," I said as he picked up the chair from where it still lay abandoned on the floor. "I've known the answer was yes for a little while, but I was just waiting for the right moment to tell you."

"That's mean," he said in a mockingly sullen voice. "I've been on tenterhooks waiting to know and you've been making me wait, to make me suffer." He smiled a cheeky grin.

"No," I said coyly, shrugging my shoulders and leaning my head to the side, "I wanted to be sure, I really wasn't being cruel. In fact, I've been thinking about us a lot recently and well…" I broke off as I reached into my bag and pulled out a small gift-wrapped box. "… well, I'd like to give you this," I said as I slid the box across the table.

"What's this?" Ed asked, a little confused. To be fair it was not his birthday, or our anniversary, so it was a little unexpected. I could see Ed turn it over, both in his mind, trying to work out if he had forgotten some occasion for which he should have also brought a gift, and physically as he turned the box over in his hands.

"Well, that's the point of a gift," I teased. "You have to open it to find out what's inside." I smiled.

He pulled the red ribbon wrapped around the small silver box. Slowly he lifted the lid, momentarily glancing up at me as he did so. Then he looked back down at the box so I couldn't read his expression. Suddenly it struck me that maybe I was overstepping the mark, maybe I had got this wrong.

I had been so focused on making sure I was in the right place to recommit to our relationship, I was so clear that Ed needed to do the running to get us back to where we were, that it had not occurred to me that he might not be in the same place.

"Look, I'm sorry," I blurted out, "I thought we were in a good place and I now realise that I haven't asked how you feel. I'm sorry," I repeated. "You don't have to open it," I said, reaching out to put my hand on top of the box to prevent Ed from seeing what lay inside. But it was too late.

To my great relief he looked at me, smiling. He pushed my hand away with the hand holding the top of the box, then laid it on the table before pulling out a small silver key.

"Do you mean it?" he asked with a serious tone and expression.

"Yes," I said, mirroring his reaction. "Only, I don't just want you to have a key. I would like you to move in." Worried I might still have got this wrong, my words started to tumble out of my mouth as I spoke faster and more quietly as I went on, "Each time you come round you leave more and more in the house and every time you leave the house it feels so empty and I miss you when I don't see you because of work and…" I couldn't think what else to say. I needed to know the answer and this time it was me that was hanging on his decision. *He must be relishing this*, I thought.

I bet he hadn't thought revenge would be served to him on a silver platter, or in a silver box to be more precise, so soon.

"Well," he said slowly, trying to eke out this moment, "well now, let me think." He paused, using one hand to rub his chin and look like he was weighing up his options. All the time the key was in his other hand.

The waiter came over to ask us about our meal, oblivious to the question hanging between us.

The waiter cleared the table. Neither of us wanted to eat any more. Ed asked the waiter to give us a moment before deciding on whether we wanted another bottle.

I felt some relief that he hadn't just asked for the bill. That wouldn't have been a good sign.

When we were alone, well, as much as you can be in a busy pub, his free hand sought out mine. He picked it up and beamed at me. He finally put me out of my misery. "I would be honoured to move in with you. I thought you would never ask, again," he teased.

This time two wooden chairs clunked to the floor as we embraced once more to the surprise and amusement of those around us.

The waiter came back once we had resumed our places at the table.

"Champagne!" Ed ordered. "Yes, I think champagne is needed to celebrate this moment."

The waiter looked slightly confused. Glancing at my left hand he couldn't see a newly placed ring. He then glanced at Ed as he was adding the key I had given him to his keyring.

Shrugging in a nonchalant, I don't really care, kind of a fashion, he wandered off to find a cold bottle of champagne and two flutes.

We laughed a lot that evening and we talked about how and when Ed would move in, where he would put all his belongings in my already full little cottage. In the end we decided he would move in with his personal belongings but all the furniture would go into storage until we could figure out what to keep or lose from each other's possessions. No one needs more beds than there are bedrooms or multiple dining room sets, sofas, chairs and more. It also meant he could move in sooner than if we waited to shift excess furniture.

But it wouldn't be this weekend, as we would be travelling north to see Dan and Emma.

In the meantime we celebrated at the pub, we celebrated back at home and we celebrated in bed that night.

The next evening Ed moved in with a suitcase and plans to hire a van and move the rest in a couple of weeks.

I was on cloud nine. I was like a teenager in the first throes of a romance. I was giddy with happiness. Work, well, I went to work that week but I don't remember it. Nothing could touch me or upset me that week. I did my hours. I did what I had to do and I disappeared home as soon as the clock struck 5pm.

This was unusual behaviour for me. Normally I worked as many hours as I needed, arriving early, taking a short lunch and working late.

Over the years I had shared my home, or a home, with several boyfriends. Sometimes it happened quickly, sometimes it took time. Sometimes it was my decision, sometimes I was asked and sometimes he just stopped going home. Sometimes it was exciting and filled with hope of a 'happy every after', which is how it felt with Ed. Sometimes it came with a realisation that this was the wrong thing and I was already trying to work out how to escape. Sometimes I just resigned myself to the 'it's better than being alone' mentality and just got on with it. Once, I had been in the process of writing a 'sorry it's over' letter which began with 'You said some really mean things which I'm sure you didn't mean, but they still sunk in…' Before I had time to finish it he had arrived with bags in hand and being a coward, or more accurately, not being the type of person to cause a fuss or to create a scene, I just accepted it and I thought I could live, literally, with the situation. How many years of my life have I wasted on relationships that would never have a fairy-tale ending?

Not that it mattered now that I was with Ed and he was the miracle I had been waiting for, searching for, for so long.

And so the honeymoon period began, again. We politely stepped around each other's little habits that were cute in short spurts when he stayed over, but having moved in they were no longer short spurts and with time these little traits, like leaving car and bike magazines piled up on the floor, would eventually become an annoyance. Again with hindsight I had been too soft in the past, tidying up after my boyfriends so either they came to expect me to do it, or worse, thought it was my job to do so.

I resolved that with Ed I was neither going to make the same mistake nor to let these traits become bad habits and gently nudged him to make them a good habit by asking, "Would you mind popping your magazines in the rack over there for me." Soon he was storing them all there and only picking them out to read them, or to recycle them when they were finished with.

There were many other traits – some I loved and encouraged and others I put to bed as quickly as I could. I was also guilty of having bad habits. I had been living alone too long and they had taken root. So I kept my eyes and ears open for signals of dissatisfaction and tailored my actions accordingly and, of course, I asked questions, checked how he felt. This was a two-way street after all and no one is perfect.

That aside, the early days were glorious. I felt the warmth of love surrounding me.

Soon the weekend came and we headed north. We had arranged to meet Dan and Emma at a National Trust property that had been their family favourite when they were young. It was a large parkland with a farm attached, ideal for family days out.

We had arranged to meet at 12.30pm at the courtyard cafe. When we arrived we found we had missed a text from Dan. He had heard the car park was closed due to flooding. We looked around us in the dry car park and laughed. There were a lot of leaves piled up at the bottom of the slope – not unexpected after all the wind and rain of late.

Dan's text had gone on to suggest we meet at a garden centre nearby. We tried calling several times to find out which venue we should head for but the call kept failing.

Eventually Dan called Ed and after a quick chat, Ed confirmed that they would drive over and be with us in ten to fifteen minutes.

It was still drizzling so we donned our raincoats and decided to check out the shop while we waited for them. We walked around the outside of the large square building that would once have been a very grand stable and cart building for a mansion. We made our way in through large, arched doors into the courtyard.

There was a second-hand bookshop in one corner, a plant shop in another with produce spread across the yard to great display, making it all very appealing and tempting to a serial buyer of things I don't need.

Further round the courtyard was a place I had to avoid at all cost, containing fudge and cakes. The smell wafted out and hit our nostrils. We quickly turned to our right and made our way into the shop.

Perusing the shelves I was tempted by so much, but none within budget and nothing I actually needed, so I desisted and removed myself from temptation and we returned to the courtyard.

There was one more corner we had yet to venture into, as that was the location of the cafe. As we made our way over we were greeted with a chalkboard that informed us 'Cafe Closed'.

"Oh dear," I said, looking to Ed for guidance.

We agreed to go back to the car park and wait for Dan and Emma and give them the bad news.

When we saw them draw up and park next to us we went over and greeted them. Emma gave me a loving hug and a heartfelt, "Hello. It's wonderful to see you," and I genuinely thought she meant it.

We told them about the cafe and decided to drive back to the garden centre in convoy although, in truth, it was an easy journey, right, right, right and then it would be on the left.

The garden centre was of medium size and typical format: a small gift shop, large indoor plant and furniture area and a long cafe that ran across the back. The lights were on in the garden area but the cafe was in darkness except for a few lights in the chiller cabinets.

The manager informed us that there was a power cut. We tried to reason that if there were lights on elsewhere then it was not a power cut, but she insisted and we didn't want to appear rude.

They couldn't make any hot food or coffee, but cold food, drinks and strangely tea were available if we wanted.

We took a moment and decided as we were all hungry and time was marching on to order four quiches with salad. Two goat's cheese and leek, two mushroom and stilton, and four cups of tea. We were surprised the salad cost more than the quiches, but we wanted to talk about the wedding so took some comfy chairs near a window to provide light.

We laughed as Ed remarked that the cafe was becoming more and more like Fawlty Towers, especially when the two mushroom and stilton quiches turned out to be bacon and caramelised onion.

There was a slightly awkward moment, as we were not sure how to proceed. I decided to break the silence. "I'm so sorry that I took so long to reply to your very kind wedding invitation. I really am thrilled that you invited me and I can't wait. Is there anything I can do to help?"

Ed reached over and held my hand, a silent thank you.

"Me too," Ed said. "What can I do, what do you need?"

Everyone smiled, and there was a visible relaxation around the small table.

Before we could get into the details our £3.50 quiches

and £5 pile of lettuce, tomato and beetroot salad drizzled with French dressing were placed in front of us.

We talked and ate, making conversation stilted at times as questions were posed just after mouths were filled with food. With the wedding so close most arrangements were in place. In truth, I don't think Dan and Emma needed us to do anything, they just wanted to reconnect with me.

I sat back in my chair and smiled at each of them, with my large cup of coffee nestled in my hands, made possible by the power finally being reconnected, we had taken the opportunity to get more drinks.

The conversation was relaxed. The best man and bridesmaids had been picked and outfits bought. As the wedding was close to Christmas they were going with a warm feel with a mix of whites and deep red.

The venue had been booked whilst I was with them earlier in the year, but now the details had been finalised, the food and drink selected, the wedding dress – no details were given with regard to its look in keeping with tradition – was being adjusted to fit Emma perfectly, the table decorations and seating arrangements all in place.

"It sounds like it's going to be a fabulous day. I can't wait. Is there anything I can do?" I asked again, wanting to be a part of the wedding and make myself useful. In a way I wanted to be needed.

"Well," Emma said a little hesitantly, "we are hoping…" Emma glanced over at Dan for reassurance. "Would you be kind enough to do a reading?" she asked.

"I'd love to," I gushed my response. "Do you have a specific reading you would like me to do or would you like me to find one?"

Dan looked at his dad. "Dad, we were hoping you might be kind enough to do a reading as well." Ed nodded his agreement, slightly choked to have been asked.

Emma continued, "Chloe, would you be kind enough to do a religious reading and Ed would you do a non-religious reading? We're not particularly religious so we don't have any specific pieces in mind, but the vicar has given us a list of popular ones at weddings or you can pick something you like if you have something in mind."

Ed and I must have looked like very proud parents, honoured to be given a role at such a wonderful, happy occasion. We both spoke at once. "Yes, yes, I'd love to." We looked at each other and laughed.

After that the conversation turned to the more mundane: 'How's work?', 'Have you seen this person or that?' The only sticky moment was when Ed asked after Clare. It was an innocent question, one asked a million times during get-togethers, but now it felt awkward. We all stiffened a little and Dan gave me a furtive glance. I smiled to reassure him. I had held my breath as Ed uttered the words, but now I realised I was the one that had to make this a natural enquiry again. If I didn't, none of us would move on, none of us would get back to the happy place we were in the last time we met. And that was something we all needed and wanted.

"She's good," Dan said slowly, deliberately. "Mum and Steve have a week away booked before the wedding. Steve is going to be in charge of the ushers at the wedding." Now the furtive glances were directed at Ed.

"That's great news." Ed sounded more jovial than any of us really felt.

"And Clare, does she have a role at the wedding?" I asked, trying to sound interested but hoping I was not going to find myself locked in a room with her preparing flowers or creating table gifts.

Emma and Dan glanced at each other. "Yes, she's in charge of the bridesmaids. Some are rather young and can be a bit of a handful, so she'll be keeping them in check and making sure they are in the right place, at the right time, in the right clothes."

The conversation rumbled on, more relaxed now that the 'Clare' situation had been covered without incident.

After we finished the second round of drinks we returned to the National Trust property, purchased tickets for the park and went for a hearty walk to work off lunch.

We were all wrapped in our raincoats, hats and scarves, our feet adorned with sturdy walking boots against the wet and mud hidden beneath the fallen leaves. Dan and Emma held hands and Ed picked up my hand. Despite the age gap we felt very much like we were at the same stage of our relationship. I hoped.

It was a delightful walk through the autumnal parkland: the spider webs suspended between the branches glistening with the raindrops still clinging to the magically strong threads of the web; the deer off in the distance gently grazing on the wet grass, yet alert to movement and potential danger.

Dan, it turned out, was a keen photographer like me and we both stopped on many occasions to snap nature in all its glory.

"Autumn and spring are definitely my favourite seasons," I said to Ed later as we were driving home.

"Why?" he asked.

"Well, spring is full of hope, of the warm days to come, flowers starting to poke through the soil proving life goes on, that soon the land will be emblazoned in colour. The joy of the tiny, delicate snowdrops, followed by the riotous daffodils, leading to the pink and white blossom as the months roll on.

"Then of course autumn, could be seen as sad, as everything starts to die back, but there are still warm days and the colours are just stunning. All around are greens, yellows, reds, the vibrant purple of the Michaelmas daisies, grapes fat on the vine, the stove being lit on cold evenings and the promise of Christmas. What's not to love?"

Ed chuckled next to me as we neared home. "I've never really thought about it," he said. "So why not summer or winter?"

"Well, I love the sun, as you know, but often it can be too hot and it's miserable being stuck in the office when the sun is blazing outside. The office is stifling. And the winter is the opposite, it's cold and wet and there is the fear of snow. I loved snow when I was little, as it meant no school and we'd go tobogganing down a nearby hill hoping to be stopped by the scrub and bumps at the bottom of the hill, otherwise you'd bump across the path and over the edge of the bank, landing with a splash in the icy river below. But it's not the same as an adult, you're still expected to turn up at work, and driving in the snow scares the heebie-jeebies out of me," I confessed. "Besides, spring and autumn can't be my favourites if I like summer and winter as much."

He couldn't argue with that logic. "True. And I can help with the driving in snow, we have a test centre where we can simulate all weather conditions. I'll take you down there if you like?"

I turned in my seat, well, as far as my seatbelt would allow, and smiled at Ed. I couldn't believe how lucky I was to have him in my life.

I reached out and touched his arm. "Thank you," I said. "I'd love that, it would certainly help my confidence."

We arrived home half an hour later and slumped into the sofa. We chatted about the day, about how well Dan and Emma were, how excited we were about the wedding. We even went online to start looking for appropriate readings for the two of us. We had a light supper and climbed the stairs, falling into deep sleeps just a short while after flopping into bed in each other's arms.

seventeen.

Time to face my demons

Over the next few weeks we got used to living together. We got used to shift working and seeking out time together to go for dinner, to go for walks, to do the mundane shopping and chores, and to do the extracurricular activities we loved so much.

We also spent time selecting and then practising our readings, either alone or taking it in turn to practise in front of each other.

As time went on I became more and more nervous. Luckily I only knew three people at the wedding, but they were the most important: the bride, the groom, and the most important person – well, to me – Ed. At that point I had not even met the groom's mother, the infamous Clare, or her husband, Steve.

I doubt Ed was nervous. He was so confident, he projected his voice, speaking slowly and clearly, and he certainly never said anything about how he was feeling. But then neither did I.

We spoke to Dan regularly, confirming our readings so they could be printed in the order of service.

It was such a happy time in my life. We had a wedding and Christmas, our first Christmas together, to look forward to.

We went to work, we did what we had to do and we came home to be with each other.

The next weekend that Ed had off work we popped into our nearest city to shop for outfits for the wedding.

I had the foresight and respect to check with the bride's mother, Ruth, as well as Clare, what designer and colour they were wearing to ensure we didn't wear the same clothes. Not that it was likely, they were both tall, slim and elegant. I was not, but it was the courteous thing to do.

I already knew Emma's colour scheme. She was going down the traditional route and wearing white, and her bridesmaids were wearing a mix of white and a deep velvet red.

Ed was easy to attire. We hired a traditional morning suit. He looked so handsome, I physically swooned when he stepped out of the dressing room all dolled up. I could feel myself getting hot. I had to fan myself with a handy brochure I found on the small table next to where I was sitting.

On the other hand finding something for me took a lot longer. I wanted to look nice, but it's very bad form to outshine the wedding party. Not that I could. Right then all I wanted to do was find something pretty, to make Ed proud to have me on his arm and introduce me as his girlfriend.

We trawled the shops, trying lots of dresses, separates, jackets, but nothing was right and Ed was clearly getting bored. Who could blame him, so was I, so we called it a day and I decided to return the next weekend while Ed was at work, and shop until I had an outfit in hand.

On Thursday, while I was at work, Ed moved in officially. He loaded his furniture into a van and took it to a storage unit, continuing to my little home with clothes, personal items and knick-knacks. It was not much, but when I arrived home I was both excited that he had finally moved in, but a little surprised to be met by a wall of boxes in my cosy front room and a hot and sweaty Ed.

"Sorry, sorry," he said as he saw me come in and no doubt read my slightly perplexed expression. "It's taken me longer than I had thought. I'd been hoping to get it all put away before you got home."

"That's okay," I reassured him, walking across the room and planting a big kiss on his lips. His arms wrapped around me and I could feel him physically relax.

"How was your day?" he asked, genuinely interested. It was so, so wonderful to have someone to greet me when I got home, but more than that it was so amazing to have someone who cared enough to ask. It sounds like a triviality, but I had had men in my life that seemed to take no interest in me, my work, my health – mental or physical. They only cared about their own problems, expecting me to be there for them at all times, always offering them help and support. It always surprised me how divorced they could be from me and from having the same care for me.

I looked longingly into Ed's eyes and replied, "It was okay, I've managed to set up a meeting with a national journalist who I've been chasing for some time, which is great. But the best part of today has been coming home to you."

I smiled and continued, "This can wait." I nodded my head towards the pile of boxes, picked up his hand and led him to the stairs.

"Yes, ma'am," he said and trotted up the stairs behind me. For a second it occurred to me that the bedroom could be in disarray with clothes everywhere as part of the unpacking process, but luckily as I led Ed through the door the bed was clear and pristine. Not for long though.

We had a light supper and curled up on the sofa to watch TV. I was always sensible on a work night and although Ed was not working on Friday I had to go to work. It was going to be hard to leave him in bed in the morning, but I was starting to get used to that.

On Saturday I drove back into the city, fighting the traffic, queuing into the central car park and regretting the decision to drive past the park and ride and not take up the opportunity – both faster and cheaper. But I sat in the traffic and eventually got myself parked.

Another day of pounding the streets, I had resigned myself to a day lost in dressing, undressing, redressing as I tried on one outfit after another.

In each shop I piled up the clothes on my arm and marched into the changing room to try all manner of combinations, only to be disappointed and increasingly dejected.

As I was beginning to give up hope I chanced upon an independent shop whilst making my way from one high street name to another. Not designer, I couldn't afford designer and would never spend that much on an outfit for one day, however important that day was.

The shop window was a riot of autumnal colours and it

made me stop in my tracks and gaze in wonderment at the display.

I could see some gorgeous clothes inside and looked up at the name of the shop. It didn't give anything away. I had no idea if they had clothes in my size or if I could afford them even if they did.

This could be very uncomfortable, I thought as I opened the door with trepidation. I feared I might be confronted by a plethora of beautifully turned out shop staff, with perfect makeup masking flawless skin, looking a little bewildered as to why I would think this shop would have anything that would fit me.

I shook the idea from my mind and mustered all the courage I could. Head held high I entered the clothes emporium.

Inside there was a lovely, sweet smell of perfume. I drew in a sharp breath of air as the inside of the shop assaulted my senses. As well as the glorious, heady smell, there was colour everywhere. The walls and racks were filled with every colour imaginable. Large ornate silver-gilt-framed mirrors broke up the racks but reflected back more colour. Large chandeliers hung overhead, throwing twinkling light around the shop, picking up the silver mirrors and sparkling sequinned tops.

It was the most magical shop I had ever been in. *How have I never seen this shop before?* I thought as I slowly progressed further into the shop, my hand trailing through the clothes picking up velvets, silks and cottons as I passed, mesmerised.

I was a little taken aback when the shop manager suddenly appeared in front of me. She had an unassuming face lightly touched by subtle makeup. She carried herself with an air of confidence that was infectious. She had plump cheeks and an engaging smile. Her long hair was pulled back from her face by an intricate silver band. A few strands had been allowed to fall free, both softening the look and veering her away from looking austere. She was wearing a fitted, floral dress that was incredibly flattering and gave me the confidence that this was the woman who could help me find the perfect outfit.

"Can I help you, my dear?" she asked.

"Oh, I do hope so," I said with relief. "I'm going to my boyfriend's son's wedding and I need an outfit. I know the colours that the bridesmaids, the bride's mother and the groom's mother are wearing. I need something that looks good, but not be showy, I need something that works well both day and night, and…" The words had gushed forth and I found myself just staring at this kindly looking lady, pleading with my eyes for help.

"You want your boyfriend to be looking at you and not his ex-wife, whilst being respectful to all those in the family with more seniority than you?" she half asked, half stated, having perfectly summed up exactly what I wanted and needed. I smiled.

"Well then, my dear, let's get started." I rattled off the colour schemes, likes and dislikes as she guided me to the back of the shop where three ceiling-to-floor, deep red velvet curtains were held back by wrought iron hooks to reveal identical fitting rooms, each with a small leather armchair, dressing table with mirror and more silver gilt mirrors on either side. I was shown into the central fitting room, feeling like I didn't live up to the sumptuousness of where I found myself.

"In you pop," she instructed. "Undress down to your underwear and pop on the dressing gown on the hook behind the chair. I'll bring in a selection and we can find your style. Then we can go from there. One step at a time," she said, taking control of the situation. She let the curtain fall silently across the opening and disappeared.

When she returned she asked politely if it was okay to come in and then swept into the room laden down with a multitude of styles and colours thrown over her arms.

"Now, let's find you that outfit," she stated as she expertly lined up the clothes on an empty rack, moving items around to create different looks.

I was starting to feel hot and tired as the multitude of clothes came and went from the room. Eventually, though, I found the one. I turned slowly to look at myself in the mirror and involuntarily drew in a sharp breath. I had never felt so amazing. I could have hugged the shop manager.

It was a princess-cut dress, red with white swirls and beading. It closely followed the contours of my ample breasts and then flowed out beneath, hiding all my imperfections below the folds of the material. It was floaty. It was glorious. It was perfect.

A few moments later it had been teamed up with a lightweight, black bolero jacket, a fascinator (I have never been one for a hat), sturdy black heels to help me walk with confidence, even after a glass or two of bubbles, and all topped off with a slim black silk handbag. The outfit was complete.

The shop manager smiled. Not a 'Wow, I'm going to make a big profit today' kind of smile, but genuine satisfaction at a job well done. She had every right to feel proud, she had done an amazing job.

I smiled back. "I'd love to take it all," I said hesitantly, "although I have no idea how much all of this will come to."

"Don't worry, dear, I'm sure it will be within your budget. Now then, you get yourself back into your own clothes. Leave the outfit in here and I'll get one of the girls to pop in, remove the labels and pack it all up for you so it doesn't get creased or scuffed." She had clearly got the measure of me, so I did as I was told and met her by the till at the front of the shop, heart now in throat as to the size of the bill I was about to be presented with.

"There you are, dear, what do you think about this?" she asked as she pointed at the price displayed on the front of the till.

"£175?" I said in disbelief. "Oh, sorry, that is just the price of the dress," I said, feeling foolish.

"No, dear, that is for everything. I rung it up whilst you were getting dressed. Is that okay for you?"

"Oh my goodness!" I exclaimed. "That can't be right. That is for everything, the dress, jacket, bag, shoes and fascinator?"

"Yes, dear," she said, now sounding a little disappointed in me. "I did tell you it would be affordable." For the second time that day I wanted to hug her, the counter between us keeping our relationship strictly professional.

"I don't know what to say, that is amazing, you are amazing, thank you, thank you," I said.

"Well, dear, if you like my little shop, don't forget to pop by again, and of course don't forget to tell your friends about us too."

"I will, I will," I assured her as her assistant handed me a beautifully wrapped box with handle to make it easy to carry.

As I left the shop I turned back and gave the two smiling women a heartfelt wave, before heading back into the town bustle.

I couldn't wait for Ed to get home that night, to tell him about my day, and, if he asked, which he did, to show him my outfit.

I stood before a silent Ed, then gave a twirl which threw out the hem of the dress. I felt like a princess, I couldn't stop smiling.

"Wow," was all he said, but his face said it all. His smile matched mine as he strode over to me, taking my face in his hands and kissing me long, hard and passionately.

"Wow," he said again as we separated. "You look beautiful," he said as he took my hand and led me back to the bedroom. Unusually I undressed slowly, taking the time to carefully return the dress to the box, interspersed with tissue paper to keep it safe.

*

This blissful life, full of love and laughter continued apace. We fell into routines of chores, shopping and work. But we also made sure that we had date nights, and when our work schedules allowed we would go walking during the days and love-making whenever and wherever we could.

As the wedding approached we had regular calls with Dan and Emma, updating us on the wedding plans: seating arrangements, food, drink, flowers, gifts, order of service, parking, hotel accommodation, set lists for the DJ and much, much more. Not that I complained, it was fantastic to be included and involved.

Despite all this joy there was an elephant in the room, growing bigger by the day, and both Ed and I knew it and knew we needed to get rid of it before the big day.

One evening Ed decided to face the demon.

"Chloe," he said with trepidation, "we need to talk about Clare." He looked at me sideways, trying to gauge my reaction.

"Yes, we do and I suspect we are thinking the same thing. That we should meet her and Steve before the big day and just put everything to bed, so to speak."

Ed let out a big sigh. Obviously he had been building up to this moment for some time.

"Thank you. I'm off this weekend, we could ask if they're free and pop up and see them?" It was more of a question than a statement, but the relief in his face and voice melted my heart.

"Sounds like a good idea," I said, trying to make my voice steady and confident, when in reality I could feel the fear beginning to rise from within. At least it would be over in a few days and if it went well it would mean the wedding itself would be a lot more relaxing. Well, it would be as soon as I had completed the reading.

Ed picked up his mobile and went into the sitting room, leaving me at the dining room table. Alone. It seemed a little strange that he decided to make the call out of my earshot, but I told myself to calm down and busied myself tidying up our dinner plates and cooking implements.

A short while later Ed returned and sat at the table.

"All arranged," he announced. "Clare has invited us to lunch on Saturday. She has also been thinking it would be good to meet. It's only a couple of hours' drive, but I was thinking we could drive up on Friday night and stay nearby so that we don't have to start too early on Saturday morning. What do you think?"

"Sounds like a plan," I said, smiling. It would be a welcome distraction.

I managed to get away from work a little early on Friday and found Ed already at home when I got there.

I was a mixture of emotions. I was excited about our night away but nervous about the impending meeting with Ed's ex-wife, the woman who tempted Ed and re-awoke old feelings in him. Feelings he thought he wouldn't feel again. Even though nothing happened then, I was still fearful that her very presence might make Ed realise that he didn't have the same feelings for me. *Better to know now than at the wedding*, I thought. *Bad form to break up during your son's nuptials.*

In hindsight we all had something to fear about the meeting – Ed, Clare, Steve and of course me. But I didn't realise it as we sat in the car chatting as we sped north.

Ed had been coy about where we were staying that night. He had promised it was a hotel and we were not about to turn up on Clare's doorstep. That wouldn't have been a popular choice. Other than that I had no idea.

A couple of hours into the journey and starting to feel rather hungry, I asked, "Are we nearly there yet?"

Ed laughed. "Yes, not much further now."

I looked out of the car window, not recognising the surrounding countryside. As far as I could tell we were miles away from anywhere. I was intrigued.

A few miles further up the road, Ed started indicating to turn right. I couldn't see any hint of where we were staying.

This had better not be a campsite or even a glamping site, I silently prayed. *That really would be the last thing I need, to turn up looking a mess after having camped out.* I reassured myself that we hadn't packed a tent so was hopeful my fears would not be realised.

We drove down a smart paved driveway and even though it was dark, the edges of the road were illuminated by elegant, discreet white light that stretched out ahead of us. I could just about make out the trees, dark and menacing, just eluding the reach of the lights.

I was starting to feel excited. A campsite wouldn't have a driveway like this. The road bent round to the left and suddenly in front of us, lit up like a Christmas tree, lights twinkled from behind curtains and blazed through uncovered windows. Outside big uplighters illuminated the whole facade of the nineteenth-century manor house.

"Wow," was all I could utter as I stared at the scene before me, gobsmacked.

Ed looked like the cat that got the cream. He was looking really chuffed with the surprise and his decision to book into this hotel.

"Have you stayed here before?" I asked, a little worried that he had brought someone else here in the past.

"No, I haven't," he reassured me. "I've known about it for some time, but living nearby I never had a reason to stay. The food is meant to be great."

"Oh good, I'm starving," I said.

"Let's get checked in, drop the bags in the room and then we can get some food."

"Sounds great."

We got out of the car and made our way in through the

large, arched, stone porch into a warm and welcoming hall. I instantly looked up to the ceiling, the elaborate plasterwork picked out by the dark blue background paint. It was stunning.

Ed had moved ahead of me to the reception desk on the far side and was in the process of checking in.

I did a slow, small-step-by-small-step, 360-degree rotation, taking in this amazing building and all the period furniture, some of which was showing its age but looked totally in the right place.

I caught up with Ed as he picked up the key from the desk, which he now dangled enticingly in front of me.

The receptionist had given Ed instructions on where to find the room and he had led the way up the enormous oak staircase that rose from the centre of the hall. At the first floor we turned away from the staircase and entered a wide hallway, flanked with expensive-looking antiques perched perilously on small wooden side tables and life-size paintings in oversized gilt frames of men and women of bygone ages. It was decorated like a stately home, giving guests the feeling of opulence and grandeur but without the expense of its upkeep.

The route to our room was a journey of discovery. Ed had stopped in front of a door just a few steps ahead of me. He was looking at me, beaming. I caught up with him.

"This is it," he said, unlocking the door and swinging it open, wide. We peered in. It was a large sumptuous room dominated by a four-poster bed with curtains, to one side. On the other side of the room was a large, slightly saggy sofa and a door which I assumed led to the en suite bathroom.

"Shall I carry you across the threshold?" Ed broke the silence.

"I think traditionally that is what a new husband and wife do, so let's not tempt fate. And anyway I don't want you to put your back out," I replied.

We opted for a romantic, but less nuanced, position of Ed leading me in by the hand. "Wow," was all we could say as we stood in the middle of the room turning in a tight circle to take it all in. It was like a dream.

I sat on the edge of bed. It felt warm and comfy as I sank into the deep bedding.

Ed put the overnight bag on the trunk at the end of the bed and sat down next to me.

We kissed, a contented, happy kiss, not a passionate one, but that would come later.

Eventually my stomach rumbled and we looked at each other and laughed.

"I guess that is our signal to get dinner," Ed announced, continuing, "Shall we leave the unpacking until later?"

"Good plan," I concurred.

Back in reception we were directed to the restaurant. We made our way through the bar. It was a massive oak counter that ran the entire length of a wood-panelled room, the back wall a riot of bottles every colour and shape containing every type of alcoholic beverage: gins, whiskies, vodkas and more. The other side of the room was neatly laid out with well-worn leather sofas and wing-backed chairs set out in formal groupings around low tables. It looked like how I imagine a gentleman's club might do.

We walked hand in hand through the crowded bar, although we barely noticed anyone. We entered the restaurant to see a very smart maître d', a tall, grey-haired gentleman in the second half of his century, decked out in black suit, crisp white shirt and russet-red bow tie. His thin hands held the sides of the wooden lectern in front of him. He looked at us over the top of his half-moon glasses.

"Good evening," his deep, rich voice somehow in discord with his thin appearance. "Table for two?"

"Yes please." Ed spoke for us both.

We were led to a small round table near the window, looking out onto the floodlit grounds. We could see the terrace give way to the formal lawn just beyond the stone balustrade and steps. Beyond the lawn we could just make out a moonlit lake and beyond, the blackness of a wood.

The table was very formal: starched white linen with a red runner across the centre and expertly polished silver cutlery laid out either side of swan-shaped napkins sitting tall and proud in front of us.

The maître d' held the chair out for me, gently edging me closer to the formidable swan. In a deftly quick, much practised move, he elegantly lifted the swan by the head. Mid-air he gave it a sharp flick and finished the move by gently placing the now flat napkin in my lap. He repeated the same move for Ed, handed us menus and vanished into the background.

We made polite conversation as we perused the menu. To my horror it was all in French and my language skills really were not up for the translation of such a refined menu. I scowled at the page, somehow hoping that would solve the problem.

Ed leant forward across the table. Picking up one side of the menu he turned the page. "It's in English on this page," he laughed.

"Thanks," I said, rather put out that he was laughing at me, rather than with me. "I didn't know."

"To be honest, I got a lucky break, it opened on the English and when I saw you scowling I thought there must be nothing on there that you like, then I turned the page and realised your concern. Sorry, I didn't mean to laugh."

"That's okay," I said grudgingly, before conversation picked up on food choices, now I could see what they were, and whether we would indulge in a starter or not.

Magically, the minute we put the menus down and started up the conversation a waiter appeared at the table. Surprisingly there was no notepad. Apparently in this establishment the waiters were expected to remember the guests' requests.

I ordered steak, medium-rare, with rich béarnaise sauce, swapping the chips, sorry, to be accurate, the 'shards of crispy potato', for a green salad. Ed followed suit with the steak but opted for a peppercorn sauce and kept the 'shards'.

"And to drink?" the waiter enquired.

"Prosecco?" Ed asked.

"Don't mind if I do," I replied.

As one bottle became two we chatted and laughed as we ate the melt-in-the-mouth steaks.

After dinner we took a quick walk around the gardens, following the low lights either side of the path, but not being able to see much further into the darkness beyond. We walked hand in hand in silence, my thoughts turning to the next day.

We climbed the stairs to bed, where we curled up, entwined in each other's bodies, but it went no further than that. We didn't speak about it, but we just needed the comfort, support and closeness rather than the passion.

*

It was wonderful not to be awoken by an alarm the next morning. We lay in each other's arms for some time before dragging ourselves through the shower and downstairs for a huge, satisfying and fortifying full English breakfast with all the trimmings, especially an endless supply of strong coffee, a requirement after a double-Prosecco night.

It was a leisurely affair. No need to rush, as neither of us was in a hurry to get to Clare's, even though that was the purpose of us being in this elegant hotel. There were a few furtive glances between Ed and me. We didn't vocalise our concerns or thoughts, but clearly we were both a little on edge.

We reluctantly returned to the room to pack, acknowledging that we would have to get this over and done with at some point, like pulling off a plaster.

As we were leaving, Ed took me in his arms and kissed me. "It'll be okay," he tried to reassure me as he pulled me close and squeezed me, trying to fill me with the confidence that right at that point, when I needed it most, had abandoned me.

I leant back, enough to look him in the eyes. "I know," I said softly.

We checked out. Loaded the car. Started the journey. Hearts were heavy.

As we made our way slowly down the drive I pulled down the sun visor and looked in the mirror at the gradually disappearing grand house. *I'll be back*, I promised myself.

"Ready?" Ed asked.

"Yeah. How far is it?" What I meant of course was not 'How far is it to Clare's?' but, 'How long do I have to steel myself for this?' I could feel sweat starting to prickle my face and neck despite the coldness in the car as the heating finally kicked in.

Great, I thought, *Clare will no doubt be as beautiful and elegant as I've seen her in a picture on Ed's phone and I will be a red, sweating mess. Ed may well regret his decision to be with me.* Ever the pessimist.

"Not far, about twenty minutes," he said, glancing over. "Are you okay?"

"Yeah. Sorry, if I'm honest I'm feeling rather nervous about today and I'm having slight palpitations to tell the truth. Sorry, you don't want to hear this. I was trying to be strong and pretend it doesn't matter, but, well, sorry."

Ed pulled the car to a stop just before the end of the drive. Handbrake on. He turned in his seat to face me the best he could within the confines of the seatbelt.

"I'm nervous too," he said, holding my hand in his and stroking the back of it. "Not because I'm nervous at seeing her again, or because I'm worried about you. But the truth is, beyond you, Clare and Emma are the most important women in my life. I know you and Emma are tight, and I just hope you and Clare can get on well too. We are a small family, but we are very close. Sorry, that probably hasn't helped with your nerves. We really should have spoken about this before, but I don't think either of us could face having this conversation. Now we have to, as we will be there soon."

"I'm sure it will be okay. Well, fingers crossed."

We drove on in silence until Ed announced our imminent arrival.

I looked at myself in the mirror again. Luckily the sweating had abated before too much damage had been done to my appearance. I stared myself in the eye. *Right, you,* I told myself, *be brave, be funny, be polite, be considerate, be yourself.*

We pulled into a narrow suburban road which ran down the side of a larger property. The 1980s detached houses lined up on one side of the road. We drove to the end of the road, the palpitations starting to build with every yard that passed. Fight or flight? Fight or flight? In truth I have never been one to opt for flight, nor was it possible or appropriate on this occasion, but I could have opened the door and flung myself out if it had been an option.

We came to a stop on the drive of the last house. I got out, straightened my clothes. *This can't be as bad as some of the presentations I've given,* I tried to reassure myself. *This is going to be okay. This is going to be okay,* I kept repeating to myself as we made our way, with weighted steps, to the front door.

Ed squeezed my hand as he lifted the other one to ring the bell.

A few moments later we could see movement behind the door, before it was pulled open enthusiastically to reveal a beautiful, demure, perfectly turned-out Clare standing in front of me and her handsome husband, Steve, standing behind her with a protective hand on her shoulder. Clearly this was not just about Clare and me, but also about Ed and Steve.

I would have liked it more if Clare had answered the door looking a state, with dirty clothes and dishevelled hair, with a splattering of flour on her unmade-up face. But she didn't.

We smiled at each other, warm, friendly smiles. In truth, how could you not like a woman like this?

"Welcome, welcome," Clare said. "It's wonderful to meet you, I've heard so much about you from Ed, Dan and Emma. Come in, come in." Clare and Steve stepped back to leave space for us to enter single file, stopping briefly for an awkward greeting, to shake hands or kiss cheeks? We both leant in for the cheek, Clare withdrawing after one. I had foolishly already committed myself to a second cheek peck and clumsily stumbled into her cheek.

"Sorry, I always go for two." We laughed.

Steve, having seen the encounter was prepared and our greeting went much more smoothly. Ed following behind repeated the two with Clare. As I watched out of the corner of my eye I might have been mistaken but he seemed to linger on the second cheek a moment longer than was entirely necessary. He straightened and opted for a firm handshake and back slap with Steve.

I stood in the hall, unsure where to go in this unfamiliar house.

"Follow me," Steve instructed as he strode off down the hall. I fell into step behind him, leaving Clare and Ed to follow on.

We were taken into a warm and comfy front room. A fire was blazing in the open fireplace.

"Do sit," invited Steve. "What can I get you to drink? Wine? Fruit juice? Coffee?"

I piped up first, aware that Ed wouldn't be drinking as he was driving, and still slightly befuddled from the drinking the night before I replied, "Coffee, if that's okay?" Ed followed suit and Steve disappeared to make a pot of filter coffee.

Mugs in hand, Ed and I sat opposite Clare and Steve, across the low wooden coffee table with its tray of coffee, milk, sugar and biscuits. Clare and I struck up a conversation, nothing in particular, small talk, the getting-to-know-you chat of new acquaintances who just happen to both love, or have loved, the same man.

She was my competition for Ed's affection and I could feel the palpitations starting again. I calmed myself down and focused on getting to know her. We covered all the usual topics and I found myself not only relaxing but also starting to enjoy the conversation and to like Clare.

I followed her into the kitchen to help her finalise lunch and lay it on the table.

Ed and Steve had, unbeknown to us, walked in and were standing inside the door watching us.

I saw them and jumped. "How long have you two been there?" I asked.

"Not long," Steve said. "We came through to see if we could help but couldn't get a word in, as you two were gabbling on so much," he teased.

"Sit down, boys," Clare instructed them. "We're all ready. Chloe, Ed, you sit yourselves on the other side of the table and we'll sit this side so we can get in and out."

I did a quick blood test as Steve topped up our mugs and Clare brought the dishes over.

Ed had clearly briefed Clare that I was avoiding carbs,

as she had made a delicious chicken Caesar salad. It was fresh, light and delicious. Of course the boys accompanied theirs with bread rolls drowned in proper butter.

"This is delicious," I complimented Clare. "Thank you."

I jumped slightly as I felt my knee being squeezed and looked at Ed who was giving me a cheeky smile.

Conversation continued to flow as we moved on to cheese and biscuits, fruit and more delicious coffee.

As Clare and Steve cleared the table Ed leant over, kissed me on the cheek and whispered, "Thank you," followed by the best three words in any language: "I love you."

"I love you too and thank you."

He looked at me surprised. "Why thank me?" he asked, perplexed.

"Well, for a few things really. Firstly, thank you for bringing me here today, it will make the wedding much more relaxed. Secondly, thank you for introducing me to, and welcoming me into, your lovely family. And thirdly, thank you for saying you love me."

As Clare brought over more freshly brewed coffee, there was a knock at the front door and Steve went to answer it.

A minute later Emma, Dan and Steve walked into the kitchen. We all stood and hugged and kissed cheeks and made room at the table for them to join us.

Anyone looking in through the patio doors would have seen a very happy lunch party, smiling, laughing, chatting – a close family and good friends.

Dan and Emma didn't stay long, they had only popped in to say hello as they were passing. We wouldn't see them again until the wedding.

Before they left, Dan took Ed aside. I found out later,

he had asked Ed if he might be kind enough to put some money towards the honeymoon. The wedding costs were mounting up and they were a little short to pay for the holiday. Ed, of course, agreed not only to supplement it but to pay for it in total so they would have some spending money and wouldn't have to miss out on anything while away.

As everyone was up saying farewell we decided to make our move as well. We had achieved what we had come to do and as the adrenaline ebbed away we were both feeling tired and still had the drive home.

Dan and Emma left ahead of us. As they walked down the drive I turned back to Clare. "Let me know if there is anything I can do to help with the wedding. I'd love to help if I can," I said with genuine affection and meaning.

"Thank you," she said, smiling warmly. "I will let you know."

The drive home was much more relaxed than the drive up had been. The radio was on and we sang along to songs, chatted about the hotel, lunch and the wedding.

Arriving home in the dark we made supper, ate in front of the TV with a well-earned glass or two of wine and then hit the hay, exhausted but excited about the days and weeks ahead.

eighteen.

Procession to the processional

The next couple of weeks flew by. We practised our readings, walked, talked, danced around the kitchen and made love as often as we desired.

And then it was here. The wedding. I felt relaxed about seeing everyone, but nervous about getting up in front of them for the reading.

We had booked the Thursday and following Monday off work to give us time to travel up and a leisurely recovery time afterwards.

It was close to Christmas, it was cold and the days were short.

As we left the town on Thursday afternoon the large county church stood proud on the hill looking down on the town. It looked almost magical in the sunshine. It was a good omen for the weekend.

Ed gave me potted histories on the wedding guests as the miles passed under the wheels of the car. Finally, he drew in a deep breath and said, "And of course my mum and dad will be there."

Wait. What? I thought as the familiar palpitations once more made themselves present.

"They can't wait to meet you," he continued.

I was stunned into silence. Of course they would be there, at their grandson's wedding, why had I not thought of this? Ed had told me a lot about them during our time together, so stupid, stupid Chloe.

I tuned back in to Ed's voice as he said, "So we're meeting them for dinner tonight," oblivious to the mild panic starting to grip me. It was an unnecessary reaction. I had met boyfriends' parents before and had always got on well with them. I sat in silence trying to make sense of my feelings.

Ed was looking at me, clearly waiting for a response, or reaction, to something I had probably missed him saying.

"Sorry, that will be great. I'm looking forward to meeting them, after all you've told me about them, and it will be nice to meet them before the big day."

"Are you okay? You've got that look on your face again, the same as you had before we had lunch with Clare and Steve."

"Yes, yes," I stuttered. "I, well, I hadn't realised I'd be meeting them, I'm feeling a little nervous if I'm honest." Not totally honest as I was, in fact, very, very nervous.

Again the reassuring knee squeeze.

"They'll love you, as I do," he said.

"I hope so." I paused for a moment then continued, "It's going to be a hell of a weekend." I forced a smile and rested my hand on Ed's thigh, trying to convey I was happy. Trepidation was closer to the mark.

Thankfully there were no more startling revelations

over the course of the journey, much to my relief. Chatting distracted me from my concerns and I settled back into my seat.

"Mm-mmm-mm-mmm-mm." I hadn't realised but I had started to hum a tune as I looked out of the window at the wintry landscape. I was brought back to the present by the sound of Ed's laughter.

"What was that?" he asked.

"Sorry, I didn't realise I was doing that. It was meant to be a song but I'm no good at remembering words or tunes. I'm guessing you couldn't tell what it was."

"Um no, can you give me any clues?" Ed's words reaffirming my complete lack of musicality.

"Unfortunately I can't remember its name, whatever it was, it seemed apt given the time of year."

Ed chuckled. "Well on that note, whichever one it was, or was meant to be, we're here."

I gave Ed a mocking laugh at his pun and looked up at the beautiful, expansive facade of the hotel.

"It really is the most beautiful setting for a wedding," I said in appreciation as I brought the conversation back to safer ground.

"You're not wrong," he replied as we disembarked the car. I collected Ed's suit and my outfit, which were hanging up in the back of the car, while Ed retrieved the weekend bag from the boot, and made our way into the lavish hall.

"Welcome, welcome," a voice called out behind us as we stood at the reception desk. We turned in unison to find Mary, the wedding planner, marching towards us, right arm and hand outstretched already anticipating the handshake.

"It's wonderful to see you again, how was your journey?" she asked, the perfect hostess.

We moved towards her as she approached. Ed took her lead, meeting her hand with his and smiling back at her.

"Very good, thank you. Are we the first to arrive?" he asked.

"Yes, we're expecting Dan and your parents and in fact a number of friends later today. Emma and her family will arrive tomorrow morning keeping to tradition that the bride and groom will not see each other until the wedding.

"Everything is ready and in place for the big day," Mary continued as she collected our room key from the equally smartly turned-out receptionist.

Mary, it seemed, was totally at the disposal of the wedding party as she personally escorted us to our room. On the way we took in all the Christmas decorations, the giant tree dominating the hall, the garlands running up the staircase, the oversized red, gold and silver baubles suspended from the ceiling. Delicate white lights twinkled from all around. It felt and smelt like Christmas.

"As father of the groom," Mary told us over her shoulder, "you have been assigned a suite on the top floor." It was palatial: bedroom, sitting room and, of course, bathroom.

"Well," Ed said after hanging up our outfits in the wardrobe, "we have a few hours before we meet my parents and Dan for dinner, shall we go for a walk, take in the wintry landscape as your song suggested earlier?" He was clearly still amused by that.

"Sounds like a great idea," I confirmed.

*

We whiled away what was left of the afternoon. Following the walk we returned to the room for a 'rest' before freshening up and then heading downstairs to meet the rest of Ed's family.

Ed reached down and found my hand as we entered the bar. I glanced over to the full-height doors which opened out onto the terrace where we had enjoyed lunch in the sunshine earlier in the year, closed now to keep out the cold. The room was comfortably warm, fed by the glowing fire in the magnificent stone fireplace, the mantelpiece adorned with a Christmas garland that complemented those in the entrance hall.

Ahead of us I saw Dan, who rose to his feet as he saw us approach. He was beaming from ear to ear. In front of him with their backs to us, two more people rose from the low sofa. They turned to greet us. I stopped in my tracks and drew in a sharp breath of shock as I looked at who I assumed were Ed's parents.

Ed turned to me, but before he could speak I moved forward and stuck out my hand.

"Hello, Joan, how wonderful to see you again."

"You too, Chloe, it's been a long time."

We dispensed with the handshake and instead leant in for a warm embrace. Joan was just as I remembered: thin and elegantly turned out.

I turned to the man by her side. "You must be David," I said as I leant in to kiss him on both cheeks.

"Yes," David said, also unsure of who I was or how I would know his name.

Dan, David and Ed were all staring at us in bewilderment, clearly unable to speak. I put them out of their misery as I chuckled.

"As you may have realised we know each other. I don't know why I never made the connection. After I finished my degree I stayed on at university to undertake research, but I needed money to pay for my living expenses. I got a job at a toy factory where I worked during the day, and then went to campus in the evenings and weekends to continue my studies. Joan was my boss. We did manage to keep in touch for some time," I looked at Joan and she nodded her agreement, "but with house moves and job changes we seemed to lose touch," I concluded.

Joan replied, "I hadn't made the connection either. To be honest Ed only told me your name was Chloe so there really was no reason for me to think it could be you."

Ed interjected, "So, that would have been when you were living in Nottingham, where I met you the first time."

Now it was time for Joan to look confused.

"Oh my goodness, yes, how weird that I knew you both, well, only briefly in terms of you, Ed. What a very, very small world," I said.

"It certainly is, it feels like we are coming full circle, like this is meant to be," Ed said with a sly smile. I looked at him curiously, unsure what the smile meant but determined not to burst the bubble.

I felt a huge surge of relief as what might have been an awkward meal with strangers suddenly turned into a light-hearted and amusing walk down memory lane whilst creating new memories as the evening drew on.

We ate, drank in moderation, and retired to bed early, contented and aware of the big day ahead of us. The next day we heard of some drunken tales from the bar, but we were glad to have kept clear heads.

We were rudely awoken at 8am the next morning when the phone on the bedside table next to Ed began to trill. I looked at the phone in confusion and sat bolt upright in the bed, my heart pounding. For some reason I had a feeling of dread clutching my heart.

Ed was more relaxed and reached out and lifted the receiver without even moving his body, putting the phone to his ear.

Lazily and groggily he said, "Hello," then a series of sounds, "mm, mm, mmm," in response to whatever was being said to him, ending the call with, "Thank you."

Slowly he opened his eyes and reached out a hand to me. "It's okay," he reassured me, "it was just our wake-up call, no need to worry. I forgot to mention I booked it last night to make sure we were up in time. Let's throw on some clothes and grab breakfast, we can come back and shower after that." He threw back the duvet and got out of bed purposefully, clearly taking command of the day.

In the bathroom I took a moment to compose myself, throwing water over my face to wash away the sleep, and buried my wet face in the soft cream towel, pressing it into my face as reassurance. I repeated my old mantra from my more stressful work days: 'It's going to be a good day. Everything is okay. It's going to be great.'

I stared at my reflection in the mirror and repeated the mantra a couple more times before re-joining Ed and making our way back to the dining room.

In just a few short hours this room would be transformed into the wedding venue and later transformed again for the reception. But for now it was as it had been the night before: crisp, white linen tables laid up waiting for diners.

Dan joined us in the queue for the breakfast buffet. It was a sumptuous spread all neatly laid out, from cereals, yoghurts, fruit, through meat and cheese platters, to hot silver warming trays containing all the elements to make up a full English breakfast.

I felt sick, nervous sick. I knew I needed to eat something both from a diabetic point of view and to steady my nerves. Next to me a confident Ed was reassuring an equally nervous-looking Dan. Ed reached out and put a hand on his son's shoulder. "I'm really proud of you, this will be a very special day, we are all here to support you." Seeing Ed with Dan made my heart soar with love. I had never had the privilege of being a mother, but I felt a real swell of pride in both of these men before me.

We all turned back to the feast in front of us and made our food and drink choices, returning to an empty table to eat a leisurely meal, accompanied by several return trips to the buffet to refill empty mugs. Eventually realising that time was marching on we returned to our rooms to get dressed, with promises to Dan that we would join him in his room an hour before the wedding.

As I entered the bedroom having showered, made-up and with my wedding outfit on, Ed, who was sitting on the edge of the bed doing up his cufflinks, looked up.

"Wow," he mouthed as he rose to his feet and strode over to me where I stood rooted to the spot.

He picked up my hands in his and leant in and kissed me hard and passionately.

"Wow," he repeated. "You look amazing." He meant it too.

He stood holding my hands, staring deeply into my eyes, smiling.

"Although," he said slowly as I held my breath, "you might need to reapply your lipstick."

We laughed as Ed wiped the lipstick from his lips and I reapplied it to mine.

As we were leaving the room a short time later, Ed looking incredibly handsome in his formal morning suit, he stopped me by the door.

"I can't wait to get back here later," he said with a cheeky grin.

"Me too," I laughed.

Ed tapped his pocket for reassurance, satisfied that his speech and any other valuables were safe inside. I checked the contents of my clutch bag for the umpteenth time to check that the reading, printed in very large, bold font, was inside. It was, as it had been every time I had checked.

We walked hand in hand down the long hallway, silent, running through what we needed to do on that auspicious day.

We heard laughter before we got to the door of the suite where Dan and his best man were getting ready.

"Sounds like they are in good spirits," Ed said as he knocked on the door.

"Coming," a cheerful Dan called out from behind the closed door.

Dan appeared, with a half-full, or half-empty depending on your persuasion, glass of champagne in hand and a beaming smile on his face, all the earlier doubts and concerns clearly dispersed by the love and support of friends and family, and no doubt also eased by the champagne. It may not have been his first glass.

Dan stepped back and beckoned us inside. "Come in,

come in. Tim," he called to his co-conspirator, "pour a couple of glasses for my dad and his girlfriend, Chloe." We shook hands before Tim was released to carry out his task.

It was a beautiful suite. We gathered in the sitting room with window seats below tall windows overlooking the garden.

The coffee table was adorned with champagne glasses and three bottles of champagne cooling in an elegant silver bucket full of ice. Clearly one bottle had already been consumed. Tim popped the cork on a new bottle and filled glasses, which he handed to us with a mock bow as he did so, then turned and topped up Dan's glass and his own. They were clearly on a mission.

"Sit, sit," Dan called over his shoulder as he went through the double doors into a sumptuous bedroom, the huge bed of starched white sheets and pillowcases adorned with lavish red and gold velvet throw and cushions. "I'm nearly ready."

Tim sat on the sofa opposite us.

Ed struck up conversation. "Lovely to see you again, Tim. It's been a long time. What are you up to these days, still in the City?"

"Yes, for my sins. I keep thinking about getting out of the rat race, but I haven't a clue what I would do instead," he admitted.

Dan returned to the room, his shirt still undone at the collar but now wearing a colourful, tailored waistcoat which reflected the reds and golds of the bedroom. He was carrying a red tie in his hand.

"We're ready a little early," he said as he sat down next to Tim, "but that's no bad thing, I guess."

"It's good, Dan, always good to be prepared," Ed assured him.

"Is there anything I can do to help?" I asked.

"No, no, everything is under control. Mary, the wedding co-ordinator, has the ushers checking everything is in place and are poised to meet guests as they arrive," Dan said, switching into controlled confident groom.

I sipped at the champagne, not wanting to slur during the reading, or fall asleep mid-afternoon. I'd never been good at daytime drinking.

"Would it be okay if I order a coffee?" I asked to no one in particular.

"Good idea," Ed said as he tapped his pocket. I was wondering whether it was a lucky talisman.

Dan looked a little disappointed. We were not admonishing him but we both feared what a state he would be in if he kept up the rate of consumption of the champagne.

"Anyone else like coffee?" I asked as I walked over to the phone on the small round console table by the door.

"Get a large pot," Ed advised. "I'm sure it will all be drunk."

Whilst we waited we went through all the plans for the day, making sure we all knew what to do and when. I was looking forward to being able to relax as soon as the reading was done, but for now I could feel the nerves starting to attack my happy mood. The palpitations. The sweat prickling my forehead and hands. The slight shake that was only visible to me.

Ed sensed my stress. "It won't be long now, and you'll be fabulous. I've heard you practise and you practically know it word for word without referring to your sheet."

I smiled nervously back at him, not feeling the confidence he was demonstrating. Ed tapped his pocket.

An hour later we gathered ourselves, buttoned up shirts, waistcoats and jackets, did final checks in front of the mirror. The boys all patted each other on the back – strong, manly slaps for courage and reassurance – before we made our way down to the transformed dining room, now set up with rows of chairs either side of a wide aisle that led down to the massive fireplace, to the left of which was a small lectern from which we would do our readings. The outside edge of each chair that lined the aisle was adorned with a small bouquet of fresh flowers, white against the green of the foliage.

The room looked magnificent.

Most of the seats were already full of animated friends and family chatting to neighbours either side or on the row in front or behind. It was a joyous sight and something to lift the heart.

A couple of ushers handed us our order of service and took us down the aisle to the reserved rows on the groom's side of the room. Ed tapped his pocket.

Clare, Steve, Joan and David were already seated and stood as we approached. We all kissed and shook hands. Dan, now starting to look a little nervous, was reassured by his parents. He looked at me and said, "Thank you."

"For what?" I asked, unsure.

"For the coffee," was all he said before he and Tim turned and took their place in front of the registrar, who was smiling at the assembled throng. We took our seats. Ed tapped his pocket.

There were no musicians but music struck up from

somewhere, piped through from an unseen sound system. We all took our cue and almost in unison we took to our feet and turned towards the aisle as the resplendent Emma, arm in arm with her father, who was clearly bursting with pride, entered, accompanied by her four bridesmaids in matching gold and red evening dresses: an adult, two teenagers and one small child with small flower basket in comparison to the bouquets that the others carried.

I turned to look at Dan. He looked like he would explode with love. I had never seen anyone look so much in love and so unreservedly happy and I felt the love emanating from him wash over me like a wave.

Ed must have felt it too, as he put his arm around my back, resting it on my hip and pulling me in close to his side.

I looked at him and smiled, returning the love that his eyes were conveying. It was a magical moment.

We turned back as Emma arrived at Dan's side. She turned to hand her reverse teardrop bouquet of white, gold and green to her maid of honour. Before turning back to Dan she smiled at her parents and then across the aisle to include us as her soon-to-be-extended family.

As we retook our seats I could feel my nerves begin to get the better of me and I missed most of the first part of the ceremony as the fog in my head took hold. Ed brought me back with a squeeze of the hand and mouthed, "It will be okay."

Why the hell did I agree to do this? I thought. *I could easily have said no and no one would have thought anything less of me, but no, I said yes, and here I am. STOP*, I told myself. *It will be okay, it will be okay.*

"You're up," Ed said, nodding towards the lectern and the expectant faces of Dan and Emma.

Clutching the reading tight in my sweaty hand, I stood slowly, trying to ground myself before making my way forward. I flattened out the piece of paper, grateful for the large font as I swayed slightly with nerves. I took a deep breath and looked up to see reassuring eyes from Dan, Emma and just behind them Ed.

I smiled. Slowly, loudly and deliberately I began to read, deciding it better to read rather than try to remember the whole piece despite knowing it almost by heart. Looking at the paper was easier than meeting the eyes of the congregation.

"This reading is 1 Corinthians 13:4-13 entitled 'Love'..."

As I approached the last couple of lines I don't know what force within me raised my head, fixed my eyes on Dan and Emma and delivered the final line, now imprinted in my mind, and I smiled at them as I drew them in with "And now these three remain: faith, hope and love. But the greatest of these is love".

Dan mouthed, "Thank you," and Ed beamed with pride as I slowly folded the piece of paper and quietly returned to my seat where Ed leant over and kissed me on the cheek.

I felt exhausted as the adrenaline ebbed out of my body, but more than that I felt proud, I felt relieved and I felt joyously happy.

The ceremony rolled on and soon it was Ed's turn to take to the stand. He rose confidently, half turning to me and smiling before striding to the front of the room.

He pulled himself up to his full height and rested his hands on the top edges of the lectern. Then in his strong baritone voice he delivered *The Dove* poem. I listened to him in awe as he held the room in the palm of his hand. I had never felt so proud and so, so much in love. I wanted to leap up and declare my love to the room, but now was not the time or place.

There was a brief silence in the room and then a ripple of applause as he returned to the empty seat beside me, tapping his pocket as he sat.

I leant over and whispered, "I love you," into his ear.

"I love you too," he said, heartfelt.

The rest of the ceremony passed in a dizzy whirlwind of love, of singing, of joyous betrothal. All the time Ed and I held hands and stole furtive sideways glances at each other.

As Dan was told he could kiss his bride Ed and I watched for a moment before Ed took my face in his hands and kissed me long and hard. The assembled guests might well have questioned who had just got married.

"We had better tune this down a bit," I told Ed, fearing that we might be stealing some of Dan and Emma's limelight.

As Dan and Emma made their way up the aisle we all fell in behind them, making our way to the reception hall and on to the bar where we were greeted with waiters holding large silver trays bearing champagne flutes and glasses of soft drinks.

Whilst Dan and Emma were whisked away for the obligatory photographs, Ed and I circulated, chatting to Ed's old friends and being introduced to new ones.

At very precise intervals we were presented with delicious canapés of smoked salmon blinis and mini chicken vol-au-vents – very 1980s. The volume of noise in the room rose as guests were filled with champagne, canapés and the beautiful sound of the string quartet entertaining us.

As Dan and Emma returned to the room, Ed made his excuses. Leaving me with Clare and Steve he marched over to the newlyweds. I saw him kiss and embrace Emma and then usher them both out of the room. I thought it strange that he had not included me in whatever they were up to but, after all, I was not part of the immediate family.

I turned back to the conversation and was lost in our enthusiastic confirmation of what had, so far, been a fabulous day. When Ed came up behind me and put his arm around my waist I jumped at the unexpected embrace and turned sharply to see Ed's smiling face beside me.

"Hey, you," I said, "where have you been?"

"Just sorting out a few things with Dan and Emma."

"Is everything okay?" I asked in response to his uninformative statement.

"Everything is hunky dory," he said without any more explanation. He pulled me close and gently kissed my cheek.

The merriment continued as the dining room was reset.

I have to confess that after the stress of the reading I finally relaxed into the day and happily consumed a number of the delicious ice-cold champagnes that kept magically appearing in my hand.

It was, therefore, a relief when the master of ceremonies appeared next to our merry little group and advised us that they were forming the line-up for guests to meet the extended wedding party and we were needed outside the dining room.

Thank goodness, I thought, now in great need of some sustenance, as I tottered on my heels, arm in arm with Ed towards our designated spot.

We shook hands, smiled, said, "Hello," and, "Thank you for coming," in equal measure as the guests filed into the dining room and found their seats.

As I turned to follow them Ed held my arm, stopping me.

I turned to him. "Is everything okay?" I asked.

"Yes, yes," he stumbled. "You know I spoke to Dan and Emma."

I nodded, fear starting to rise and the palpitations returned.

He smiled at me to reassure me it was nothing to worry about and then continued.

"I wanted to check they were okay for me to do something I've wanted to do for ages and today just seemed the perfect time, but I wouldn't do it without their consent."

Now I was confused. I had no idea what he was talking about or where this was going. I caught Dan and Emma out of the corner of my eye. They were standing in the double doorway with the Christmas garland above their heads. They were smiling at us.

"Okay, I don't know whether to be nervous or what," I confessed.

Ed tapped his right pocket again and then his hand delved into it to retrieve whatever had been secreted there all day. As he pulled his hand from the pocket he sank to one knee.

I looked at Ed, and then up to Emma as she yelped and jumped up and down like a child.

I looked back down at Ed who was now opening the box lid to reveal a beautiful, princess-cut diamond set in a platinum ring.

Ed looked up at me. All he said was, "Will you marry me?"

"Yes," was my simple, but heartfelt reply. Finally, here was a love that would never to be lost.

Note from the Author

The medieval town depicted in the pages of this book is real. Saffron Walden, in north Essex, nestles into the protection of nearby Hertfordshire, Cambridgeshire and Suffolk.

Most of the shops, cafes, restaurants and landmarks are real too. The bookshop is Hart's Books, the cafe that Chloe and Ed visit on their first date is Maze Bar & Grill, and the bike cafe where Chloe bumps into Ed's friend is Bicicletta. All of the places mentioned in the book can be found on the way into, or in, the town centre, where you will also find a gorgeous gift and furniture shop, Angela Reed, full of wonderful things to discover. These are all places I love.

The wonderful campsite in Le Mans is run by a company called Lycian Events which I thoroughly recommend if you ever want to experience the thrills of twenty-four-hour racing.

As the world, hopefully, starts to generate a new normal, to reopen and to meet again as we rebuild our lives post-pandemic, it is more important than ever that we support our favourite places so we can continue to enjoy them for years to come. So, if you are ever in Saffron Walden, please visit the shops and eateries I have described and maybe, just maybe, you will bump into me whilst you are there. I hope you will love them as much as I do.

Finally, a couple of words of thanks. Thank you to all my family, friends and colleagues who have supported and encouraged me on this journey. Particular thanks to Richard, Andy and Tracey, who provided me with invaluable advice and guidance. And, thank you to 'Doris' (Sue) for your enthusiasm and kind words, especially during my moments of doubt.

About the Author

Loves Lost and Found is E V Radwinter's debut novel. Inspired as a child after visiting the library where Evelyn Anthony wrote her books, Loves Lost and Found was born out of the encouragement given to her by her beloved, but now departed, Mother and Grandmother.

E V Radwinter was born in London and grew up in Essex, although she has lived in some of the liveliest and most beautiful places across the country she is now back to north Essex where she lives with her partner.

E V Radwinter has worked in Marketing and Communications for most of her career and has a passion for writing.

E V Radwinter has just started work on her second novel.